CHARLIE —
Hope you Enjoy
the Book

Rod Harris
"The Hawk"

Live Long
Live Well

FRANK-3 ENROUTE

The Streets of Las Vegas

Rod Harris with Norma Hood

authorHOUSE®

AuthorHouse™
1663 Liberty Drive
Bloomington, IN 47403
www.authorhouse.com
Phone: 1-800-839-8640

This book is a work of fiction. People, places, events and situations are the product of the author's imagination. Any resemblance to actual persons, living or dead, or historical events, is purely coincidental.

© 2010 Rod Harris with Norma Hood. All rights reserved.

No part of this book may be reproduced, stored in a retrieval system, or transmitted by any means without the written permission of the author.

First published by AuthorHouse   11/16/2010

ISBN: 978-1-4520-8726-9 (hc)
ISBN: 978-1-4520-8727-6 (sc)
ISBN: 978-1-4520-8728-3 (e)

Library of Congress Control Number: 2010915653

Printed in the United States of America

This book is printed on acid-free paper.

Certain stock imagery © Thinkstock.

Because of the dynamic nature of the Internet, any Web addresses or links contained in this book may have changed since publication and may no longer be valid. The views expressed in this work are solely those of the author and do not necessarily reflect the views of the publisher, and the publisher hereby disclaims any responsibility for them.

OASIS IN THE DESERT

The desert sun rises hot, heavy and glaring over the glittering lights of the city that never sleeps and unceasingly performs. Its scorching rays pound relentless and unforgiving on the sidewalks and the pavement. It is already in the 90's as I emerge after my 07:00 hrs. briefing, ready to tackle another day on the streets. The sun's blistering shafts assail my head and shoulders sucking beads of sweat to my forehead and down my back. I patrol my area alert and observant, preserving the peace and protecting the inhabitants of the Naked City, Las Vegas, Nevada.

It is my job to confront those who do evil or wrong, to bring them to justice and to discourage one human from hurting another. I instruct others in how to oppose dishonesty and corruption, to repel unjustness and acts of malice, and in how to go home alive and to feel they have done their job, one day at a time. I am one of many, Las Vegas's finest. Officer Rod Randel by name, AKA The Hawk. Preventing crime is my game; I am a major player! And God, I love what I do!

The dazzling lights, painted ladies, celebrities, casinos, slot machines and gambling houses are our city's main attractions. The Las Vegas strip and downtown attract people from all over the world. The jingle of coins, the clack of a stack of chips, and the shuffle of cards draw you like steel to a magnet. Others, the discouraged, the lost and the forgotten, forage, live on the streets, eat from dumpsters, and sleep in crevices and alleys. Some make their living on the street, trading their bodies or their wares for the almighty dollar, trafficking drugs and negotiating the sale of guns, or preying on others.

As for me, I am a twenty-four-seven police officer that fights the inequities and injustices in my city. Undaunted by the heat that rises to and beyond 120 degrees, I face the world and my work with eager anticipation. Welcome to Las Vegas, the Oasis in the desert.

ACKNOWLEDGEMENTS

WE GRACIOUSLY ACKNOWLEDGE AND THANK OUR families and friends all of whom have been the catalyst and strength that kept us excited about our first writing efforts. You believed that we could do this and are still encouraging us to write our second book that has a working title, <u>The Call.</u> A special thanks to Elvis, Rod's nineteen year old, albino, Cocker-Westie-cross dog that sat patiently beside us hour after hour, occasionally offering an encouraging, "Woooof." And last, but extremely important, thanks to you the readers; we hope that you will enjoy <u>Frank-3 Enroute</u>.

DEDICATION

<u>Frank-3 Enroute</u>
is dedicated to the memory of
Rod's
grandmother, Polly Yates,
to
Ellen L. Harris,
Rod's loving mother,
to the
Las Vegas
Metropolitan Police Department
and to the officers
that faithfully serve.

CONTENTS

ROBBERY-CODE RED 1
THE NAKED CITY 5
BLUE CADILLAC 9
SPEECHLESS 13
THE OFFICE 20
BREAKFAST BURGLAR I 27
ANOTHER MURDER 32
UP AND DOWN 42
WHEELCHAIR ANNIE 45
HUGO and MOLLIE 51
LONG LEGS 56
THE CRASH 58
THE BLACK BITCH 68
MULES 73
SLAVER 77
BREAKFAST BURGLAR II 82
BACON 'N BUDDY 85
JUDGE WHITE 89
RADIO 'N ANTS 93
METER MOLLY 98
BREAKFAST BURGLAR III 107
MAC-aroni 114
PUPPY LOVE 124
GRAMMS 134
NO MIRANDA 143
DEAD WRONG 148
THE COMPLAINT 152
STOOLIE 159

BREAKFAST BURGLAR IV	161
THE CHRISTMAS PARTY	168
DEAF BUT NOT DUMB	174
COBRA ONE STRIKES	177
BLUE MULE	180
BREAKFAST BURGLAR V	183
HANGIN' AROUND	196
WILD THING	201
GEORGE AND THE ALIENS	205
CHRISTMAS	210
SCARED	214
SKINNED	220
THE NEW YEAR	226
THE CALL	236

ROBBERY-CODE RED

WILLY WELLS, MY RECENTLY ASSIGNED ROOKIE, and I had been on patrol since 07:30 hrs. and decided to stop in at the 7-11 for iced tea and a soda. The 7-11 at Oakey and Las Vegas Blvd. was close. As we approached, I did not stop but cruised slowly past as usual, and something did not strike me as right. I knew my area and I knew the regulars that worked at the 7-11's, the Rebel's and ARCO's. I pulled around the corner and asked Willy if he noticed anything wrong. He didn't think so. "I saw a big white dude behind the counter, but I didn't see Stacy, that cute little black-headed girl." I did a U-turn on Oakey and pulled to the north side of the store that had no window. "Wells, call in a 425, suspicious circumstance. Have Cheri' call the store and tell the clerk to step outside."

"Control, this is Frank-3, we have a possible 425 at the 7-11 on the corner of Oakey and Las Vegas Blvd., across from the White Cross Drug."

"Frank-3, do you want back-up?"

"Affirmative," said Wells.

I heard, "Control, this is Adam-12, enroute." I felt good that Sam Sikes, my partner of many years, would be there shortly. Dispatch then called the 7-ll. I heard the phone as it rang and rang and no one answered. All I could see when I sneaked a peek around the corner was a big Bubba, wearing a ratty, white T-shirt and black sweat pants. He did not work there, for sure.

Returning to the patrol car, I took the mike and said, "Control, be advised, a possible 407 in progress. Give me a Code Red, no lights and no sirens. Block off Las Vegas Blvd. at Wyoming." When I called the Code Red, no other traffic was allowed on the radio. All that could be heard during that time was a beep…beep…beep…as the airways remained deadly silent. Every patrol car and patrolman close by and available rushed to that location, knowing that there was a crime in progress. We needed to make sure the employees and any customers were all right and able to leave the premises. On my last look, I could see that Bubba was brandishing a revolver as he worked on the cash register, which he was having trouble opening. Still, no one else was in sight. He could have Stacy, other employees and customers just lying on the floor or he might have shot them. There was no way to tell. Definitely a Code Red, a robbery in progress.

I kneeled at the corner of the building and removed my PR-24 baton, 24 inches of *hurtcha*, holding it like a baseball bat ready to swing. Willy stood right beside me with his gun drawn. Whispering, he questioned, "Randel, where's your gun?"

I replied, "In my holster. Live and learn, Wells. When that son-of-a-bitch comes out, I'm gonna take his leg off just below the knee."

"What if he don't run this way, Randel?"

"He will! But if that bastard comes out and goes the other way, one of the other officers will nail him. I don't want to catch anyone in crossfire. Get ready now, Wells, he'll come this way. Oh, by the way, if I tell you to shoot him, you shoot to kill and don't miss."

"Are you sure, Randel?" The sound of Wells voice made me wonder if he were up to the task. *One hellava time to find out*! *He will be… He's my partner.*

Another police car arrived silently and the area would soon be cordoned off and surrounded. However, Bubba was none the wiser. He backed out the door to the 7-11 looked both ways and headed right toward me. *My luck's runnin' with me,* I thought. As he ran by, I swung my baton like a bat and hit him hard in the shin. *Ouch! What a loud crack that made. Home run!* It busted his bone in a compound fracture. Blood was seeping through his pants leg like water through a sieve. He went down, surprised as hell, and hurting like a son-of-a-gun.

His bag with candy, chips, sodas and money flew in front of him. His gun flew about ten feet from where he lay; he completely forgot about his gun and goodies. I was on him in a second, my knee on his neck, cuffing him fast. As I stood over him, he started screaming like a little banshee even though he was 30-ish and well over 6' tall. "My laig, my laig, you broke my damned laig!" He rolled back and forth on the ground yelling for help. When Mercy Ambulance and the Fire Department arrived, the medics ran to the downed robber.

"Forget him," I stated emphatically, "I don't care if he bleeds to death. Go see if anyone inside needs help first." Wells was already inside clearing the store, checking for other possible robbers and releasing the manager and Stacy from a locked storage closet. They had not been harmed.

Sam Sikes, AKA Grumpy, was there in a flash. He advised dispatch, "Code 4," to clear the radio channel. Then he hovered over big Bubba and asked me, "Randel, did this SOB hurt that little Stacy in there? If you did," he directed his comment to Bubba, "I'll hurt your other leg so bad that you won't be able to walk around in the jailhouse for a long time. Those big, dirty boys in there'll like that just fine."

The ambulance attendant, a young woman, that was standing by gasped, "Oh, no, he wouldn't hit him again would he?"

Trying to soothe her, I replied, "No ma'am, Officer Sikes won't hit him, he'll just cut him long and deep with one of his big knives."

I thought she might faint as Sikes continued, "Damn boy, lookie there, your blood's as red as mine." He pushed Bubba's leg with the toe of his shoe. "Hurts like hell don't it?" Hee, hee, hee, hee. Is that bone I see stickin' out of those pants? Hey Randel, good job!"

It seemed as if everybody arrived in unison, which showed how well Las Vegas coordinated things in an emergency. Several backups, Criminalistics and Robbery arrived. We were about finished and Mr. Kaa-Zee, the part-Asian owner of the 7-11, had thanked us at least a thousand times. Stacy, that sweet little girl, although she had been terrified and was still shaking, brought out an iced tea for me, my favorite drink. "Thank you, Officer Randel, you saved my life. I was so happy to see that it was you."

Wells stuck his head out the door and motioned with his hand to his mouth that he would appreciate a drink too. I thought, *yeah, and you're wonderin' why I got a drink before you did, when you went in first. Experience, boy, experience!* I asked Mr. Kaa-Zee if everyone could come inside from the raging heat for something to drink. I assured, "Mr. Kaa-Zee, I will be glad to pay for all the drinks."

He replied very respectfully with a semi-bow, "No, no, Offica Landel, you no pay. No! You numba *One,* much better than numba ten. All dlinks on house. Kaa-Zee belly glateful too."

THE NAKED CITY

"FRANK-3 ENROUTE!"

Dispatch called reporting that one of the girls from the Naked City had reported that someone tried to jimmy her door open during the night. I asked Cheri', the dispatcher, for the particulars so that I could go check it. I took my new partner with me.

The Naked City was a part of my regular patrol. It is a borough within Las Vegas that runs west of Las Vegas Boulevard and behind the towering, extravagant Stratosphere Casino and Hotel. Most of the showgirls lived in that area. They were just regular working girls, beautiful ladies that needed to be suntanned and gorgeous when they performed on stage. This was before all the tanning salons came about and these girls used the sun's natural rays for tanning. They resided in apartments and condos that had high, private walls around the pool areas. Picture fifteen to twenty naked women lying around a pool with nothing on but tanning lotion. *Whew, what a sight*! These girls were not allowed to show any tanning lines from bathing suits or bras. The only thing they came outside with was a towel, sandals and maybe sunglasses.

I knew most of these girls, and occasionally I would receive a call from dispatch to check on an apartment of one of the bevy of beauties. Sometimes it was an attempted break-in, or someone had tried to sell drugs, but usually it was reporting a peeping tom, trying to watch the girls. *Go figure.*

I would casually drop by the pool area to ask for the particular lady in question. Someone would jump up and say, 'Oh, Officer Randel, I'll get you some iced tea. It's brewed.' Another would say, 'Officer Randel, I made cookies this morning and I'll bring some for you.' Off they would run, naked as jay birds, their tight little buttocks showing no jiggling and with only a towel drawn up to their chin, barely covering their shapely bosoms. It was a tough job but someone had to do it. I patrolled that area for over three years. I was spoiled, oh so spoiled by these ladies.

As I said, on this particular call, I took my new partner with me. Okay, so you need to know a little about Willy Wells. He was a rookie, young, chaste and naïve, fresh out of the Police Academy. He was tall, slender and good-looking, with sandy-blond hair and not even peach fuzz yet on his face. He was far sighted so he wore prescription sunglasses. His actions showed that he thought he looked pretty sharp in his fully attired new uniform.

We strolled into the private pool area of a set of apartments to ask for Sarah. As I closed the gate behind me, I heard Willy say, "Oh God, here goes my career." I looked at him and he was looking down at the ground, trying not to see what he thought he saw and was certain he should not be looking at.

About that time four of the girls jumped up, scurried over to us, and told me one would bring iced tea, another just baked brownies and another was Sarah. The last one approached Willy, whose innocent baby face was bright red with embarrassment. This sweetie said, "Officer Randel," as she looked into Willy's face, "who is this handsome young man?" Obviously flirting, she ran her long manicured finger across his chin, and he turned his head to avert her attention and to not look at her luscious body.

I introduced Willy to all the ladies and left him on watch as I went with Sarah to look at her apartment door that had been jimmied. When I returned, Willy was sitting in a lounge chair with sweet, young, naked ladies crowded around him. He was nervous and animated but he was trying to chat normally with the girls. I let him

Frank-3 Enroute

know with a motion of my head that it was time to leave. He politely excused himself, rose, trying not to brush against any of the ladies bare parts, and made a quick exit with me following him. I assured Sarah that I would send Tony from A-1 Key and Lock to change her locks. I waved a goodbye to the Naked City showgirls and promised I would bring Wells with me again.

As we were leaving the complex, I noticed that Willy was chewing on something. I asked in a panicked voice, "Willy, what the hell are you doing?"

"Eating a brownie, Randel," he said with his mouth full.

"Where did you get that?"

"One of the ladies brought me this bag of brownies for us."

"And you just took it and are eating from it? Didn't your mama ever tell you not to take candy from strangers?"

"Yeah."

"Well, did you know that person?"

"No."

"Were you in her house?"

"No."

"Then you never saw if her kitchen was clean or nasty did you?"

"No."

"What was her name and what did she look like?"

Willy was totally horrified as he spat out the rest of the brownie on the sidewalk. "Her name was Lila. She was a tall red-head with freckles across her nose."

"Did she have green eyes?"

"Yes, I think so."

"Think so! Man, you're supposed to know so. What did they teach you at the Academy?"

"I'm sorry, Randel," he replied sheepishly.

"Don't you know that people lace brownies and cookies with drugs? Give me that bag and get in the car."

Willy, who was totally mortified and certain he might have ingested a poisonous substance, climbed into the passenger seat and sat shamefaced. I took the bag around to the driver's side of the car. I opened the bag and withdrew a brownie taking a mouthful as I opened the car door. Willy looked at me in utter shock. "You're not gonna eat one of those are you, Randel? What about the stranger and poison?"

"Oh hell," I mumbled, "I know Lila. Even been in her house. She's okay." I swallowed just before I started laughing aloud.

"Damn you, Randel, damn your hide!" Willy reached over and grabbed the bag of delicious brownies from my hand. At least he found out I had a sense of humor.

BLUE CADILLAC

I FELT SADDENED ABOUT THE WAY the Naked City had aged and deteriorated. The elderly population couldn't sell their homes and move to better living quarters. Many apartment dweller's landlords had offered to sell their accommodations to them at discounts as condominiums. Those who could purchased their dwellings and lived among the other slumlord apartments and houses. This section was comprised of low-income families with many unsupervised youth; juveniles easily led down the wrong paths of life. In my experience, poverty breeds malcontent and apathy, wont and need, and the desire to achieve life's sustenance in any way possible. For the callused and hardened that means robbing those who can't defend themselves or their possessions.

I was patrolling that sector daily and had become well acquainted with many of the inhabitants, both the innocent, and the misguided, in other words, the dirt bags. The elderly relied on the Metro Police Officers to protect them and to capture those who stole from them. One such lady was an elderly woman, about seventy-five, five foot three, snow-white hair, an amiable smile and good nature. She lived on the second floor of a building in her small condominium. She parked her aged, blue Cadillac in the parking area off the alley behind the building. She had been robbed of tires and battery several times. Each time she had reported it, another officer had come to her home, taken the report and nothing had been done about it. Consequently, she was a victim again and again. Finally, when she called Gray's Auto on Commerce for another battery, Gray told her to call the police and to ask specifically for Officer Randel because he cared about the older people and would take care of her.

She did as he said and the dispatcher called me. "Frank-3, copy a call. Mrs. Jenkins at apartment 225 at the Cincinnati Arms has had her car vandalized again. She has asked that you and only you take this call."

"**Frank-3 enroute.**" When Wells and I arrived, I knocked on the door and Mrs. Jenkins peeked out the peephole and opened the door, leaving the chain attached. "Good morning, Mrs. Jenkins, I am Officer Randel and this is my partner, Willy Wells. You called for assistance. May we come in?"

"Oh, Officer Randel, Officer Wells, please come in." She unbolted the door and ushered us into her small, spotless home. "I'm so sorry that I had to call you for help. I just didn't know what else to do."

"Don't you worry, ma'am. It's no bother. This is what we do. We're paid to work for you."

She looked more at ease. "Just a minute and I will serve you some hot tea." She toddled into her kitchen where she took petite, flowered, china teacups and saucers and brought them to her coffee table. "I made some lovely tea biscuits when I knew it would be you coming. The tea is still steeping. Do you use lemon or cream, Officer Wells?"

"Ma'am," I interrupted, "Maybe you shouldn't use your good china for Willy or me. Willy's clumsy and might break your cups and saucers." I thought, *I guess I can down one cup of 'hot' tea.* "Maybe you have a big old cup that Wells can't destroy."

Wells frowned at me, then turned and graciously told Mrs. Jenkins, "I will be extra careful with your beautiful china and, thank you, I use lemon." Joyfully, she returned with a tray laden with tea biscuits and a cute little teapot, sugar bowl and creamer that matched her cups.

Reminiscent of days gone by, I believed. "Mrs. Jenkins, can you tell us about your car and how many times it has been vandalized?"

Tears welling in her gray-blue eyes, she began, "In the last two months I have had to replace three batteries and six tires and wheel covers. That just leaves me in a tizzy when I need to go to the store. I have to call the police and Gray's Auto and then I'm afraid to leave my house. I just don't have the money to replace things either."

"Mrs. Jenkins, ma'am, after tomorrow you will not have to worry. Wells and I will take care of your problem."

"Thank you, thank you, Officer Randel. But how do you know my car won't be bothered again after tomorrow?"

"Don't you worry your pretty little head about that, ma'am. Just trust me."

After we left Mrs. Jenkins' home, Wells asked me the same thing, but in different language, "Randel, how in the hell are you gonna protect her car? Oh no, don't tell me. I don't want to know. Not if this is gonna cost me my job!"

"Don't worry Wells, just meet me at the station at five in the morning. Dress out and we'll come over here and TCB." (Take Care of Business).

That next morning we parked about three blocks away and walked toward the alley behind the Cincinnati Arms. We spotted three boozed blacks staggering back and forth against the fence near Mrs. Jenkins' car. I could see they were just hangin' out, but I sent Wells to the front of the apartment's egress so they could not run away. I walked up to the young blacks and told them to strike a pose against the fence. I cuffed first one and then another as Wells arrived and cuffed the third. "Hey man, we not be doin' nothin' to bother you about, Randel," the larger kid ranted.

"That's Officer Randel to you, bub, and how do you know who I am?"

"We all knows One Glove." It was pretty well known in Vegas that I always wore one, beige, tanned-leather glove, which, incidentally was not regulation. "That be you, man, One Glove, Randel."

I thumped him on his thick noggin', "That's Officer Randel, I said!" I took names as Wells returned for our patrol car. We brought the perps up on the MDT (Mobile Digital Terminal) and found over ten thousand dollars in bench warrants against them. "Okay, Arthur," I said to the biggest of the three, "I see you're stealing from my grandmother's car here, so to jail you go. With all your warrants and stealin' too, you'll pull 5 to 10 years."

"Sur, Officer Randel, please, we ain't stealin' no car, man. We jus' hangin'."

"Yeah, hangin' and drinkin' and usin' and who knows what else," chimed in Wells. *This boy's learnin'* I surmised.

"Arthur, I don't give a damn if you're *not* messin' with that car. What I see is three no-good, lazy mo-fos hangin' around my grandmother's car. The very car that has been vandalized six or seven times. Now, let me explain this to you. If you want to be allowed to stay on the street, you'll take care of her car from this moment on. If anything and I mean *anything* happens to her car, or to her apartment, or to her, you go to jail. No questions! Do we understand each other?"

"But how'm I gonna pro-tect her car? I can't be here all day."

"That's your problem, Arthur. See Officer Wells here, he'd love to book you because he likes my grandmother's tea and cookies." The three blacks looked frightened and unsure as we uncuffed them. "Now, get the hell out of here and do whatever you need to do to protect my grandmother's car." I scowled at the three as I shoved the youngest boy away from me. "And you, Short Shanks, no more drinkin', drugs or sassin' your mama or I'll personally send you to Juvie. That clear?" He was shaking all over and his shoes were wet, as was the ground where he stood. He nodded affirmatively and ran toward the third boy.

"Wa' he goin' do 'bout da warrant, Bubba? He dinna say nuttin' 'bout da warrant."

Bubba jabbed Short Shanks sharply in the ribs with his elbow. "Shut yur mouf nigga. He lettin' us go. Git! Now git!"

Willy and I returned to the patrol car and watched as the three reformed black boys walked away. As they passed Mrs. Jenkins' car, Arthur used the bottom of his T-shirt to buff the headlights. I felt certain that Mrs. Jenkins and her blue Cadillac would be well watched from then on. "Wells, just in case, remind me to call Tony and have him install a wrought-iron screen door with a lock on Mrs. Jenkins' front door."

SPEECHLESS

EVERY POLICE OFFICER LEARNS TO DEAL with situations entailing traffic control devices. On this particular beautiful, sunny, summer day, I was out with rookie, Willy Wells, at the big intersection of Las Vegas Blvd., Main Street, Paradise and St. Louis. This is an intersection where a red light is frequently run and there is a high accident rate. It was about 10:30 a.m. and I had been teaching Wells how to conduct vehicle stops after the driver had run the light. I had demonstrated several stops, giving Willy the opportunity to observe how I made my stops and where I placed the patrol car to insure my safety. I taught him how to report the stopped vehicle on the radio, making sure that he knew that the code was a 467 for a traffic stop. He was shown how to approach the vehicle and the safe distances and posturing to keep him out of harms way.

I informed Willy, "Okay Wells, the next stop is yours." It was not but a few minutes when we watched as a two-seat, red Thunderbird with a blond woman driver increased speed and barreled through the intersection on a red light. We had already changed driver's positions so when I said, "Okay, this one is yours, go get her," Willy turned on the red lights and the siren and proceeded safely through the intersection, following her down Paradise. The lights were flashing and he ran the siren blasts a few times before the woman noticed him and pulled over.

Willy pulled to the correct distance and placed the patrol car off center with his driver's side extended to properly protect the officer from cars that would pass from behind. Willy called control and advised, "Frank-3, copy a 467 at Paradise, just east of Las Vegas Blvd., the license plate, Baker Charlie Nora, 788, NV, occupied by one female." Wells exited the car and unfastened his holster so that his gun was ready should he need it. He waited for a few seconds, watching the driver through the back window and then he checked out the trunk of the car, tested it with his right hand and made certain that it was locked. He then walked toward the driver, stopping behind her window at the post between the door and the back of the car.

I was sitting on the passenger side of the patrol car with my door open, observing everything that Willy was doing and ready to leave my position if he needed me. Willy leaned forward as the woman opened her window and I did not see him say a word. He properly had his right hand on his holstered gun and as the lady turned far left to see him, he stood dead still for a few seconds and then started to back away. He still had not uttered a word to the woman. Noticing this, I immediately stood and loosened my gun from my holster and placed it behind my back. I looked at Willy as he exaggeratedly pointed his right index finger, moving his whole hand directly at the female. Still, he was not saying anything, but his lips were moving and I thought that he mouthed, 'Wow,' but I wasn't sure because no sound came from him. Willy kept pointing as he backed the entire way to the passenger side of the patrol car.

Totally unable to understand him or to grasp the meaning of his pointing gestures, I walked toward him. As we met, Willy, still gesturing radically, emitted, "Did you see that?" Looking from me to her, he repeated almost silently, "Did you see *that?*"

"Willy, what the hell is wrong with you, speak up!"

"Did you see that?" He still motioned toward the lady.

Not knowing what was going on, if there was a safety problem, and definitely not knowing what the circumstances were, I cautioned Willy to stay where he was. I moved forward, checking the trunk of the car and proceeding to the door post of the driver's side. With my weapon behind my back, I leaned slightly forward to observe the driver and saw a beautiful girl with nothing covering her entire body but a pair of pink, bikini panties, and gorgeous, blond hair with long tresses that dangled just below her shoulders, covering nothing. Astonished as I was, I had to admit that she looked good! I carefully holstered my weapon and in my normal, calm, nothing affects me manner, I proceeded, "Excuse me, ma'am, may I see your driver's license, registration and proof of insurance, please."

In an absolutely compliant manner she stated, "Oh sure, officer," as she jiggled her hooters at me. She immediately removed her seat belt, leaned over and reached into the glove box and took out her registration and proof of insurance. I watched carefully for anything threatening in the glove box, but I did not fail to notice her trim waistline and the dimples on the back of her buttock just above her panty-line. She shifted her large bosom back toward me as she withdrew her license from a small bag and wiggled again as she handed me all three items. "Here you go, officer." She made a complete sideways turn, extending her breasts to full view, so that she could see me and I could *see her*, and she read my badge. "Officer Randel," she continued, smiling sweetly, "Is there anything else I can do?"

Damn, I'm glad I'm wearing sunglasses so she can't see how wide open my eyes are. Now I know why Willy couldn't say a word. In a professional tone, I continued, "No, ma'am. Are you aware that we stopped you for running the red light at Las Vegas Blvd. and Paradise?"

"Oh, I did? I'm sorry."

While she was talking to me, I kept my eyes on her beautiful face, watching her expressions as she gave me her information. It was a hard thing to do, as she kept wiggling and she kept jiggling with every movement. "Ma'am, will you please wait patiently in your car and I will be right back." I backed to the end of her car and walked sideways, keeping an eye on her back, as I went to the passenger side of the patrol car to check on her identification. Willy, who was standing as if at attention at the driver's side door, commented brazenly, "Did you see 'em? Did you see 'em, Randel?"

Calmly I questioned, "Did I see what?"

"You didn't see 'em!"

"See what?"

He exclaimed, making hand gestures about the size of cantaloupes, "The front of her, her hooters!"

"Yeah, I saw them, but what does that have to do with the ticket?"

"Uh, I ah, don't know."

I instructed calmly, "Let's run her up and see if she has any outstanding tickets or warrants." Willy told me that he had already run the license tag and it was clean. Further checking with NCIC and local revealed no previous tickets, and no warrants. I explained to Willy that she had told me that she was a dancer and was on her way home after work. I asked her where she worked and she explained that it was at Crazy Horse Two.

As I sat in the patrol car and started to write the ticket, Willy looked at me in amazement. "Are you writing her a ticket?" he questioned in disbelief.

"Yes, I'm writing her a ticket for running a traffic control device."

"You're really gonna ticket *her?*"

"Yes!"

"I wouldn't," he conceded.

That's when I had to teach Willy a lasting lesson. "Did we ticket the young man that just ran the light before she did?"

"Yes."

"And did we ticket the other drivers that we stopped for running a traffic control device?"

"Yeah, but..."

"So," I interrupted, "If we ticketed the others for failure to observe the red light, who are we going to ticket here?"

"Her, I guess," Wells uttered sadly and rather pitifully.

"That's right. There can be no favoritism when we are enforcing the law." I finished the ticket and approached the driver's side of the Thunderbird where Miss Wagner was waiting, tapping her bright, long fingernails on the steering wheel. "Miss Wagner, you are receiving a ticket for failure to safely observe or execute the directions of a traffic control device, a red light. Please sign here." I advised her that signing the ticket was in no way an admission of guilt. "It says that you will appear in court on said date and time. Failure to do so means that a bench warrant will be issued for you. Do you understand?"

I handed her the ticket pad and she signed it very cheerfully. "You don't have to worry, Officer Randel, you won't have to appear in court. I'll just pay the ticket." She bounced lightheartedly as she handed me the book. "You know what, Officer Randel, I really like you officers from Metro."

"Thank you Miss Wagner," I professionally replied as I handed her the ticket, her license, registration and proof of insurance. "Have a nice day, ma'am." In my mind, *Wow! You already made my day.*

She thanked me with a nice jiggle and a sweet smile.

"Please drive carefully. We wouldn't want to see you injured or killed because of failure to yield to the traffic signal."

"Maybe I'll see you again, Officer Randel. Come down to the Crazy Horse Two sometime and watch me work," she invited as she started her engine and drove slowly away.

Willy questioned, "You're gonna void that ticket aren't you Randel?"

"No, Wells, I'm not."

"Well, did you get her phone number?"

"Of course not, Willy. You can't take a phone number off a legal document and use it for personal interests. What if she's really angry and you called her? She could make a complaint to the department and you would be disciplined severely or fired. It's not worth the risk, and it just isn't right. Let's get some lunch, while I explain the rest to you."

We hit Don Pedros at Charleston and Las Vegas Blvd. and had delicious Mexican food. Maria, the cute little Hispanic waitress, greeted me pleasantly and had my iced tea ready immediately. Wells commented that she had not been as friendly to him as she was to me. "That's because she doesn't like you, Willy. She only likes me," I chided.

"I don't understand why all the waitresses like you, Randel. You're impatient and rude about your ice tea."

But I'm really not! "Yeah, but they still love me and so do you, Wells," I offered with my genuine and friendly grin. Wells did not say another word but shyly smiled back at me. I continued my tutelage about fairness and discrimination between the sexes and the boy took it all in. I was sure that Willy was still dreamily pondering the fact that he would have rather had her phone number and not have given her a ticket.

Shortly after we resumed our duty, we were ordered to the sheriff's office because there had been a complaint lodged against us. Wells immediately lamented, "There we go again. There goes my career, because of *them*!" He held out his hands mocking the size of the bosoms he had seen earlier.

"Willy, don't worry, it's no big deal. That may not even be what the sheriff wants to see us about."

"No, no. It is a big deal, Randel. You always say it's nothing, but I'm forever getting called in with you. I'm still a rookie, and I have my whole life in front of me. And every time I turn around, we're being called in for something. I don't know how you do it."

Sheriff Morgan greeted us and asked how we were doing. I informed him that we were fine and had been taking care of his city. He expounded, "I got a strange call today, Officer Randel. By the way, who is this young officer with you?"

"This is Willy Wells, Sheriff Morgan. He is a rookie from the Academy and is new to the department. I have been working with him for a few weeks as his FTO." (Field Training Officer)

"Welcome to the department, Officer Wells. You have the privilege of training under one of the best officers that Metro has to offer. What do you think of all this?"

"Thank you, sir, but I'm still not sure what this is all about or what is going to happen to me."

Sheriff Morgan laughed heartily and assured Wells that he would enjoy the department. The sheriff explained, however, that he had received a complaint from a young woman that had been stopped and ticketed by an Officer Randel and a young officer wearing glasses. He asked for verification and I reassured him that we had properly stopped, identified, and ticketed the woman in question.

I asked, "Did she complain about the ticket?"

"Oh no, Randel. She said that you were very polite and courteous, and that she would just pay the ticket. But she wanted to know why you didn't complement her on having a nice body, and I want you to explain that to me."

"Well, Sheriff, she didn't have anything on but a pink pair of panties."

Surprised, he offered, "Oh, I didn't know that."

"She did have a very nice body, but I had to take care of business and give her that ticket. 'Cause if I was looking at what she didn't have covered we'd be in a lot of trouble. But, Officer Willy got a good look at those hooters," I admitted.

Willy's baby face turned as red as a beet, and he couldn't even defend himself. All he could say was, "Sheriff, I was…I was…I was…" Finally, he uttered in complete supplication as he indicated with his hands, "But you should have seen 'em, sir, you should have seen 'em."

Sheriff Morgan, the best man there was around, was an officer that had come up through the ranks and he appreciated a good joke. He admonished Wells by saying, "You'll go far Officer Wells, just keep those eyes forward. Good job, Randel. You two have a good day."

As we exited the building, Willy professed, "Oh dear God, Randel, I was sure he was going to fire me when you told him I was looking at her boobs. Why the hell did you say that?"

"Just because you are a rookie, Willy, and you can still get away with shit like that. A trained officer can never see what he is not supposed to see and is supposed to see everything else. I knew that today you had sure seen a wonderful sight with those young eyes of yours. I'm sure that if you go to confession you'll have to admit that you've never had the opportunity to look so long at such a delicious sight before."

"Yeah," Willy smiled broadly, "and I have to confess, Randel, that I've never see anything like those hooters before."

Shaking my head in agreement, I thought, *I'm sure he'll never see anything up close like that in church either!*

THE OFFICE

THE OFFICE WASN'T WHERE MY DAY began or ended, but it was the place where I went to have a few minutes to myself to think and to work on reports and to dictate. Not too many people visited me there, except my partner, the sergeant and occasionally the captain. We had recently lost our secretary of six years when her husband was transferred to another city. My partner and I had a great working relationship with her and I hated to see Sandy go; I was afraid she was irreplaceable.

It was about 08:00 hrs. when I stomped into my cubicle and flopped into my chair. I was making my desk as neat and orderly as a non-compulsive person could make it. I was staring at my recent orders when my partner, Sam Sikes, sidled into the doorway, leaned heavily against the frame and crossed his long legs at the ankles. Sam, AKA Grumpy, was having a bad morning. I don't think it had to do anything with the fact that the sergeant had told him that he had to pay for some food and things that he eaten. Actually, I was the one that had spent the money. "Randel," he began in his deep, raspy, rugged, gritty voice, "You gonna have that late report for the sergeant by noon?"

"What the hell are you talking about, Grumpy. I ain't doin' any report this morning."

"The one there on your desk, ass hole." He took two steps toward my desk and pointed. "I put it there with the sergeant's request. I sure as hell ain't gonna do it. I called for a typist earlier, but I don't think they're sending one."

I stood, picked up the papers and circling my desk, reiterated, "I'm not doing this, Grumpy, it's about time you learned to type." I made an effort to shove them at Sikes.

"Don't come at me with those papers, Randel, or I'll cut you long, hard and deep and watch you bleed to death."

"Like hell you will, Sam, I'll shoot you dead before you can unsheath that little thing you call a knife." It would have been the six-inch knife he wore on his belt. "You know better than to bring a knife to a gun fight, you big gorilla."

Sikes leaned silently against the doorframe and withdrew a Winston cigarette from his uniform pocket. *It doesn't matter that this is a non-smoking facility,* I rationalized. *He doesn't give a shit.* Slowly, he placed the drag between his churlish lips, revealing his teeth, yellowed from years of smoking. He removed his lighter from his pant's pocket and quickly flipped it, lighting it and his cigarette in one quick move. His age-spotted hand replaced the lighter as the noxious cloud of smoke drifted behind his wire-rimmed, reading glasses and into his eyes.

"Listen here, boy, I'll hurt you so bad your mama won't even recognize you when I'm done. Now, get to that report. I'm goin' to my office to relax and smoke while you write." He smiled smugly and went next door to his office. I heard his chair squeak as he sat in it.

"Sam," I called, "I forgot to tell you, don't sit your big butt in your chair. I taped a load of C-4 to the bottom and if you get up, it'll blow you to smithereens. They won't even be able to find traces of that cigarette you're smokin'." I laid my head back and gave a great, loud guffaw.

"You dirty SOB. Your scrawny, narrow ass is mine." I sensed Grumpy cautiously feeling beneath his chair as he checked it. "Randel, I have a brand new knife and now I *am* gonna cut you and watch you bleed." I heard him rise from his chair and walk toward my office. "Hey, asshole, wanna catch some breakfast? Maybe I can poison you."

"Sure, let's go next door. They have bacon and eggs, and the food's good. Maybe I can put some rat poison in your coffee." We walked out together unaware that we had a new secretary. We returned in about an hour and went directly to our offices. On my desk was a note saying that Grumpy and I were to report to the sergeant's office.

"Randel, Sikes," the sergeant started, "I guess you haven't met your new secretary yet. However, she came down here after you left for breakfast. I asked if she had met you and she said in a very shaky voice that she didn't think that she wanted to work with you. I was flabbergasted, because nobody has ever turned you down. So I asked her why and explained that we have people that want to stay here and only leave because they get transferred. I told her that you guys are really nice. And she said, and I quote, 'Have you ever heard them threaten each other? One's gonna cut the other, one's going to shoot the other, one's gonna blow the other one up, and their going to poison each other. I can't work up here under those conditions. I'll be a nervous wreck.' I started to laugh and said, 'Aw, no way. They've been doing that for years, and you'll love them. Just go on back to your desk and give it a few days."

We walked back and Grumpy skirted around me and went to his office. I went to the secretarial desk. Sitting pertly at her station was a pudgy, short, brown headed, brown-eyed, young woman, neatly coifed, dressed and wearing high heels. She was nervously fidgeting with a pen and had a paper in front of her. I said in my most polite manner, "Hello, I'm Officer Rod Randel."

Her tender rounded, double chin was quivering as she spoke. I thought, *damn, she's gonna cry.* "I...I'm your new secretary, sir."

"What's your name?"

"Tootie Tillman, sir."

"Tootie," *I liked that name; just as cute as she was,* "just call me Rod. I'm sure we'll get along just fine. You'll meet my partner, Sam Sikes, in a few minutes. We all call him Grumpy because *he is.* If that big lug ever does or says anything to bother you, you come tell me and I'll fix him good. Understand? I'm working on a report that I'll need you to type, Tootie. Do you know where everything is?"

"Yes, thank you, Officer Randel."

"We're glad to have you here, and we're gonna make things good for you. Nobody's gonna bother you; we don't allow it. You're our number one little one. Make yourself at home, and I'll be right back. You'll like it here, I promise." I passed Grumpy in our hallway, raised my eyebrows at him, and nodded toward Tootie. "Our new secretary, Tootie Tillman. Be nice."

Boisterously, he stated, "Hell, Randel, get out of my way. This hall ain't big enough for both of us!" He arched his thick, bushy, brown eyebrows good-naturedly, and mock punched me in my solid six-pack belly.

"Suck in that big, flabby gut of yours, Sikes," I chided, "and there'll be room for the whole damned army."

"Huhrumph," he emitted through his lips as he slipped easily past me. "Ms. Tootie, I'm Officer Sam Sikes. Glad to meet you. They call me Grumpy, and you can too. You'll be working with me and with my partner, Officer Randel. You're gonna like it here, I promise. But, if that cranky boy in there gives you any grief, let me know and I'll cut him for you and watch him bleed to death." I watched from my doorway as Grumpy fiddled with the knife on his gunbelt with one hand, and handed her a paper for typing with the other. Tootie paled as she looked at him and accepted the page. "Can you please add this to the report for Randel? He's a slave driver, so watch him. Besides that, he's a one-way, egotistical, self-centered, conceited asshole. Don't trust anything he does and don't believe anything he tells you. He'll even try to hug you."

Stunned, she senselessly replied, "Oh… oh, okay."

As Grumpy turned to leave, he said, "If you need to borrow one of my knives to use on him, I've got plenty." With that, he turned and strode toward me, slapping me on the shoulder with his big thick hand as he passed. "She'll do just fine," he confirmed as he walked back to his office.

A few minutes later when I went to give Tootie the report to type, she was not at her desk. I watched for a bit and then asked Grumpy where she was. "Hell, I'm not her baby sitter, Hawk. "How would I know? You're the bird that *sees* everything."

"Well, Sam, I thought she might be one of yours, with her little round face, just like your big one, and her wide nose and thick eyebrows, just like yours, and those pudgy, petite hands, just like yours big ones. I know she doesn't look a thing like Kate, but who knows where all you've been." *I liked my analogy to his genetics, and the slur on his reputation.* "I didn't check out her ears yet, under all that brown hair, but I'll bet they're big and stick out just like yours too." *That's a good one,* I praised myself.

"Randel, now you've done it!" He was pulling his big knife from his pocket case, just as Sergeant Blake and Tootie walked into the outer office.

"Officer Randel, Officer Sikes, I hear that you've met Ms. Tootie Tillman, your new secretary. I've told her she'll really like working with you. Excuse us, Ms. Tillman." Turning back to Sikes and me, he stated, "I'd like to see the two of you in my office, *now!*"

Behind closed doors, Sergeant Blake told us that Tootie had come to him in tears stating that she could not work with us because we were violent, threatening each other with guns and knives, and she could not handle being scared out of her wits all the time. She had asked to go back to records from where she had moved. He said, "Tootie got up very quietly and tiptoed to my office and informed me that Grumpy had volunteered to loan his knife to her to cut officer Randel, and he said he had plenty of them and not to worry. Tootie said, 'I never even use a sharp knife in the kitchen.' I tried to console her and asked her to go back to her desk while I talked with you. So, you guys treat her nice and respectful and there won't be any bad words said around her. Treat her professionally; this is a professional office. You officers know that you need a good secretary and I think Tootie will make a fine one for the squad. Go easy on her for a little while so she can settle in. She's a single mother of two, and she needs the upgrade in pay. I expect the best from both of you."

"You've always had our best, Sergeant," I spoke dryly. "Don't we always come through for you?"

"I told Tootie that you and Sikes have been together for twelve or more years and have always talked like that to each other, but that you have never injured one another yet." I thought, *I still remember the time Grumpy hit me with his baton,* still not forgiving him. The sergeant was continuing, "I've asked her to give it three weeks, and if she's not happy, I'll transfer her."

"Hell, Sergeant," espoused Grumpy, "I'll treat her just like she's my very own daughter!" I swore that his down-turned countenance raised slightly and his lips almost broke into a smile as he turned and looked at me with great satisfaction, just like the Cheshire Cat. He rose his six-foot-four body and took his size fourteen feet down the hall in front of me.

"Sikes, hold up a minute," I called. "I was very nice to her, how about you?"

Grumpy said, "Yeah, I was very nice to her. I even offered her one of my knives to cut you long, deep and hard and watch you bleed to death, Randel."

I just gaped at him and suggested, "No wonder she was scared, look at you!"

"Yeah, look at me!" He arrogantly went back to his office, and I returned to mine.

After a few moments of quiet reflection, which is what I used my cubicle for, I went to Tootie and apologized, "If we scared you, girl, we're sorry. Grumpy shouldn't have frightened you or offered to loan you his knife. You'll get to like us, I promise. We'll even take you out to lunch sometimes, and we're a good bunch. Don't pay any attention to Sikes, he was born grumpy." Although Tootie only gawked at me, I felt satisfied and reentered my office.

Next thing I know Grumpy's back at her desk asking, "What did the asshole in there say to you?"

Tootie said tactfully, "Nothing."

Grumpy walked close to Tootie and held out his big hand. "Ms. Tootie," he said graciously, taking her smaller hand in his and placing his other hand over hers, "I'm bettin' you'll like it here with us." I knew his handshake would be strong and not overpowering, but as I watched, he did tend to pump her short arm a little too much.

I had to put in my two cents worth. "Don't let him break your arm, Tootie," I warned protectively. "He's tougher than he thinks. Say, we're going to lunch at the Red Lobster. Why don't you come along? I'm driving and Grumpy's buying today," I poured out the invitation hospitably. *Why not! He paid the chit for my previous lunches this morning. Ha!*

Her already white complexion paled considerably as she stammered, "Thank you, Officer Randel, but…but I already have plans for today." *We've scared this poor girl half to death,* I surmised.

"Okay, Tootie, tomorrow or the next day or so we'll all go to lunch together. We'll invite the sergeant too. How's that? That way you won't have to be afraid of my partner here."

Shyly she responded, "That will be wonderful, Officer Randel."

"Little girl," Grumpy proffered, "I'll take good care of you so this big blowhard won't bother you. Just remember what I told you earlier. "Don't you worry. I'll handle him; I'll make him bleed a really long time." He walked proudly back to his office.

I smiled and shook my head and Tootie timidly smiled back at me. It was over a month before we could convince Tootie that we would not eat her alive or kill each other, and she finally went to lunch with the two of us. Shortly after that she saw the sergeant who told me she had said, 'I love those two guys, Sergeant. They're the nicest guys I've ever met.'

BREAKFAST BURGLAR I

07:00 HRS. SATURDAY MORNING BRIEFING. THE lieutenant informed us that there were several homes that had been broken into by a burglar or burglars in the Rexford area. The graveyard units were still out taking reports. The police officers would be detained for some time since the burglaries had just been reported in the last hour or so. The lieutenant wanted to relieve those officers so their units could finish their night and come in to fill out their reports. He wanted Sam Sikes and me to take over their investigations. I was riding with Willy Wells and Sam was working with rookie, Benson.

We left the briefing, stopping at the 7-11 for donuts and coffee for the graveyard crew. Jenny, the sweet little woman behind the counter had my iced tea ready for me. I laid a twenty on the counter and told her to keep the change. We hit the street heading to Rexford, which is just off Oakey and Las Vegas Blvd. Most of the houses in that area are occupied by senior citizens. Willy and I arrived at the first house and spoke with the officer that was taking a report and shared the coffee and donuts, leaving the rest for them to distribute, and we took over the case.

Inside, and according to the elderly couple, their home was entered in the early morning while they were sleeping. The aged couple,

Oscar and his wife, Tilly, both in their eighties, a very sweet man and woman, was intensely upset. The burglar had entered through the kitchen door where he had broken the door's window, reached in, unlocked the door and entered. The burglar had gone into the bedroom where the couple was sleeping, and had lifted Oscar's wallet that was lying on his nightstand next to where he slept. He had taken Tilly's billfold from her purse on the dresser. Also missing were two rings and a man's watch that were on the nightstand.

The couple was distressed because they had heard nothing and when they awoke they noticed that their bedroom door was closed. Neither had closed it and it was their custom to leave it open. When they looked around they noticed that the burglar, obviously only a single individual, had opened the refrigerator, removed link sausages, eggs, bread and butter. He had made a pot of coffee, fried the sausages and eggs and had made himself some toast. He even treated himself to Tilly's homemade strawberry preserves.

He was neither a neat nor an orderly burglar as he left the stove dirty with egg dripping down the front and shells on the stovetop and on the floor. The dirty dishes were on the table, crumbs on the floor and he had cracked Oscar's favorite coffee cup, which he left with several teaspoonsful of sugar in the bottom. The uncooked food had not been returned to the refrigerator. He had, however, left the couples credit cards on the table next to where he had sat. Tilly reported that her mother's hand-embroidered pillowcase from the other bedroom had been taken off the pillow and it appeared that the burglar had used it to take the stolen items. He had apparently left through the same door that he had entered.

I called for Criminalistics and when Maggie arrived, I asked if she could dust carefully for prints and to look for any clues that would help us to discover who this criminal was. The couple, Oscar and Tilly, were quite beside themselves. They could not believe that they could sleep through someone entering their home, and were frightened that they had slept through his cooking and eating while they were in their bedroom.

Wells and I left Maggie to finish her investigation and went to the second house. Again it was an elderly couple whose house had been broken into, except this time, the burglar had actually kicked in the kitchen door. He had removed like items, wallets, billfold, jewelry and a small clock radio. He did not cook, but removed milk from the refrigerator, poured a glass and left the milk sitting on the kitchen cabinet. His glass was sitting on the counter next to the sink. I asked Maggie to dust for prints and she advised me that the burglar had left no prints at either home and that he wore some type of soft, cloth gloves.

'Damn,' I cursed under my breath, *'can't I ever get a break?'*

At the third house, the couple, a little younger than Oscar and Tilly, was very irate. They wondered how the police could allow this to happen in their area. Where were the police when they needed them? We assured them that we would be looking for the burglar and would do everything we could to assure their safety. The old woman was most angry that not only had the burglar destroyed their kitchen door, but that the 'bum', as she put it, had used the restroom and had left the seat up and had wet on her clean floor. She informed me that her husband was better trained than that, and that she had scolded him for making the mess when she went into the bathroom. Of course, he denied it, and then he discovered that the scoundrel had brushed his teeth with the man's toothbrush and had used his Sunday-go-to-meeting expensive cologne, Old Spice, before he left.

Grumpy arrived at the third house as I was talking with that couple. Seeing that the little lady was so upset, he offered, "Ma'am, you can rest assured that I will find that sucker and I'll cut him long, hard and deep, and make him bleed for dirtying your pretty little house." The woman seemed appeased after Grumpy's reassurance. The old gentleman walked outside with us and thanked Grumpy for placating his wife. He said that he did not know how to quiet her when she was so upset and he thought he might just go for a long walk after we left to give her time to straighten the house and to calm down. *I wonder if he will ever come back.*

I sent Willy and Benson to check other homes in the same area. They asked if anyone had seen a strange man in that area, or seen anyone lurking around in the area near the homes, or following anyone in the past week or so. No one had seen anything. At one house, however, the man said that he had heard a dog barking around four or four thirty that morning, but that it did not bark for long. We cautioned each homeowner to watch for the Breakfast Burglar, as we started calling him, and warned them to call the police if anything suspicious happened.

Grumpy and I, along with our partners, spent the rest of the morning and early afternoon stopping people in the area, asking for identification, social security, date of birth, and where they lived. We were hoping to put some shred of evidence together so that we could start to solve the mystery of the Breakfast Burglaries. Despondently, Grumpy grumbled, "The seniors are depending on us, Rod. We have to catch this SOB." However, we came up with nothing that would serve us. We returned to the homes of the elderly that had been burglarized.

Tilly had been crying all day because she realized that the burglar had stolen a special ring that Oscar had given her just a few weeks past when they celebrated their seventieth wedding anniversary. It had been especially made in gold to look like a Cracker Jack ring that he had given her as his first pledge of love when she was twelve and he was fourteen.

Grumpy swore that he would keep an eye on all the pawnshops and that if the ring were found, Tilly could be certain that he would personally return it to her. Tilly gave Grumpy a warm hug and a kiss on his cheek that she tiptoed to reach. I could tell that Sam was touched as he quickly bid her goodbye and went outside to smoke a cigarette. He did not accept affection very well, but I sensed that he really cared about the elderly folks. He told Willy, "I'm gonna catch that SOB. Ain't nobody gonna hurt my Tilly. I'm gonna stab him so bad when I find him that he'll be lookin' at all the knife holes that I leave in his damned body as he's on his way to hell. I'll cut him so long and so hard and deep that he'll bleed out in five seconds, and even the crows won't need to peck his eyes out, 'cause they'll already be lyin' on the street."

I had never seen Grumpy so emotional over a burglary before. Maybe that was why he avoided hugs and kisses and terms of affection. *But, they work every time for me too.* We all went to IHOP for our breakfasts and Grumpy was quiet and sullen. We were all mad, but I could tell that he was not going to let go of this series of burglaries until he had the culprit in jail. Willy and I checked everything in the area that day, dumpsters, alleyways, trashcans, gutters, doorways and pawnshops for any evidence, all to no avail. We were all hoping that the Breakfast Burglar would not come to any of our folk's homes for breakfast again.

ANOTHER MURDER

IT WAS MY DAY OFF; I was doing a ride-along with U. S. Marshal Boston Hoy. We were on Interstate 15 headed south about thirty miles outside of Las Vegas. Hoy was delivering a prisoner to the state penitentiary. We were clipping along at about seventy when Hoy suddenly pulled to a fast stop at the side of the road. He turned on his flashing lights and started backing. He went about the length of two football fields, slowed and backed further. Then he eased off the highway and stared out the windshield. "Look at that piece of turquoise clothing caught on that bush. It isn't even dirty and those are fresh skid marks on the road. Randel, look at those tire tracks leading into the desert. Someone was in a hurry to go nowhere. There's nothing out here. What do you think?"

"Want to take a look-see, Boston?" I asked, as curious as he was. Instead, he checked his odometer then drove forward for half a mile or so until we reached a mile marker. Taking note of its number, he turned around and sped back to the skid marks, pulled a note pad from his pocket and wrote down his position. Then he called in to advise dispatch that he was driving off road with his prisoner secured in the back seat. He gave his position using his proximity to the mile marker ahead.

Careful not to drive over the tire tracks, he bounced the vehicle over rough desert terrain until he reached a shallow ravine. Hoy exited the car and walked toward the ravine, then motioned for me to join him. I rolled down a window then reached over and turned off the engine, removed the keys and opened my door. From the back seat, our prisoner, Mr. Jasper Murdock, bellowed, "You can't leave me in this oven in one hundred degree heat. I'll fry, man!" Ignoring him, I strode to meet Hoy. I mentally noted that an unknown vehicle had driven along side the ravine. Someone had exited the vehicle and walked around to the passenger side, then walked to the edge of the ravine and returned. The vehicle then reversed, turned around and drove back out of the desert. I noted that the single set of footprints leading to the ravine was more deeply imbedded into the sand than those footprints returning.

"Over here, Randel," called Hoy, pointing into the ravine. I covered the distance to him in three long strides. Looking down into the ravine, I saw what appeared to be a naked body of a young woman. *Damn!*

"Why the hell is someone dumping a little girl out here? It doesn't look like she's been here long, Hoy. Let's see if she's still alive." The marshal carefully approached the girl, mindful not to disturb any evidence. He placed his fingers on her neck and shook his head.

"No, and she's still in rigormortis, so she hasn't been dead long either. I'll go call this in, Randel, while you look for anything of note."

This was a young white female, maybe fifteen years old, strawberry blond hair, probably a pretty girl, but not showgirl quality. Her throat had been slit but she had not bled out here. That meant that there was a crime scene somewhere else and only God would know where that was. Some vehicle might have traces of her blood, hair and skin, depending how she was transported. Her fingernails were broken and jagged, and it looked as if she had put up a real fight. Searching the perimeter, I did not find anything of note except that the sagebrush at the ravine had been driven over by the vehicle. If a suspect vehicle were found, it could have sagebrush in the tires or under its body.

I reentered the car as Hoy was talking on the radio with the coroner. She and the crime lab fellows would be along shortly. Hoy ordered another car to transport our prisoner and two other officers to escort him. We would remain on the scene until Homicide arrived.

"Damn, I hate to see something like that," I commented. We'll have to check missing persons and see if that child has been reported. I sure feel sorry for her folks."

"Do you find many bodies dropped like this in the desert, Randel?"

"Once in a while, but they're usually pretty putrid, mostly decomposed, no face left, or eaten by coyotes and hard as hell to identify."

"You guys are gonna make me puke my guts out if you don't quit talkin' like that," Murdock protested.

"You should have thought about things like that before you tried to kill our city council woman, Jasper. Then you wouldn't be sitting here with us in the desert with the sun beating down on your delicate, little body. Just put a sock in it and let us do our jobs," Boston replied.

"That council woman is a real bitch. Never cares about us little guys. She only wants to clean up the city, to make the city more beautiful for tourists and run for mayor. What about us citizens that live in the city?... I'm tellin' you, man, I gotta get outta this car. I'm so hot, I'm sick and I need to take a leak. Help me out here, fellas."

"Do you want room service with that order, Jasper," I rejoined, looking at Hoy with a smile. "I'll help you as soon as the other officers arrive so we can watch you. We can't have you lost or wandering around the desert by yourself. And we sure as hell don't want you screwing up our crime scene."

"Oh, go to hell, Randel," he retorted, sitting back and laying his head against the back of the seat. I knew he was probably spending his time figuring how he could use this stop to his advantage to initiate an escape. Not likely!

Poor Jasper Murdock! He was born the tenth boy in a family of sixteen. His mother was so tired and worn out that she couldn't think of a proper name for him. The midwife had placed 'boy' Murdock on the birth certificate, thinking that the family would name him appropriately later. Well, it seemed that no one took it upon himself or herself to change 'boy' so he was Boy all his young life. That may have had something to do with his lack of self-esteem and the reason that he failed at everything he tried.

He had been in and out of juvie so many times that the guards assigned a special room for him. He felt comfortable there, but when he turned eighteen, he could no longer stay. Boy failed at everything, even being a thief. His rap sheet showed nineteen arrests by the time that he was twenty-one. Always doing something stupid that led us immediately to him, he would smile when we arrested him and confess to either Wells or to me. He would say with pride that we were his favorite police team.

Jasper was twenty-one the last time he stood in front of Judge White for a petty misdemeanor. Just before the judge found him guilty, Boy asked politely if the judge could change his name. Smiling down at Boy's arrest record he asked, "Boy, what would you like your name to be?"

Boy stood there, thinking real hard, but couldn't come up with a name. "I can't decide on a name, judge. Can I think about it and tell you the next time I see you?"

"Does that mean that you intend to appear before me again, Mr. Murdock?" There was snickering from the back of the courtroom. "I think we had better decide on a name today."

"Could the bailiff come over here so I can read his badge?" The judge gave a signal to the bailiff who approached. "What does that say?" he asked.

"Jasper Cordell," replied the bailiff.

"Jasper, that's a fine name. I would like to be Jasper Murdock, judge."

"So it shall be, Mr. Murdock. Do you want to keep Boy in your name? It could read Jasper Boy Murdock."

"That has a purty ring to it, don't it!" he stated with pride. "Yes sir, that'll do just fine."

"All right then Mr. Murdock, the court clerk will take care of the paper work and you should receive a formal birth certificate with that name. Now for the matter before the court, I find you, Jasper

Murdock, guilty of a misdemeanor and sentence you to ten days in county jail and to forty hours of community service. Next case."

Less than two weeks later, Willy and I answered a call about Jasper. He had tried to commit suicide with an old, dirty, 22 calibre rifle that probably had not been fired for years. Jasper had placed it in his mouth and pulled the trigger. His grip must have slipped, for when we arrived he was holding his jaw and his face with a towel and he was bleeding profusely. The wound had entered sideways in his mouth and exited after blowing off his left jaw near the ear. "Offither Randel," he mumbled, "I can't do anything right; not even kill mythelf."

We visited Jasper Boy Murdock in the hospital and I told him, "Jasper you're great! Do you realize that you hold the record for the most arrests and convictions in such a short time in the whole state of Nevada? Imagine, *the record*!" I laid the praise on real thick. Jasper sat more erect and showed a sense of pride.

Jasper slurred past a swollen tongue, "No thit man. No thit! That's thumthin' to be proud of, huh, Offither Willy?"

"Yeah, Jasper, real proud," offered Wells.

On this day, Marshal Hoy and I were transporting Jasper to the state penitentiary for a two-year stint. He would not return to society as naïve as he left and I was sure his rate of recidivism would be as long as his adult rap sheet.

We watched as police units arrived from both directions, sirens blaring and lights blazing. The Coroner's vehicle, a less glitzy, plain-wrapper, gray sedan with small writing on the side door panels, was close behind the cars from Las Vegas. The press had not yet arrived and we were anxious to finish the examination before they came with their cameras and reporters.

I helped the Coroner, Ms. Doli Leija, from her vehicle and kept a hand at her elbow to steady her in the uneven desert. "I hadn't planned to walk in the sand today or I would have brought my tennis shoes. These high heals are not good for this terrain. Thanks, Randel."

When Leija reached the body, she was all business. Her team knew just what to do and what not to touch until she had done her cursory evaluation. "This woman has been strangled before her

Frank-3 Enroute

throat was cut. However, the knife injury appears to be the cause of death. Look at the numerous print marks on her neck. Then look at these marks, like something, a scarf maybe, was tightened around her neck. Whoever it was wanted her dead, and she put up a hell of a battle. Don't let any of these facts out to the press, Rod." Basically, Doli reconfirmed my theory that it was a single person who carried her to the ravine. The crime boys made plaster casts of shoe prints and tire tread marks. Pictures were taken of the corpse and the whole area surrounding her. "I can give you more information when I do my autopsy, but it appears that she has been sexually molested, her inner thighs are bruised, and her vaginal area is distended, raw and bloody. Her ankles and hands have been tied at one time. Her lips are swollen and she has cuts on her lips and her face. That poor little Jane Doe went through hell before she died, Randel. I hope you catch the son of a bitch who did this."

"I'm not assigned to this case, Doli, but I would like to come by tomorrow and see what you found. We're on our way to the pen to drop off a prisoner. But thanks for coming right out. You could have sent an assistant and not ruined your day."

"Well, I was in a boring meeting, and when the dispatcher called and told me you were out here, I chose to take the call. You know I always love to give you a challenge or two, Rod. I'll see you back at the coroner's office tomorrow after four."

"I'll bring the pizza," I chuckled. I always felt ill when I went to the morgue or the coroner's offices. The odors there, no matter how they tried to obliterate them, stuck in my nose for days. I escorted Doli back to her vehicle and as she was turning to sit, I asked her for her shoes. She smiled and let me take her pointed-toe sling-pumps off her tiny feet. I brushed them and slid them back on after I also dusted her feet. There aren't many women I would go to that length for, but Doli was special to me. We had worked together for several years and had become good friends. Her petite, five-foot stature and her ninety-pound soaking wet little body was always wired for action. She was a beautiful, chestnut-brown, American-Indian lady who wore her coal black hair slicked back from her face with a French twist at the back. She always wore dangling earrings and very little makeup. What I found most attractive about Doli was her grand smile and eyes that twinkled making her whole face glow. Her smile was ready 24-7 and we felt good just being around her, in spite of her chosen profession. She joined our group many times for the fellowship, and with her quick wit was the life of the party, but always a lady. If she ever needed a ride, she would ask me to take her home. She was rearing two young children alone; her husband had abandoned her and the children for a younger, more buxom dame. He sure as hell never realized what a jewel he had forever lost.

Hoy changed our route, leaving the other team to deliver Murdock. During our exchange, I heard Jasper tell the other officers that he knew who the murderer was. *Sure you do!* I thought cynically. He offered to tell the name if they would assure him that he could have a reduced sentence.

"Hell no, Murdock," responded the officer, "we aren't taking any confessions today. Get in the back and let's go."

"I still need to take a piss," he extolled. "Randel promised I could take a leak, didn't you?" His eyes looked as if they might be swimming, at least half full.

"Sure, let him go, but watch him," I cautioned.

"How can a man take a leak with his hands behind his back?"

"Okay, cuff him in front. Stay with him," Marshal Hoy ordered.

"I can't go with you starin' at me," Jasper whined at the officer. "Turn your head the other way." *Yeah, you just want a chance to run away while nobody's lookin', you stupid little punk,* I guessed. *Ain't gonna happen!*

The officer said, "Walk no more than ten steps forward, Murdock, and pee. I'll watch and if you have to go bad enough, you will."

Jasper had no more than started his mission when he yelled, "Dear Jesus, Mary and Joseph, Randel, I'm surrounded by rattlers. Help!"

"Don't move," I countered. "Are they coiled?"

"Yeah! What do I do?"

"Stand perfectly still, Boy," I reverted to his old name. "Medic," I hollered to one of the EMT's from the ambulance. "Give me a bottle of anything that's flammable, a soft cloth and a cigarette lighter, pronto! Jasper, look at your shadow. The snakes will move toward your shadow to cool themselves. Are any of them rattling like they're gonna strike?"

"Yeah, man. I'm gonna die. I'm gonna die!"

"You won't die, buddy; just hold on. I'm makin' a bottle rocket. When I throw it, I want you to turn away from your shadow and run like hell in the opposite direction. Then you turn and run back to me. Understand?" The medic ran to me with what I needed. I soaked the cloth he brought, stuck it into the remaining liquid, and then torched it. I threw it with all my might, like a hand grenade, hoping I could reach the snake's nest. It seemed to explode in mid-air, landing right where I wanted it to go. Jasper did as he was told. Then I saw a large sidewinder loping after Jasper. "Run Jasper, one of those snakes is after you." I took the gun from the officer next to me and tried to aim at the fast moving snake, knowing without a doubt that I didn't have a chance in hell of hitting it. Suddenly from the side of me I heard a shotgun blast. I turned and saw Marshal Hoy lower his shotgun as the snake's head dropped to the ground. I cautioned Jasper, "Get over here, you little bastard, you're lucky you're not pushin' up daisies right now."

"Thanks, Marshal. I'm sorry, Randel. Now I've peed all over myself."

"I'm glad I'm not riding with you, Jasper," I said with a wrinkled nose. "However, you are riding with this nice officer who's going to have to write a report as to why he fired his weapon today. You'd better apologize to him and his partner for their trouble." The officer looked at me with a huge question mark in his eyes. "Hell, I'm off duty; I'm not even here," I chided. *Besides, I sure as hell wasn't gonna fire my own 380, Beretta.*

Hoy approached still holding his shotgun. "See me when you get back," Marshal Hoy advised the officer. "I think we can work out our reports together with something about snakes in the area. You giving your gun to Randel could get us all fired. Besides that, Randel isn't even here."

Grinning from ear to ear, Jasper extolled, "Hey, man, can I have the rattles off'n that snake? That'll make a great story to tell where I'm goin'."

"You slap-happy little bastard," growled Hoy, "get back in the vehicle before I find another live snake and let it bite you in the ass."

The other officer was cuffing Jasper behind his back, wrapping the seat belt twice around the cuffs before he snapped it into place. The first officer approached with an entire snake and proceeded to throw it on the back floorboard at Jasper's feet. "Just remember, Boy, they say it doesn't matter what time you kill a snake, it isn't ever really dead until after sundown. This sidewinder has ten rattles and a nub. He's been around for a long time."

Jasper drew his feet up onto the seat, the fear of the Lord clearly in his eyes. "They're just funnin' me, ain't they, Marshal? Randel, is it true, what you said about my shadow?"

I shrugged my shoulders, opened my hands, turned down my mouth and placed a questioning look on my face. "I don't know anything about snakes, Jasper, never seen one before." Everyone laughed.

Jasper asked, "Can I have the rattles, Marshal?"

Hoy smirked, "Sure, and we'll ask the warden to save them for you, and to keep your room reserved." Lowering his shotgun and turning to me, Hoy quizzed, "Did you really think you could kill that damned snake with that pistol, Randel?"

"I wouldn't have killed him, but I might have slowed him down some. I could just see all of us having to head for high ground, and I'd hate to run in this damned heat, especially on my day off."

As the officers were accessing their seats, Jasper shouted, "I know who done that woman, Randel, but I ain't gonna say a word, no sir, not a word."

Like I could believe anything you ever told me, Jasper, I thought.

Fortunately, we passed the members of the TV news headed for the scene just as we left. This little girl's picture would be on the news and hopefully someone would recognize her. We needed any help we could get to identify her.

It took almost forty minutes to return to the sub-station. Hoy and I parted ways and I headed down the hall to my office. My secretary, Tootie, was returning to her desk. "Oh, Officer Randel, I didn't have you scheduled for today. May I help you with anything?"

Frank-3 Enroute

"You don't see me, 'cause I'm not here, Tootie. How are they treatin' you today?"

With a warm smile she returned, "Oh, just fine Officer Randel."

"Tootie, how many times have I told you to call me Rod? Do it, girl, we're not that formal here. Now, you let me know if anybody bothers you, and I'll just go shoot 'em, got that?"

"Okay, Rod, everybody's very nice to me, thank you. Oh, Ms. Crystal Li from KTLV called for you. I told her I was not expecting you today. I put her phone number on your desk."

I thanked Tootie as I entered my office. I knew Crystal would want more information than she could garner from the site, so I called her right back. "Ms. Li, this is Officer Randel from the Las Vegas Metropolitan Police, what can I do for you today?"

"Hi, Rod, you don't have to be so formal. After all… I was just wondering what the scoop was on the murder victim that you found today. Can you share anything that we can use on the twelve o'clock news?"

"No, Hon, this isn't my case. I was just on a ride along with U. S. Marshal Hoy. I'll be glad to give him a heads up so you can contact him for any release. I'm sure they will want to get a picture of her on the news so maybe we can identify her. We have no leads as of now and some facts will not be for publication. You understand, of course, Crystal."

"Oh sure, Rod, but you know that I have to find all the facts I can. That's my job. How's Grumpy doing?"

"Grumpy as usual, Crystal, but I have him under control," I laughed.

"That'll be the day. You two always argue, but I love you both. I'll catch you later, Rod. Take care."

I left the office to try to enjoy the rest of my day off. I couldn't stop thinking of that pretty little girl, wondering who she was and what her parents would be going through when they came for her lifeless little body. I swung through the drive-in for a burger, fries and a large iced tea. I went home, pushed a shoot-em-up western in the VCR, salted my fries, doused them with catsup, ate and then slept through the end of my movie. I hated days off like this one.

UP AND DOWN

For several months, cars in the parking garages of the Mint, the Fremont, the Horse Shoe, and other garages near First and Ogden had been burglarized. A well-dressed, large black man had often been seen hanging around parked cars where victims later found items missing; money, music, stereos, radios or anything that would bring a few bucks were gone. One morning, a previous victim saw this same man loitering in the garage where he was parking his car. Suspicious, he called the police.

Frank-3, copy a call. We have a black suspect in the parking garage at the Mint. A man who was previously robbed has identified him as a possible suspect in the car burglaries. Can you check on it?"

"**Frank-3 enroute**." When Wells and I arrived, a small, heavy-set man with a mustache and white hair met us at the garage entrance.

Excitedly, he pointed upward and declared, "He's on the second floor now, officers. He's breaking into a blue sedan *on the second floor*. I've been trying to keep an eye on him for you. Hurry! Go catch him!"

I drove cautiously, without squealing tires to the second floor where I spotted the culprit reaching through a broken car window.

Ebony-black, approximately 5' 10", large, string-bean frame, short, black, kinky hair, lots of gold jewelry, flashy, gold watch, white-knit short-sleeved, sports shirt, tailored, gray slacks, black leather belt, black and white Adidas... and one tan pillowcase apparently filled with loot. Wells and I were quickly out of the car and running up the ramp. The big son-of-a-gun spotted us as we approached. He started running from us even though I ordered him to freeze. Up he went. Third floor, *I'm gonna catch you, you SOB, and when I do, you're gonna pay. Puff*...fourth floor, with Willy and me hot behind him. And I mean *hot*. Hell, it was already 90 degrees in the shade. Then winding up to the fifth... Willy's longer legs were gaining ground on me. *All this equipment is holding us back, but you don't have anywhere to go you sucker...puff...puff.* When he topped the fifth floor, our perp realized there was nowhere else to go. He turned and pompously looked at us as if to say, 'Hell, you pinko-cops think you've got me. Ha!' Without looking over the side, he put both hands on the top of the south wall and swung his feet over, jumping sideways, like he was just jumping a fence. I saw the pillowcase he was carrying fly over the edge with him.

Willy and I reached the ledge just in time to hear him scream, to see the panic-stricken whites of his eyes and his empty hands clawing the air, along with his feet and legs traveling ninety-to-nothing, trying to save himself. He had no idea that he was five-stories high. There was no place to land except onto the grassy knoll at the bottom of the garage. *Opps!* We watched the hideous sight as our unlucky suspect plummeted down, down, down five stories and hit his head on the only granite boulder on the grassy area next to the sidewalk. His head split gruesomely along with the pillowcase, splattering gray matter, blood, jewelry and radios onto the tailored lawn, leaving his lifeless, twisted body for us to reclaim. Wells, though white as a ghost, did not puke. Instead, he complained, "Oh damn, damn! My career! My poor career! I hate you, Randel."

I wondered, *why's he mad at me? What did I do?*

Wells and I stood by while homicide cleared us of any wrongdoing and the coroner's office sent their people to take custody of the body and to determine the cause of death. Believe me, a rock is always harder than a head. That poor bastard, his parking ticket finally punched, proved the universal theory of gravity. What goes up must come down.

Wells and I decided to catch some lunch after he declared that he was hungry. I thought that as usual he would not want to eat for hours after what he had just seen. However, we went to Tony Roma's where Willy sat, sucking up spaghetti, *made me think of gushy brains*, and I merely drank iced tea. I still could not believe how that guy's head had busted. "Wells," I inquired, "did we say anything to that guy to cause him to jump? Wasn't I polite to him? Called him sir?" I couldn't remember.

Our waitress, Janie, told me I had a telephone call. It was dispatch. "Randel, sorry to disturb your lunch, but we just took a call from the Horse Shoe about Wheel-Chair Annie. Can you take it?"

I knew Cheri' wouldn't call me during lunch unless she had no other choice. "We're on our way." We left a twenty on the table and headed for the car. I was still thinking about being polite.

WHEELCHAIR ANNIE

I'M KNOWN FOR BEING A POLITE guy. My mama and my Grandma Polly taught me manners and told me if they ever heard of me not being polite they would whack me over the head. And from experience, I believed them. I even have a few knots left on my head to prove they meant what they said. So as a police officer I always treat people with respect. It doesn't matter what kind of low-life, scum-suckin' bottom-feeder I'm dealin' with, I always call them sir or ma'am.

As a matter of fact, Wheelchair Annie was a prime example. Annie was one of the nastiest old panhandlers to ever work Fremont St. She arrived every morning, of all things, in a chauffeur-driven, black limousine. The chauffeur would take out her wheelchair, help her into it, hand her the bag that was full of cans, pencils, erasers and her money box, then leave her to work the area from the Sun Dance to the Four Queens. Annie had staked out that area as her own and had run off everyone that tried to infringe on her territory. She would beg passersby to buy a pencil. If they did, she would grin at them with her wrinkled, toothless mouth and thank them. If however, anyone did not buy, she would spit on him or her and call them filthy names. But that was not the worst of Wheelchair Annie. She had a bad habit of goin' into one of the casinos, takin' an elevator, locking it down and doing her business inside. When she was through, Annie would exit, leave the door open and wheel herself back to the street. At least once a week, we would receive a call on Annie.

"Frank-3, copy a call."

I guess it was just my day to answer the casino's call. "**Frank-3, enroute.**"

My partner, Willy, and I arrived at the Mint Casino where security had detained Annie. She was screechin' and cussin' and makin' a scene for all the patrons to observe. There were three security guards standing around her so she couldn't leave. She was running her chair into first one and then another and spitting on them and on anyone else she could. She looked and acted worse than Betty Davis when she played Apple Annie in <u>Pocketful of Miracles</u>.

Willy and I approached and I asked, "What seems to be the problem here?" *Okay, Annie, I know the problem,* I thought. Well, I didn't have time to draw a breath before Annie started in on me.

"You filthy pig! Don't think you're gonna get your dirty hands on me. Let me outa' this lousy hole. I gotta make a livin'."

"Wait just a minute, ma'am," I said in my most convincing polite voice. "Let me speak to security and find out what the problem is, please." With that I turned to the security chief who informed me where Annie had sullied their premises. I proceeded to the elevator where a janitor was washing down the walls and the floor. The evidence was still reeking like shit, the same putrid smell that was all around Annie. I returned to Annie and stated, "Ma'am, you've crapped in their elevator and I am going to issue you a citation to appear in court."

"I ain't appearin' in no damned court even if Clarence Darrow's the Judge. Let me the f... out of here!"

"Excuse me, ma'am," I proceeded, coming as close to Annie as I dared. "Please drop your voice so we can get on with our business. You will have to appear in court, ma'am, or we'll have to arrest you."

With that, Wheelchair Annie hocked a big fluggy and spit it in my face. Thoroughly disgusted, I drew my handkerchief from my pocket and wiped away the slime. Then I politely stated, "You have just battered an officer of the law, and we are going to arrest you, ma'am."

With a big guffaw, Annie cackled, "You won't arrest a poor old lady in a wheelchair. You'll be the laughin' stock at the jail."

"Well, ma'am, that's just what we're gonna do. You've given me no choice. I'm gonna have to book you." I spotted a squad car that had arrived and told her, "Those nice officers will be happy to drive you to the jail." I'm thinking, *I sure as hell don't want your stench in my car.*

"I'm not gettin' outta my wheelchair and you can't make me." She tightly gripped the arms of her chair.

My partner, Officer Willy, had had almost enough of Annie, too. "Annie," he said, "maybe if you apologize to Officer Momma for spitting on him, he won't arrest you."

"Apologize! In a pigs eye! Lean over here you asshole and I'll lick your whiskers clean." Annie stuck out her tongue and rolled it around. Next she snickered and snorted, blowing snot from her nose, and then licking it, she smacked her lips. The long hairs on her protruding chin wiggled like whiskers on a giant rat.

I wanted to puke right there. But, thinking better of it, I turned to Willy, "Let's wheel her out to the sidewalk and call for the paddy wagon." I instructed the other officers, "You can go ahead and clear."

She hollered, "No! Help! Police brutality." We started pushing her and she dragged her feet.

"Okay, ma'am," I responded. "You can stay in your wheelchair." "Willy," I asked, "do you have your handcuffs?"

"Sure do, Jo," he replied.

"Good! Snap your set on her left arm and to her chair. I'll take the right side. Annie, you can stay in that chair as long as you want; we'll just take you to the jail in the wagon. You'll sit there, handcuffed, until I have my apology. Is that perfectly clear, ma'am?"

We called for the paddy wagon and waited until it arrived. Annie seethed and cussed and ranted, but no one paid her any attention. The onlookers had tired of her foul mouth, security had returned to their stations and Willy and I ignored her. She could not move her wheelchair with the cuffs hooked from her wrists to the arms of the chair. We lifted her into the wagon, hooked her to the side rail and followed the wagon to the parking structure at the jail.

We were parked on the ground level and had to walk down to the lower level. As we made our descent, Annie started slipping out of the wheelchair. "Stop, stop, you bastards. Lift me back in my seat. You're hurtin' my gawd damned back."

"Sorry, ma'am," I cautioned, "we can't do anything to help you. We can't touch you until after you're booked, and we have witnesses that we aren't abusing you." Willy gave me a questioning look and shook his head, but he was smiling.

By this time, the fronts of Annie's shoes were dragging on the concrete and she was hanging on for dear life. The incline was pretty steep as parking garages go. "Just let go of me! Go ahead you dirty pigs, kill me."

Suddenly, we hit a protruding, water-drain grate that abruptly stopped all of us. Annie was teetering on the brink of turning over sideways or spilling forward. She was totally at our mercy. "Ma'am," I spoke, in my most mannerly tone, "You really need to apologize for spitting on me and this could all be over. You'll still be charged with a misdemeanor; I can't help that, but we don't have to proceed with the battery charge."

"Go to hell, you bastard!"

"Well, ma'am, I have another solution. I'm just gonna leave you here, stuck on this grate like you are. The first driver that comes down that ramp above you won't be able to stop fast enough to keep from running over you and splattering your carcass all over the street. Of course, Officer Willy and I will be on the side to observe the accident, we'll remove the handcuffs and it will be a very sorrowful event. What do you think about that, Willy?"

"Well, if she won't apologize, that's fine with me." *That's out of character for Willy. Guess he's had enough too!*

Turning to walk down the rest of the incline, Willy and I abandoned Annie. We heard the screech of tires above and knew that we needed to act. However, Annie heard them too. "Okay, Okay, Officer Jo. I'm damned sorry I spit on you. I won't ever do it again. Now can you get me the hell outta here before I get run down?"

"Certainly, ma'am," I responded. "I'd be most happy to oblige."

We wheeled Annie to the side, saving her from a descending squad car and placed her on the walkway at the edge of the garage. We removed our handcuffs and turned to walk away.

Annie struggled to adjust herself in the wheel chair. Angrily she fumed, "You can kiss my sweet ass, you gawd-damned dirty sons-a-bitches. You're gonna pay for this. I'll sue your sorry asses, do you hear me?"

Right then, Willy shook his head. "Oh, here goes my career, Randel," he complained, imagining what I would do next.

I walked another few paces, stopped, counted to ten, and did a slow one-eighty. My face and my eyes scrunched up, and I was boiling. I was breathing hard, my fists were tight, and I approached Wheelchair Annie without compassion. I placed my angry face right up to her putrid nose. I was eye to eye with her swollen, beady eyes. Her rotten breath assaulted me. I raged, "You dirty hag. Your ass is so nasty that no polecat within five hundred miles would even want to sniff you. Get your foul-smelling self and your chair out of here. If you ever see me again, Annie, you'd better say 'yes, sir, and no sir' to me or I'll drag your bare ass all over town behind my squad car. Do you understand? Just say, 'yes, sir,' now and get the hell out of my sight."

Looking shocked, Annie murmured, "Yes, sir."

Straightening my well-composed self, and stepping away from her, I smiled and politely countered with, "Have a nice day, ma'am."

Willy and I had walked half way to the station entry when he questioned, "Uh, Randel, did you write out her ticket?"

"Oh hell," I grimaced. "No. Didn't you?" I was hoping my partner had covered my ass. Willy shook his head from side to side. "Well, I'm not about to tackle that bitch again. Maybe we scared her enough for one day." I looked back only to see Annie laughing with satisfaction as she flipped me a finger.

When Willy and I checked in later that afternoon, the sergeant asked, "Randel, do you have your name tag on?"

"Well, of course, Sarge, right there," I said pointing to it. "Why?" I gave him a stare that included a slight smirk.

He told me that a woman in a wheelchair came in ranting and

raving and wanting to file charges against an Officer Jo Momma. She said that Officer Momma had treated her badly, had cuffed her to her wheelchair and tried to push her to her death in the parking garage. "I told her we don't have an Officer Momma, but she said she wasn't blind and that she could read the damned badge. It clearly said, 'Jo Momma'. I didn't think it could be you, beings how you're such a nice guy, but I had to ask. Willy was behind me shaking his head and holding his breath. "What's wrong Wells?"

Willy muttered, "Nothing." I knew he was thinking, *'What now?'*

"Randel, wear your real name tag for the next few days and stay out of Wheelchair Annie's way."

Being the polite guy I am, I saluted the sarge, smiled and replied, "Yes sir!" Willy and I retreated quickly but proudly.

HUGO AND MOLLIE

SOMETIMES I WONDERED ABOUT THE STREET people and what paths brought certain ones through the portals of Las Vegas. One person that seemed amiable, mild-mannered and not at all dangerous was Hugo. He lived on the streets and usually caused no problem. I learned that this great big barrel of a man that stood six-foot six, came to Las Vegas on vacation, met a strikingly beautiful show girl and stayed to marry her. They lived together for only a short time when she became very ill and suddenly died. Hugo was devastated and went wild with grief. Then one day, he gave up everything he owned in the city and moved to the streets.

As the story goes, he came from a very wealthy family in the Miami area. His family tried to persuade him to return there, but he could not leave his beautiful, loving wife's grave. After he turned to the streets, the family sent him four or five thousand dollars a month on which to live, but Hugo would only pocket the money and never spend more than a few dollars a month. He slept and ate on the street. There were dumpsters behind several of the large Casinos, the Fremont, Mint and Horseshoe, where he would forage for food. Through the years, restaurant staff started leaving good food as garbage for him on certain nights of the week so that he, along with one other friend, was well fed.

That other friend of his was the one thing that got him into trouble. His friend was Mollie, an invisible little dog. If any one approached Hugo, who incidentally was kind of squirrely, he would become very agitated, start screaming at them or fighting them accusing them of mistreating or stepping on Mollie. We would get a call from dispatch declaring that Hugo was at it again, causing a disturbance because of some mistaken reasoning of bystanders. I would respond to the calls, tell Hugo that I had Mollie and that she was just fine. Sometimes, I would say, "Hugo, I have Mollie right here. Are you feeding her enough? She feels a little thin." I would cradle the invisible dog and pet her and as Hugo clamed down, I would hand her to him and the ruckus would be over.

You need to understand that Hugo was large enough to take me apart, hook, line and sinker. He must have weighed nearly three hundred pounds and it was all brawn. His arms were as muscled and big as Popeye's after the spinach. His legs were as large as Bluto's and the combination was formidable. I was not willing to try to tackle Hugo alone and neither was any other officer that I knew. Grumpy and I had learned to talk him down and to ease his anxiety. Once, even though I was holding Mollie, he would not calm down, so Grumpy in his best and kindest form told him to quiet down or he would have to 'cut him long, hard and deep.' However, he did explain to Hugo that Mollie would be left homeless, with no one to take care of her. Hugo quieted down, even though I thought at first he might be tempted to take on Grumpy. I assured Grumpy that using his knife would not be necessary, as I persuaded Hugo to sit down and hold Mollie.

Many times I coaxed Hugo into renting a motel room for a night or two so he and Mollie could get a good night's sleep and he could shower and shave. His head was as bald as a billiard ball so he never needed a haircut. Hugo always wore lightweight, khaki pants with a good leather belt, docker shoes without socks and a white T-shirt with a button-down collared shirt that was never tucked in. I don't remember him ever looking ill kept or dirty and I don't know how he stayed so clean living on the street as he did. Maybe he just bought new clothes when his were soiled. Hugo would hang around with his cronies, those who knew and loved Mollie as he did, cause no trouble, eat out of the dumpsters and sleep in the park, in an alley or on the street, depending on the weather. I finally talked him into opening a bank account at the Bank of America so he could be safer on the street, but every time I had to search him he tried to show me his wad of bills. I never had him remove his money so that no one would know that he carried so much cash.

"Frank-3 can you copy a 416 at Fourth and Fremont? Police officers are trying to arrest Hugo and cannot hang on to him."

"**Frank-3 enroute,** send Adam-12 as backup."

Willy and I arrived in less than two minutes and were out of the car. Police officers had PR-24s drawn and doing a major beat down on Hugo, who was getting the best of all five of them. I yelled loudly, "Hugo, I have Mollie. Here she is and she's fine." Hugo's body went limp and he stopped struggling.

"Officer Randel, is that you? Let me up fellows, Officer Randel has Mollie." The officers stopped battering Hugo and turned questioningly to me. I was standing there with the invisible dog in my arms, petting her and talking baby talk to her and telling her how sweet she was. All the time I was making head movements to the other officers to back off. Finally, I said, "Hugo, I'm handing Mollie to Officer Wells so I can see if you're all right." Wells looked at me in stupefaction as I pretended to hand Mollie to him. "Talk to her and pet her, Willy," I admonished quietly. "Make Hugo think you have her." Wells clumsily feigned holding a little dog and I didn't think he looked very convincing, but I went to talk to Hugo. "Hugo," I insisted, as the other officers stood back, sheathing their PR-24s, "I'm going to have to arrest you for disturbing the peace. If these nice officers want to though, they can take you in for assaulting an officer. What do you think we should do, Hugo?"

"They was hurtin' Mollie, Officer Randel. I had to protect her. You understand!" Hugo spoke with a gravelly, garbled voice that sounded like a foghorn with a cold. "I'm guilty, if you say so. But what will I do with Mollie?"

Grumpy and I took the officers aside, some of them rookies trying to make a good impression, and told them Hugo's situation. They decided, with Grumpy sternly and critically looking at them, that Hugo had not really hurt any of them and that disturbing the peace would be fine. None of them, however, wanted to be the one to attempt to transport or to book him. Therefore, as the fracas ended and the police cars cleared, I cuffed Hugo; it took two sets of cuffs because of his size, and told Wells to drive us to jail. I took the back seat next to Hugo and I held Mollie, petting and crooning to her as we traveled.

When we booked Hugo, he wanted to know what would happen to his dog, and a likable police woman told him she would kennel her and feed her and that Mollie could come to visit him once a day if he were a model prisoner. I instructed the officers to place his money in his envelope and to say nothing about the amount to anybody. Hugo went peacefully with the guards to his cell. Later, the booking officer told me that Hugo had over ten thousand dollars in his nice, leather money belt.

When we went to trial for Hugo's case, he had been provided with a public defender. However, when the judge asked how he pleaded, Hugo spoke up and admitted, "I'm guilty, your honor."

"Wait a minute, sir," cautioned the judge. "Your counsel will speak for you."

"No, sir, judge," Hugo continued shushing his lawyer, "Officer Randel said I'm guilty, so I'm guilty, right, Officer Randel?" Hugo looked at me expecting me to substantiate his plea.

"The court will take a brief recess. Officer Randel, Counselor, I will see you in my chambers." Hugo sat quietly, petting Mollie as we adjourned. "Randel, what's going on?" The judge was perplexed. I explained the situation, the invisible Mollie and the struggle that no officer wanted to press charges about, and asked the judge to find him guilty as charged. I asked how many days he had already served and was told fifteen and so started to ask the judge, who interrupted, "I know, Randel, I'll sentence him to time already served. But, can you guarantee that he will not cause any more trouble?"

"I can't guarantee that, your honor, but he has always been peaceful. I'll look after him as much as possible and ask his buddies to do the same."

"Randel, I have always heard that you are a real tough cop, and now I see you with a soft spot for this bum and it makes me wonder if the stories I have heard are true."

"Well, sir, I don't know what you've heard, but I've always had a soft spot for dog lovers." The judge smiled wanly and we went back to court.

It wasn't but about three months later that I got a call to respond to a 421, an injured person in an alley.

"**Frank-3 enroute**." Grumpy and I were riding together that morning just after briefing and we arrived to see a small crowd of local street people huddled around a downed figure. There on the ground lay Hugo, his enormous body battling for a breath of air. Hugo's comrades told us that a gang of hopped up street punks started taunting Hugo, wanting his money. He had fought them until they had sliced open his belly with a stiletto, rolled him, stole his bankroll and had run away.

Gramms, a tall, black panhandler, about fifty years old, and one of our infamous street people, was there trying to stop the bleeding. Gramms cried, "He thought they were hurting Mollie and he fought them. He couldn't understand that they wanted his money. He would have given them anything they wanted; he just didn't want them to hurt Mollie."

Sirens alerted us that the ambulance was on its way. As I knelt beside Hugo who looked up at me in grave distress and with a tear in his eye, he barely whispered, "Officer Randel, will you take care of Mollie for me?"

"I will, Hugo." I felt as if I had somehow failed that colossal human being. "Hang in there, help is on the way. I have Mollie right here, see." Hugo moved one bloodied hand from his gaping belly wound, reached out tenderly for Mollie, his hand shaking pitifully, as he emitted his last, feeble, dying breath.

"Damn them, damn them to hell," I muttered, thinking *I won't rest until Hugo's killers are caught, tried, convicted and sent away for taking the life of this gentle giant. And, I will repeat his name now and again so that I never forget Hugo.* And to this day, I have never forgotten, after all, I still take care of Mollie.

LONG LEGS

She had legs as long as an Olympic sprinter's. I swear they went all the way up to her neck, and I had to chase after her. *Not good!*

It started with a call from dispatch, "Frank-3, copy a call. Be advised we have a tall, black female that just ripped off the change girl's money at the El Cortez Casino." The thief had been anxiously pacing outside and security was keeping an eye on her. However, as the change girl passed inside, the black woman opened the door, ran in and snatched the money container. Then she took off running across Fremont.

Wells and I were across the street at the Orbit Inn having a quick lunch. I had finished eating and Willy had a few bites of his sandwich left.

"**Frank-3 enroute!**" I informed dispatch that I had this one covered and told Wells to finish and follow me. Putting on my sunglasses, I stepped into the light of day, looked to my left and saw this tall Amazon in shorts and a halter top running toward me, almost at the corner.

Legs spotted me and quickly turned to the right headed southbound on Seventh Street. *Damn*, I thought, *I hate to run. I hate to run in stinkin' 110 degree heat and glaring sunshine, and this bitch is fast.* I felt the weight of my gun, my PR-24 and the lunch I had just consumed. But, I kept fit so I was hot behind her. She ran westbound on Carson to Las Vegas Blvd. Folks on the street were cheering me on, "You can catch her, Officer Randel. Do you need any help?"

"I've got her, thanks," I managed, waving at the onlookers. I was close on her tail, but I could see those long legs and the bottoms of her sneakers beginning to leave me behind. She ran in and out through six lanes of traffic on Las Vegas Blvd., dodging as she dashed between screeching car after car. Then she was back on the sidewalk. All the way she was losing bills and change from the container that was crammed into her shorts. She was northbound on the boulevard as I sped behind her onto the curb. I could see that I wasn't going to outrun her so I paused, panted and yelled, "Stop now," *pant,* "or I'll turn the dog loose!"

Legs instantly turned, treading backward, to see where the dog was. Her gait strayed sideways to the right, and as she turned forward she headed straight into one of three signs that line the sidewalk near the curb. She jolted backward then toppled forward to her knees and went down, landing face first on the steaming concrete. *Ouch!*

I was cuffing her as two backup police units arrived. I asked that pictures be taken of her and the bills and change that was strewn about halfway up the block. When Legs came to and moaned, she muttered, "W'ere's the damn dawg?"

I questioned, "What dog, ma'am?" Laughing to myself, I thought, *thanks again, Elvis, my imaginary, highly trained and efficient attack dog.*

At the hearing for Legs, it was reported that she still had over six hundred dollars tucked into her shorts when she was arrested. I watched as an erotically dressed, attractive black woman, long legs sexily crossed, gave her captivating testimony. She blinked her long eyelashes at the judge and coyly accused me of sending my partner around the block to confront her. Supposedly, he had hit her in the face with his nightstick. She lifted her exquisitely long manicured hand to her forehead and told how he had cracked her skull, and (real tears appeared) had broken her nose. However, there were plenty of citizens that gave statements to the contrary, and one of the photos showed the blood on the bus stop sign, about head high for her.

This was not Legs first offense. *Honey,* I thought after the judge handed down her sentence, *you found the bus stop sign but you missed the bus. We'll be sure you catch the bus that takes you to the pen though, so you won't be usin' those pretty long legs for runnin'.*

THE CRASH

My shift was over about 16:30 hrs. and I had survived another day on the streets of Las Vegas. I was heading up Fourth Street toward the station located at Stewart and Las Vegas Blvd. As I approached the intersection at Carson, I was suddenly slammed on the driver's side of my vehicle. My whole police car decided to go sideways. At that same moment a call came over the radio, "All units, be advised a 407 has just occurred at the Bank of America located at Third and Carson. The suspects were a white male in his fifties wearing blue jeans, a green shirt and black shoes, and a skinny white girl, approximately twenty-five, with unkempt brown hair, wearing a denim mini skirt, a white blouse and three inch, red high heels. They had robbed the bank and left in an older, maroon Cadillac.

It just so happened that the driver of the maroon Cadillac had rammed me in the intersection, careening both vehicles into the middle of the street. The driver had hit his head on the steering wheel and was knocked out. The woman's head hit the windshield and she was stunned. I tried to exit my patrol car and I realized that I could not open my door. I had to crawl over my MDT machine and the center console and past my shotgun to reach the passenger's side door. As I stood, I was suddenly hit with a severe pain in my left side below my ribs. In spite of the sharp pang, I proceeded to the driver's side of the car where the man was coming to consciousness. I saw a Bank of America bank bag lying on the seat between the two. On the floorboard next to the young woman's feet was a gun. Thinking fast, I jerked my handcuffs from my back and cuffed the man's left wrist to the steering wheel. In the meantime, the girl realized what was happening, and she grabbed the moneybag, opened her door and exited the car, running southbound on Fourth Street.

During this mayhem, the sun-protected windows of the Justice Court that is located at Fourth and Carson were filling with onlookers. The bailiffs and the occupants in the building were looking to see what the crash was about. I took off running after the woman. As she ran past the windows of the court, the bailiffs were pounding on the window, cheering me on. One of the bailiffs, Rocky, came out and ran behind me, but we were well ahead of him and he was an older man. I appreciated his efforts, however, and told him so later. I chased the woman another block when she tried to cut across a lawn at a lawyer's office, and twisted her ankle and fell. I jumped on her immediately. We had a bit of a tussle where she tried to scratch me and bite me. I managed to turn her over and told her, "If you try to bite me again, Bitch, I'm gonna bite you back."

She stopped struggling for a moment and yelled at me, "You pigs are all alike." By this time, I had one handcuff on her. She tried to kick me with her high-heeled shoe. I've never been kicked with high heels and I had no desire at that time either. However, she brought her heel back and caught me on the back of my head just above my left ear. That made me mad. I shoved her head into the grass, which incidentally had recently been watered and was slushy and muddy. She quit fighting me because she was struggling to breathe with her face mashed into the wet grass, the mud and a clump of dog dookie that was being sucked up her nose. I hooked her other arm and made her stand. Meanwhile, she was spitting and sputtering, trying to get rid of the doggie poop that was in her mouth and nose. I wouldn't let her spit on me, but she complained that I was cruel and had pushed her head into the shit on purpose. I explained that I did not have anything to do with where she fell or what she fell into. *At this point, I really appreciate that big dog, and his master,* I thought.

Rocky and some other officers came to help me with the arrest. I asked them to call Criminalistics so we could take pictures of the bank bag that was sitting where she had lost it when she fell, pictures on the lawn where the woman's three-inch heel had been imbedded into the grass, and photos of the woman's face, showing where she had banged it into the windshield. Maggie arrived and took all the pictures and turned as she was leaving and observed, "Officer Randel, I think you really run around with shitty women."

Some sense of humor, girl, I speculated. "No, Maggie, I think some of these skuzbags eat a lot of it though. Thanks for coming by. Maybe we can have lunch one of these days. What you doin' tonight?"

"I hope that's not an inference to what I just said, Randel," she chided.

"No, I was just on my way to check out. I'm through with my shift."

"Sure, where do you want to meet?"

"How about Tony Roma's at 7:00?"

"See you then, Randel."

That went pretty well, I lauded as I watched her leave. Just then, my friend and partner, Grumpy, arrived on the scene. He brought a witness from the bank to identify the woman. She told us that the woman was definitely one of the suspects and we proceeded with her back to the maroon Cadillac.

Meanwhile, my patrol car and the Cadillac were still in the intersection of Fourth and Carson. Motorcycle officers had arrived at the accident to control the situation and had ticketed the man that caused the accident. One officer told me that they asked him if he always drove with handcuffs hooked to the steering wheel, and a gun lying on the floorboard. He commented, "No, an ugly lookin' police officer put the handcuffs on me, but I didn't do anything. Let me loose, okay?" The bank clerk identified that man as the bank robber and the vehicle as the get away car. The police took statements from the other witnesses. Sgt. Bill Hightower of motors read the couple their rights and took them to jail where they would be booked for robbery and resisting arrest, plus a ticket for the man for running the red light. Sgt. Hightower booked the gun and moneybag into evidence. By the way, the gun was loaded.

The pictures of the woman's face and the pictures of the three-inch heels I hoped would help me if the woman filed a complaint that I had knocked her down. It would be apparent that she had tripped because of her heel sinking into the wet, muddy grass. Her face, on the other hand, I felt, could be a bone of contention. *I did not shove her head intentionally into the dog poop, but I'd give that big dog a bone if I knew where he was!*

I was busily looking into my wrecked patrol car to retrieve my things since my vehicle would have to be towed, and the last thing I recall was lifting my ditty bag from the center console. I passed out, and the next thing I remember was coming to in the hospital, needing to go to the bathroom.

Ambulance personnel, nurses and doctors surrounded me, all trying to take care of me at once. Sam Sikes stood by and the first thing he said to me was, "Randel, you are one lucky and very spoiled son-of-a-gun. When that amb-o-lance crew saw it was you, they boarded you up and put you on that gurney and took you to Sunrise Hospital. They said that UMC was not good enough for you. Unh Huh! You went directly to Sunrise. They weren't taking you to where they took criminal and ner-do-wells." That ambulance crew stayed with me until I was placed in a room, then content, they took their leave.

My attending nurse allowed me to go to the bathroom, but with constant surveillance and assistance. When I started my flow, it was as red as a stoplight; I was pissing blood. The nurse immediately took me back to the bed and advised Doctor Snyder, who quickly ordered tests run. Of course, they were concerned about a renal contusion, damage to my left kidney, and possibly my spleen, and wanted to take X-rays after they injected me with IVP dye that had iodine in it. I was allergic to the damned dye and puked my guts out after they took the X-rays. So they filled me with Benadryl and epinephrine that made me loopie.

My nurses were very nice to me, even though I was acting as if I were drunk from the drugs. I then explained that I had vomited bile and guck and had not eaten all day. I told them that I sure could go for some prime rib, a baked potato, salad and some iced tea. They calmly explained that I could not have anything to eat or drink until my tests came back. They brought me a toothbrush and toothpaste. *Hell, I even thought about eating the toothpaste.* Finally, one sweet little nurse's aid snuck me three crackers and some ice cubes; one cracker was for the prime rib, one cracker for the baked potato and the other for the salad. The ice cubes had to suffice for the iced tea. I was very thankful and careful and was trying to open the crackers with no noise.

However, the shift had changed and Big Bertha, an amazon centurion came stomping into my room. She must have had super-sonic hearing because she marched in and demanded that I give up whatever I had in my hand, and ordered me to tell her where it came from. Being my honest and truthful self, I never lied and told her that I found it on the bedside table. That little nurse's aid did not deserve what Big Bertha would have done to her. Bertha waddled out of my room very satisfied that she had obliterated any chance that I had of receiving sustenance until she said I could have it. I listened as her panty-hosed, fat legs rubbed each other going swish, swish, swish as she and her big behind left the room. She heard my cracker paper rattle, but she couldn't register the noise her thighs made as she walked. *Amazing! I'll remember that noise and hide my stash if I hear her coming again. I'm not stupid, and by damn I'm still hungry! I'll fix that.* I lifted my bedside phone.

Grumpy arrived about midnight with two Whoppers, fries and a fifth of Jack Daniel's. He stepped into my room as if he were God Himself, and blessed me with manna from heaven. He was not happy that I had called him in the middle of the night, now that he knew that I was not dying. I ordered him to bring me something to eat and to drink, and here he was. A true friend is always a friend that'll stick with you no matter how much trouble you are in, and usually be right there in the middle of it with you. I had unwrapped my first Whopper after gobbling a couple of fries, when I heard Big Bertha's loud Marine Drill Sgt. voice rumble down the hall. "I smell food in my unit. It smells like hamburger and I'd better not find one in any room." *Damn, she has super-sonic smell too!* I quickly chomped two big bites and was chewing them when she swished into my room.

"Officer Randel, I smell hamburger and fries in this room. What do you have beneath your sheet?"

Swallowing quickly I elaborated, "Now, ma'am, you shouldn't ask a red-blooded police officer (no pun about my pissin' condition) what he has beneath the sheets. You might be surprised. I could just cuff you to the bed rails and show you."

"Why... why... you can't talk to me like that, Officer Randel. That's disrespectful. Now fork over that food."

Grumpy tried to save me. "Ma'am, I just had a burger and fries that I ate on the way in here. That's what you're smelling."

"I'll have security escort you out, fella, so don't try to cover for your buddy here." She came to the bedside and threw back my sheet, with me in that tiny thing they call a gown. She revealed a bag with one Whopper, my fries and one hidden hamburger partially gnawed on, only two bites shy of being whole. Man, I was pist. She dropped a fry and I grabbed it and stuffed it into my mouth. "Officer Randel, how could you? We're here to take care of you. What if you have internal injuries and have to go for surgery. They couldn't operate because you just ate. What would we do then?"

"Well hell, Mrs. Butts," *Mrs. Butts?* (I looked at her nametag. It said Butts! For real!) *Big Bertha Butts, or should I say Bertha Big Butts. Ha!* "Mrs. Butts," I continued, looking at the smirk on Grumpy's face and almost busting out laughing, "I ain't goin' for surgery, and I sure ain't gonna starve to death in here either. I need to eat. All I've had all day is one iced tea."

"Well, let me see what I can do." She set about adjusting the draw sheet and replacing my sheet after she confiscated the burger and fries. She stepped to the other side of my bed and commanded, "Roll over, Officer Randel."

"Can't we do this later? I want to visit with Officer Sikes and I don't feel like moving right now."

"I said roll over," she demanded, physically placing her hands and arms under my arm and my butt. That was when she felt the fifth of Jack that I had sneakily placed under my right arm, and beneath my right side. "Officer Randel," she cautioned shaking her amazon arm and the bottle of Jack. "I will take this as the policeman's donation to our nurse's Christmas party. Thank you very much," she rejoined smugly. "I am too old to be fooled, even by the police." As she finished tucking me securely into bed and raised the side rail, she smiled brazenly at me and at Grumpy and whooshed, whooshed out of the room. *Man, I hate to see that Jack Daniel's leave the room. I would have enjoyed a Coke and Jack before I went to sleep.* Big Bertha was back in the room in an instant and addressed Grumpy, "Sir, you look old, tired and worn out and it's time for you to leave. Visiting hours are over and I have a hospital to run here."

Grumpy mumbled something under his breath, I think it had to do with a knife, but I wasn't sure. However, Big Bertha stood with her hands on her wide hips almost daring him to stay in the room. Finally, Sam Sikes, the grumpiest man I know, gave Big Bertha a warm smile and offered to buy her a cup of java at the nurse's station. That seemed to please that big broad, and Grumpy winked at me as he said a good, "Good night, Randel, see you in the morning."

I have to give Nurse Butts credit. She was gone about fifteen minutes and she returned with some red jello. Now I don't like red jello. I don't like orange jello. I don't like jello of any color or flavor. I explained in no uncertain terms what I thought about that jello and what she could do with it. I told her again that I had not eaten all day, that I was dehydrated and that I only had one iced tea all day. *That was the third or fourth time I had told the nurses that.* "Well hell," I spoke curtly, "I need to eat. And if I can't get something here, I know how to take care of myself. Take this damned needle out of my arm, or I'll do it myself. I'm getting the hell out of here."

"Officer Randel, please calm down," Nurse Butts pleaded as she hit my nurse's call button. "You can't leave. It is against hospital policy. You would be leaving AMA."

"What the hell does the American Medical Association have to do with whether I stay or go," I complained as I hung my feet over the side of the bed that did not have a railing lifted. I tried to stand, but I felt woozy from the medications that I had been given. I hung my head down to relieve the dizziness.

She corrected, "No, that's *'Against Medical Advice'*. Please, Officer Randel, lie back down before you fall down, and I lose my job." About that time another nurse came in and Nurse Butts said one word, "Sedative!" The nurse turned on a dime and was back in an instant with a long needle that Butts stuck into the IV. Suddenly, I was lying down, down, down, and feeling very relaxed. "Thank you, Officer Randel. You'll feel much better in the morning. Officer Sikes is just outside and wants to say good night and pick up your badge and other official items that he said cannot remain in your room. You may come in now, Sam."

Grumpy came into the room and questioned Nurse Butts as to where my things were. She walked hastily to the narrow closet and opened the door. As she was doing so, Grumpy slipped something under my mattress, and was standing almost at attention when she returned with my belongings. "Oh, Randel, I see that the other officers have already taken everything they need back to the sub station. Okay, buddy, I'll see you in the morning. Don't give Nurse Nancy any more trouble. She's a nice lady and will take good care of you."

I was drifting and I didn't seem hungry any more. *What the hell is this Nancy and Sam business?* I slipped into a deep sleep and slept until some damned technician came in to take my vitals. Didn't they understand that it was vital that I slept now? *Hell, they won't feed me, and now they won't let me sleep.* By 07:00 hrs. I was up and dressed, and had removed my IV. I was going home, AMA. It was my day off, and I sure as hell was not going to spend it in some place where I could neither eat nor sleep. Anyway I had realized that I had stood Maggie up for our dinner date at Tony Roma's and that I needed to talk with her. It seemed ill fated that we would ever have time together.

After the nurses had changed shifts, Nurse Butts came in to say goodbye. She informed me that I was one of the most difficult, surly patients she had ever taken care of, but she informed me that it was still a pleasure to tend to me and she wished me well. She commented, "Officer Randel, you have a very good friend in Officer Sam. I came back in after you were sleeping and I noticed something sticking out from your mattress. I laid the bed back and felt underneath and found two ham-and-cheese sandwiches from the nurse's station tucked there. He is one sneaky fellow, but I enjoyed getting to know him too. He thinks a lot of you and said that you have been friends for years. Now, sir, I think that we can probably dispense with the IV, so will you please get back in bed and I'll bring you some iced tea and crackers right away, and if you like, I'll stay while you eat and you can tell me more about Sam."

Sam is it? What a rascal! He had her eating out of his hand. I relented because I really hurt like hell and I stayed two more days. I called and had a large fruit basket with little cakes and candies sent to that floor for all the staff to enjoy. Nancy Butts was very happy when I was allowed to leave with medical consent. She kissed me on the cheek and gave me back my fifth of Jack, but confessed that she and another nurse had enjoyed the two Whoppers and the fries that night after Grumpy left.

After three days I returned to work, even though I was pissin' blood for two weeks. At briefing I was awarded an Atta-Boy, which is a commendation for being at the right place at the right time and catching the bank robbers. Actually, it is a damned piece of paper that tells you how great you are. It turned out that the woman had fifty thousand dollars in warrants for prostitution and warrants for failure to appear in court. Three days later, Sheriff Morgan and Under Sheriff Collins caught me as I was going to ride along with Officer Wells. Sheriff Morgan commented, "Great job, Randel, you're always at the right place at the right time."

Under Sheriff Collins informed me that my vehicle had, however, been totaled. He said, "I'll get you a new one, Randel. No, on second thought, we'll get you an older one that runs well. You seem to be hard on cars."

"That's fine with me Sheriff. I hate to have to take care of a new car. It makes me nervous thinkin' that I'll put the first dents in it. Give me an older, broke-in vehicle that I can rely on to get me there, and I be happy as a pig in a puddle."

I didn't know why he thought I was especially hard on cars unless he was referring to an incident a couple of months earlier. I had rammed a get-away car with my patrol car to keep a killer armed with an AK-47 from heading downtown into a heavily congested area. I received an Atta-Boy for that capture too, but I caught hell from Lieutenant Dan (Benedict) Arnold who felt I should have used more resolve and ingenuity. *I'd like to ram this next patrol car up that SOB's ass,* I thought as I thanked the Sheriffs for my new, used car. *Nah,* I reconsidered, *I'd still be drivin' it and my car would come out lookin' and smellin' worse than that bitch I arrested with dog poop all over her face.*

THE BLACK BITCH

In Las Vegas, the city is cut into different patrol areas. I usually worked in Frank area and Sam Sikes, Grumpy, usually patrolled in Adam area. On this particular day, I heard a call come in to dispatch. "Control, this is Adam-12. I'll be making a 468 (a pedestrian stop) at Seventh and Stewart. Is there a unit that can back me?"

I was clear so I responded, "**Frank-3 enroute**."

Control asked Grumpy, "Adam-12, can you give a description of the pedestrian?"

"Yeah, control, I'm stopping a big black bitch that's crossing the road." There was utter silence on the radio. You could hear yourself breathe and nothing more for a brief pause.

Control came back and remarked, "Adam-12, can you repeat that?"

I'm certain that dispatch did not think that he would repeat what he said, or that it had been misunderstood. Grumpy came back, "Yes, I have a big black bitch, about 150 pounds, right here in the street."

About that time, another call interrupted on the radio, "This is 320, what unit was that, control?"

I don't think you want to tell him, dispatch, but you have to 'cause it's the lieutenant. "That is Adam-12, sir."

Lt. Dan Arnold, who is Sikes and my archenemy, came back and asked for Adam-12's location. Dispatch told him that it was at Seventh and Stewart. "I will be enroute there, control. Go ahead, arrive me."

Well, Grumpy's my friend and partner and I knew that I had to arrive before the peevish, ill-tempered lieutenant. I put the pedal to the metal, speeding only *ever so slightly*. I got there a couple of minutes before Arnold did. Sam was out in the middle of the street hanging on to a big black bitch all right. That's exactly as he stated. This bitch had four legs and a long tail, and she was whimpering. It was a beautiful, black, lab-cross dog. I advised Grumpy, "Lieutenant Arnold will be here in a minute. He's already enroute. I think he's pist." I advised dispatch that I had arrived and that Grumpy did have that individual stopped. About that time, with screeching tires and flashing red lights, here came Lieutenant Dan Arnold.

The first thing he commanded was, "Randel, watch that dog. Sikes, come here! What the hell are you doing coming on the radio and saying that you were stopping a black bitch?"

Grumpy, in his blatantly complacent, insolent manner calmly pulled out his six-inch long pocketknife and started cleaning his fingernails. "Sir, a female dog is a bitch, and in this instance, she is a big black bitch." Arnold was so confounded that he couldn't even speak. He turned crimson red as his cheeks puffed out like a bullfrog's. Finally, he let out a big puff of air, filled with malice and declared, "I'll see you at debriefing," another deep breath, "Grrr-umpy."

Grumpy, feeling his oats, replied, "Excuse me, lieutenant, that's not police protocol. I am Officer Sikes, or Officer Sam Sikes to you, sir."

At that point, Arnold said nothing more. He peeled off down Stewart toward the Boulevard. *That man is a basket case,* I observed. He was so bamboozled that he forgot to turn off his redheads. He had cars stopping everywhere and he was looking at them, and jerking his vehicle first one way and then another around them. Then I heard this voice that sounded like Grumpy's come on, "320, your reds are still on. You're stopping traffic everywhere. You might want to shut 'em off, sir."

Grumpy looked at me and went, "Hee, hee, hee, hee! I got him, huh!"

"Sikes, you're in trouble now," I warned. "You do realize that bastard has tried to get me fired twice already."

"Aw hell, I ain't worried. Let me get this bitch out of the street before she gets run over. Come on, baby, let's see where you live." The dog was panting heavily and whimpering, looking at her back end. She tried to turn circles, but Grumpy held her tightly, so that she could not run away. "Randel, I think she might have been hurt. I should call animal control." Grumpy checked her collar for her tags. Her tag had the number of the Vet's office. "Hawk, help me out will you. Call the vet while I get her to the grass over there. The dog was tugging hard, twisting her head and trying to continue up the street as Grumpy tried to take her to the curb. Suddenly, she broke loose and bounded away from Sikes. Hurrying after her, Grumpy called pitifully, "Here, doggie, here doggie, doggie," to no avail. Then the dog stopped and went in circles trying to reach her backside. "Here doggie, doggie. Stop, you black bitch! I ain't gonna chase you; I'll shoot you first!" The dog ran back to Grumpy and circled his legs, sat at attention at his feet, then jumped up and tried to lick him. "Get down, you crazy bitch." She circled him once more and then lay down at his feet, whimpering again. "Randel, look at this, she has something hanging out her rear end. What is it?"

"Oh shit, Sikes, I think she's trying to have puppies."

"What the hell do I do now?" Grumpy was nervous and excited.

"I don't know, Grumpy, I'm just here as backup. It looks like you have everything under control, so I think I'll advise dispatch to clear me."

"Randel, you sorry SOB, don't you dare leave me. I'll poison your iced tea if you do. Call that vet, buddy, please." I could tell he was anxious. Dispatch came back with a call from the vet's office that was no more than two blocks away. I explained the situation and they suggested that we transport her to their office. "Randel, we can't transport her; I think it's probably against Lt. Arnold's regulation."

"Then you'd better walk her down there, Grumpy. It's only two blocks."

"Too late, Rod, lookie here, somethin's coming now." A black and bloody sack containing a tiny four-inch puppy passed onto the ground. The dog immediately began to bite, lick and clean the pouch from the puppy as she stimulated it. Suddenly, she left the puppy and dropped another sack. Lying there, she tried to clean both puppies. Grumpy and I watched in amazement as she brought both to life. Then came another puppy. "Hell, Randel," complained Grumpy, "What are we gonna do? We've gotta take care of her." The dog looked up at Grumpy with fawning, honey-brown eyes; then she licked his hand.

After that, Grumpy was right there helping her deliver and clean the rest of the black mongrel puppies. I advised dispatch that Sikes was helping with a delivery and that I was staying as backup. Cheri' wanted to know, as did other officers, just how many puppies there were. Grumpy sat on the grassy knoll and placed the tiny newborns in his lap and caressed each of them, then placed them where they could suckle, then retrieved them again until she was through. I simply conducted the flow of traffic and waved on the curious. It took about forty minutes before the last of six puppies was born. By that time, animal control had arrived and they safely placed the black bitch and her snuffling, whimpering newborns in their van.

I contemplated, *I'm not sure that Grumpy wants to let go of those puppies.* He was petting the mama and her babies and saying goodbye to them all. I felt kind of sorry for that big lug of a policeman that threatened everyone with his knives and prattle, knowing deep down that he had a heart of gold. "Excuse me," I said to the driver of the van, "Where are you going with the dog and her puppies?"

"We're taking them to the shelter. The owner will have to claim them there."

"And if they don't?" queried Grumpy.

"Then we'll have to put them down. We keep them for thirty days and try to find homes, but then we are forced to euthanize them."

I had a very strong feeling that Sam and Kate would be the proud owners of at least one black puppy, if not the black bitch and all her off spring.

That evening when we attended debriefing, Lieutenant Dan

(Benedict) Arnold already had the incident written up stating that Sikes would receive disciplinary action and would be suspended for three days without pay. About that time, Lieutenant Eugene (Mean Gene) Germain walked in. He asked, "Arnold what the hell are you doing with Officer Sikes?" Arnold in his whining, piss ant, sarcastic way tried to describe the situation. Germain looked Arnold straight in the eye and declared, "Look, you idiot, that's what you call a female dog; she is a bitch. If you don't have anything better to do, you go ahead and write up Officer Sikes, and I'll write you up. You lazy, worthless piece of shit."

Lieutenant Arnold grimaced at Germain's words and touted, "I don't have to take that from you."

Mean Gene smiled maliciously and answered, "Yes, you do. Anytime you want to do something about it, you just let me know and I'll punch your heart out and send it on to hell."

Lieutenant Arnold left the debriefing and never said another word about the black bitch incident. Lieutenant Germain however, looked at Grumpy and admonished, "Sikes, don't you ever say anything like that over the radio again, do you understand?"

"Yes, Lieutenant. Thanks!" Sheepishly, Grumpy replied, "I love you. By the way, sir, would you be interested in adopting a cute little black bitch in about eight weeks?"

MULES

I KNEW WITHOUT A DOUBT THAT he and his bitch were mules. Every weekend or every other weekend they would travel across the Arizona border bringing tar heroin that would be distributed on the streets of Las Vegas. I made up my mind that I was going to sit in wait for them on the next Saturday. Sure enough, I watched as the ten-thousand-dollar, black and gold Harley rolled past the corner of Sahara and Boulder Highway where I was patiently waiting on a side street out of their view. As they passed my patrol car, I hit my reds and siren, and pulled out behind them. They did not stop, but speeded up and made several quick twists and turns trying to lose me. *Aha! You dirty bastard,* I thought, *your ass is mine, and you and your bitch are goin' down. I'm sick of you bringing that shit into my town and I know it's being distributed to little kids, even on the school grounds.* I alerted control, telling Cheri', "**Frank-3 in pursuit** of a motor west bound on Fremont from Sahara." I gave my location and the address of the house that I knew they would run to and asked for backup. I also gave the license plates of the Harley and descriptions of the suspects.

That Harley Davidson Motorcycle was sweet, one of the sharpest of its kind that I had seen. I wished that our traffic guys could have such great rides, but the department bought Kawasakis and swore that they were better quality motors. That baby cornered like a dream, even with that broad butted bitch riding loose behind the driver. I was not to be lost, however, as I skirted around corner after corner in hot pursuit. The driver picked up speed on the straightway of Charleston, kicking it up to sixty. Traffic was light for an early Saturday morning and the motorcycle swayed masterfully in and out of the other vehicles. Cars pulled to the side, allowing me a more direct route to pursue the suspects.

Suddenly, the cyclist made a sharp right turn on Nellis and headed about three blocks forward until he came to an abrupt stop in front of a rundown house that had no fencing and only a dirt-covered front yard. The woman jumped off the motorcycle and immediately ran into the house, carrying a bag with her and calling to others who were inside. The man dismounted his cycle and looked cynically at me as I drove onto the dirt yard keeping him between the house and me. I exited the patrol car, with my PR-24 in my hand and ordered, "Tell that bitch of yours to get her ass back out here now. If she's not here in ten seconds with that bag of heroin, you're gonna feel pain, because I'm gonna hurt you."

About that time several people filed out of the house, making derisive comments, and stood aggressively watching me to see what I would do. Undaunted by the threat of the gang of assholes, I moved close to the cyclist and continued, "If that bitch doesn't get her fat ass out here, with that stash, I'm going to take you out." At that point I hit the motorcyclist in the jaw with my one-gloved fist, knocking him down.

Two patrol cars careened into the dirt yard. It was my backup, Adam-12, Grumpy, and Frank-4, Marie. Grumpy walked toward the man that I had decked and removing one of his long knives, rejoined, "You'd better stay on the ground you SOB or I'll cut you where it hurts. I'll change you from a stud to a bitch." The culprit stayed on the dirt. Grumpy sheathed his knife and cuffed the bastard.

I was watching the Neanderthal rat pack that stuck to the porch, making obscene gestures and touting me. Surprisingly, the mule bitch walked out and joined the pack. "Get your smelly ass over here now," I commanded, "or I'll tow this piece of shit bike down the street behind my car and your boyfriend with it. There won't be anything left but blood and guts, and nuts and bolts when I'm through with them." My backup Marie was shaking her head at me as if she were having a case of apoplexy, but hiding a smirk; I ignored her. I was hot under the collar and I wanted to confiscate that tar heroin, which I knew the bitch had probably already flushed. *Damned good thing, too,* I surmised. *One batch that won't hit the streets.* About that time three of our patrol units arrived and we brought the rat pack to the dirt covered front yard. I advised control that we were entering the dwelling, and Grumpy and I searched the house. We found no stash of heroin, which was what we expected, but we found bong pipes and other drug paraphernalia used by druggies. All we could ultimately do was to run the man and his bitch in for failure to stop for a police car, for speeding, and for reckless driving. I called for a hook and had the mule's bike towed. I was making a point with the cave dwellers.

When I went in for debriefing that evening, Lieutenant Germain took me aside and told me to sign a paper that he presented to me. "What is this, Lieutenant?"

"You are being reprimanded, Randel. Just sign right there," he directed, pointing to the line.

"What the hell am I being reprimanded for, sir?" I queried.

"That gang of dirtbags that watched you this morning all came to the sub-station and lodged a complaint that you were verbally abusive to the man and woman that you arrested. You called her a bitch, but that didn't seem to bother them as much as you calling the Harley a piece of shit." Smiling he continued, "I believe that they care more for their set of wheels than they do about their women. Now, sign that paper and consider yourself reprimanded for conduct unbecoming a police officer." I signed the paper.

The next morning at briefing, Lieutenant Dan Arnold called me aside and told me he was going to take disciplinary action against me for my conduct with the mule case. I suggested that he speak with Lieutenant Germain first. "Randel," he sputtered, "You think you run this department and do things your way, but you'll find out differently. You're consistently embarrassing this office with behavior unbecoming an officer of the police force, and I won't have it. A week off duty without pay might straighten your line of thinking. I'll see you at debriefing."

I dropped by to see Lieutenant 'Mean' Gene Germain and told him what 'Benedict' Arnold was going to do, and he instructed me to hit the streets and to not worry about it. "You have already been reprimanded for your actions, Randel. There is nothing further to be done about this. Incidentally, we had to let those assholes go with misdemeanors only. Don't worry, though, we'll get them one day. You're a good officer, Rod, but watch yourself. Arnold is out to get you for anything he can."

That evening at debriefing, Arnold was waiting for me. He was madder than a swarming nest of hornets. Lieutenant Germain had gone to him and told him to back off as I had already been reprimanded, and that he had cleared it with Undersheriff Collins. "Randel," Arnold fumed, "I am going to the sheriff on this. I won't have this kind of behavior on the department."

"Yes, sir," I answered politely, "do whatever it is that you have to do for the department's sake, sir."

'Mean' Gene was immediately behind me. "Arnold, you go over my head, and you're in deep shit. The captain has already signed off on the reprimand that Randel accepted last night. If you even think about writing out a complaint, I'll ram it down your useless throat. If you have any problems with that, see me later. Otherwise leave my officers and me alone and go do something like real police work. I won't put up with this petty jealousy that you have because my officers out class and out work yours. I didn't realize that you had so little to do; I'll have to talk to the undersheriff." 'Benedict' stomped out of the office. Gene placed a supportive hand on my shoulder and commented, "Randel, have a good night. See you tomorrow at briefing."

SLAVER

Monday morning rolled around and I was still steaming about losing the arrest on the two mules, so when a call came in from control, I was ready to roll. "Frank-3, copy a call. The principal at Charleston Elementary is reporting that an older man in a gray El Camino pickup is sitting in front of the school watching the children as they enter the premises, and trying to talk with them. Can you check him out?"

"**Frank-3 enroute.**" *That bastard had better not be a pedophile, or I'll kill the son-of-a bitch.* I pulled up behind the car, placing my vehicle half way in the street, and ran the plate. The car had been reported stolen. I asked control to send a backup, and Adam-12 responded that he was in the area. I drew my gun as I exited the patrol car. I advanced to the doorpost of the El Camino and knocked on the window. The man inside jumped as if I had completely startled him, as he reached to place his already running car into gear. I grabbed the door latch and opened the door, switched my revolver to my other hand, elbowed him in the chest and reached across, placing the vehicle in park and retrieving the keys. I observed that his trouser fly was open and that he was actively masturbating as he watched the children. I shoved him forward, hitting his face on the steering wheel, and I ordered, "Hands on the wheel, you pervert. Now, place your left hand behind your back, palm up." He complied, as he complained that I had shattered his nose on the steering wheel. I cuffed the first hand and then dragged him from the vehicle just as my backup, Adam-12, Grumpy, arrived. I cuffed the perp's other hand and locked the cuffs, then shoved him across the hood of the El Camino.

Children were gathering to watch, and a teacher quickly ushered them to safety on the school grounds. "Randel, you got him cuffed?" asked Grumpy.

"Yeah, check out the vehicle for me, Sikes. See what this useless piece of shit is doing here." I did not question the suspect, but held him at bay as Sikes looked through the vehicle. When Grumpy opened the glove box it was totally empty without any paper work, identification or registration. He looked under the seat and then threw the back of the seat forward. What he found there made him sick. Sikes saw a multitude of little girls panties (later the count would total fifteen) and a bloody machete.

Sikes took a pen from his pocket and withdrew a pair of little girl's panties. Then he turned and vomited. At last, he muttered angrily. "Look here, Randel. Looks like we've got us a major, damned ped-o-phile."

"Sir," I stated as I shoved his head down on the hood of the car, "you have the right..." I read him his rights. I made him sit on the sidewalk with his legs straight out and with Sam watching him. I called in his description to control. "Control, he is a white male, approximately fifty years old, with graying hair and a straggly beard and mustache. He has brown eyes and a scar on his left cheek. He gave his name as, Wade Albright, DOB 7/6/1934."

Cheri' came back with information, "Frank-3, he is an ex-felon and is wanted in three states for murder and for white slavery. He has been abducting young women and little children around eight to ten years old and selling them into sex slavery in foreign countries."

"From our observation, control, he has obviously taken liberties with the little children before he sold them." The machete told a different story, one of heinous atrocities to the little ones. *Thank the good Lord that someone has spotted him before he made off with any of the children at this school. He won't last long in prison because even the worst offenders hate pedophiles and they usually meet with a terrible death while incarcerated. That could be a good thing,* I decided as I scrutinized him.

Cheri' advised, "Randel, the FBI has been called. Please wait there for their response."

"Thanks, control. Consider it done."

Grumpy and I were incensed. I was ready to shoot the bastard where he sat. I put a knuckle to his head. "Don't think of making a move, limp dick, or I'll rip your throat out, do you understand?" He tried to shake his head, and I knuckled it again. "You have a mouth; use it for something else than molesting little girls, you bastard."

He mumbled, "Okay, I'm not movin'." He understood my message loud and clear.

Grumpy, as irate as I was, went to the perp's head where the man could see what he was doing. He removed his largest knife from its sheath and then kicked the perp's legs far apart. Sam walked between the legs to the man's thighs and snarled, "I'm gonna cut you long, hard, and deep you baby killer, and watch you bleed to death before the FBI gets here. But before I do that, you sorry bastard, I'm gonna take pleasure in castratin' you. I'll say you were playing with your dick while you were trying to talk one of those little babies into your car. I'll swear that you were trying to attack me and that I had to cut you where it hurts the most." Grumpy reached down and deftly slit the man's trousers two ways at the crotch.

The man, twisting in morbid fear screamed, "No, no, don't hurt me. I'm sorry. I just can't help myself. I never meant to hurt any of them. Please, please, don't cut me!"

Sikes growled, as he held the other end of his knife on the man's undershorts, "Did those little babies that you killed plead for their lives while you were hurting them? Did you give them any mercy? I don't care if you live or die!" He shoved the blunt end of the knife into the man's testicles evoking a loud, painful scream from the offender.

I have to admit that we were caught up in the moment and neither of us was probably thinking clearly, but we did not usurp our authority, and treated the man with a fair amount of dignity, that is for the scum sucking, child molester that he was.

The school's principal rang the bell early and the children scurried so they would not be late, and only a few stragglers came past as we held the pedophile for the FBI. Grumpy had stepped away from the man and was leaning against the El Camino, smoking a cigarette as we waited. Grumpy, who was still furious at the thought of what the man might have done to the little children, threatened, "I wonder if that bastard burned those little ones with cigarettes? I wonder if he made them scream. Maybe I should burn you with this cigarette right on your eyeball!"

"I don't smoke," he avowed protectively. "Please don't hurt me."

"Yeah, maybe you don't, but I found more than one pair of little girl's panties behind your seat. What do you do, save them for memories while you jerk off?"

The man did not have time to answer as two, black, unmarked, FBI sedans arrived and four men piled out of the vehicles. When they asked the criminal what happened to his pants, he stated that he thought that they tore when he went to sit on the sidewalk. He never mentioned the conversation between Grumpy and me. He had however, wet his pants, and they chided him about that. *That must have happened when Grumpy punched him with the wrong end of that stiletto he calls a knife,* I surmised sardonically. We gave our reports to the FBI agents; they thanked us and hauled the murderer away. "Damn, that felt good, didn't it Sikes," I remarked, relieved that one less child molester would be on my streets. "Stuff like this makes it worth all the hard hours we put in. You really wanted to cut him, didn't you Sam?"

"What I saw made me puke, and I could imagine what it must have been like for those scared little babies. I was thinkin' about cuttin' him real hard just about the time those other fellows arrived." Grumpy lit another cigarette and snapped, "Oh hell, Randel, let's go have some iced tea and cool down."

That night at debriefing, I approached Lieutenant Arnold and asked, "So, sir, do you have those discipline papers for me to sign?"

"Well, Randel, I've been thinking about that. You are one of the best officers in Metro; even though your methods are sometimes unorthodox, you're still a good man. I'm gonna let this one slide since

Lieutenant Germain and the Captain have already signed off on it. But watch it, Randel."

Yeah, like you aren't scared shitless of 'Mean' Gene. You think he might tear your heart out for messin' with one of his guys. "Thank you, sir. That's so kind of you," I replied in my most humble manner. I thought, *very kind of you? NOT!*

"By the way, good job on that child molester you caught today. You and Sikes did a good job. Made the department look good."

"Thank you, sir. Have a good night." *Well, saints preserve us, a compliment from old 'Benedict' Arnold. That's one for the books.*

BREAKFAST BURGLAR II

"We switch you now to Crystal Li for the 6:00 o'clock news."

"Thank you, Marty. Today's breaking story involves many of our senior citizens in the Rexford Area. For the second time, residents have reported a rash of early morning break-ins. Officer Rod Randel of the Frank Area tells us that the burglar, apparently a male individual, entered five different homes in the wee hours and burglarized them while the elderly slept, taking jewelry, money, small appliances and anything easily carried on foot. The burglar has the audacity to cook himself a good breakfast or to help himself to any food he chooses before he leaves the homes. He has even used the bathroom, uses shaving cream, razors and cologne. Today, he brazenly took one gentleman's freshly ironed shirt that was intended for church. As yet, the police have no leads, but they are asking all residents to watch for suspicious men lurking in or casing the area, and to report them to the police, Marty.

"Stay tuned for breaking news about a missing woman that the police say has been found in a garbage bag that was left under the I-95 and I-15 interchange. Back to you Marty."

After the commercial break, Marty returned the audience to Crystal Li. "This afternoon as the freeways were full of go-home traffic, a motorist spotted a dark van hesitate under the I-15 underpass at I-95 where a large, black, garbage bag was shoved out the side paneled door. The motorist called the police, giving the license plate number and description to the van. When the officers arrived at the scene, they found the body of a young woman that they believe to be Martha Waverly, a Las Vegas show girl that has been missing from her home since October twelfth. Police are waiting for identification, but consider Ms. Waverly to be the victim of a vicious crime, Marty. Anyone with information about the case, please contact the Las Vegas Metro Police Department, for Missing Persons. This is Crystal Li reporting the latest breaking news for KTLV channel 13 News. Back now to Marty Glory for sports and weather.

Damn, I thought, as I listened more than watched the news as I filled out my last report. I looked up and glanced at the photo of Martha Waverly that had been seen many times on the different stations, and that was posted in relevant spots around town. I made a mental note to find out more about the case.

But shit, that SOB Breakfast Burglar was going to drive us all crazy. He was operating in Frank Area. Grumpy and I had been on alert and had gone with our partners into the Rexford area where the Breakfast Burglar had intruded upon many disgruntled elderly homeowners.

He was becoming braver as he helped himself to pretzels and a six-pack of beer, and had time after the burglary to drink three beers while he sat and watched television. In another home he ate his hot, cooked oatmeal, drank coffee and ate a Pop Tart before he left. In the next, he had rifled through every drawer in the bedroom and had taken numerous items of underwear and socks of a man that dwelled alone. The man, who was hard of hearing did not hear a sound, but dreamed that his deceased wife was making coffee for him and was patiently waiting for her to bring him a cup. Here, he had left a good footprint of a heavy boot, perhaps a wading boot, size eleven, on the damp lawn of the home. However, it could not be matched to any previous burglaries.

Finally, at the fifth house, an elderly lady had arisen when she heard the sound of the back door closing. She had rushed to see a tall man in a hooded sweater, wearing yellow rubber boots that she described as fireman's boots, and carrying a pillowcase, run from her home. She had immediately called the police and the night shift had taken the call.

Grumpy and I were pissed off that there were no more leads, and I avowed that the Breakfast Burglar was first on my list. Sikes and I decided that we were going to be on duty at 04:00 hrs. every morning until we caught the son-of-a-bitch. Of course, that meant that our partners would be there with us, and we would all be losing a significant amount of shut-eye. But damn it, the folks in my area were relying on us!

BACON 'N BUDDY

SIKES AND I WERE ABOUT READY for a late Saturday morning breakfast when we heard control. "Frank-3, copy a 416 in progress. We have a family disturbance at 210 West Boston. A young man approximately ten called in. His mom is holding a sharp knife and his dad has a BBQ fork in his hand."

"**Frank-3 enroute.** Keep the boy on the line."

"We are."

"Okay. Ask him if there are any guns in the house," I elaborated. The boy did not think so, but was not sure. "Does he know what his folks are fighting about?" We were rolling as we talked.

Grumpy took the mike as we heard, "This is going to sound funny, you guys, the boy said they are fighting over a piece of bacon."

Grumpy growled in disbelief, "A piece of bacon?"

"Yeah. Can you believe it?"

"Copy that!" Grumpy grumbled, almost as loudly as his belly, "Arrive us, Cheri', we're almost there."

As we arrived at the apartment that was near W. Boston and Tam Drive, a low-income area, a small tow-headed boy approximately ten or eleven ran out the front door toward our car. Preceding him, with its tail tucked between its legs, ran a skitterish, shaggy, ragged, black and tan dog that circled behind my legs and crouched, quivering as I asked, "Are you okay, son?" He nodded affirmatively, holding back tears. "Is your dog okay?"

"Yeah! Please make 'em stop fighting, officers."

"Boy," Grumpy asked, as kindly as he could, "does anyone have a gun?"

"No, Mama's gonna cut my papa and he's gonna stab her." The long held tears welled in his eyes and spilled down his dirty cheeks.

Sounds like this one is right up Grumpy's alley, I thought. "Listen carefully, stay outside, but don't go anywhere," I quickly warned as we left him and entered the house. The dog was right on my heels but I closed the screen before it could enter. A screaming female voice and a bellowing male voice emanated from the kitchen. The mother, a malnourished, brassy redheaded woman about thirty, was standing defensively about two feet from a beer-bellied, unshaven, seated, older man that was brandishing an 18-inch, two-pronged BBQ fork above his head. Grumpy and I signaled as to who would take whom.

"Ma'am, put the knife down, right there, in the sink will be fine," I cautioned.

"This is my house and my knife. I'll do what I damned well want to with it. Get out of my house now and take that S.O.B. with you," she screeched, pointing the knife at Grumpy.

Placing my hand on my holstered gun, I warned her, "If you don't put that knife down, ma'am, I *will* kill you. Think of that poor little boy outside crying 'cause he won't have a mama. You must not love your son, ma'am, or you'd put that knife down."

Remorsefully, she laid the knife in the sink. Quickly by her side, I grabbed the knife, opened a cabinet drawer and tossed it inside. Constantly keeping her in my sight and watching that she was not looking for another weapon in *her kitchen*, I reasoned, *Out of sight, out of mind.*

In the meantime, Grumpy had controlled the man and had forcefully taken the BBQ fork from him. "Now what's all this ruckus about," demanded Grumpy. Both people started again, one screeching like a banshee and the other loudly cussing like a sailor.

"Hold it," I ordered loudly. "What's the big problem? Why are you going to cut each other up? What's your problem," I directed my comment to the woman.

"That fat pig wants to eat the last piece of bacon, and I want it."

"Ma'am, did you have any bacon?" I figured, *there has to be more to this than meets the eyes.*

"Yes. But…"

Interrupting her, I quizzed, "Sir, did you have any bacon?"

"Hell yes. But, she don't need no more bacon. She's already fat. I work for the money for this food and I get what I want."

Shaking my head, I questioned, "You mean to tell me you're going to kill each other over a piece of bacon?"

Both resounded in unison, "Yeah!"

About that time, the little boy and his dog slipped into the kitchen. The dog positioned itself next to me on the floor and the boy hovered behind me, leaning down to pet his dog. "What's your dog's name?" I asked the boy.

"Buddy," he replied sheepishly.

"That means he's your friend, right?" The child shook his head up and down. I looked at Buddy and thought, *now that's a friendly dog and that little boy loves his dog.* I stepped toward the stove where the one piece of cold, fatty bacon lay on a greasy plate. Reaching over, I picked up that slick piece of meat and inquired, "Is this the piece of bacon you were arguing over?" As I held it high so all could see it, I could feel that piece of bacon slipping, slipping from my fingers to the floor. Buddy, like a good dog, jumped to the occasion and snatched it before you could say, 'Jack Rabbit'. Then, that little pup gave me a gleeful *'woof'* and licked my hand.

The mother called me an asshole and said, "I saw that. You did that on purpose."

The father, rising from his chair, called me an S.O.B. and shouted, 'That was my bacon!" Grumpy grabbed him by the shoulder, forcing him back into his seat, and cuffed him.

"Shut up, sir," he reprimanded. "You're going to jail."

"You too, ma'am," I informed the woman as I handcuffed her.

"But my baby," she sniffled.

Like she cares, ha! "You should'a thought about him before the bacon," I sneered. "I'm sorry, young man, is there anyone you can stay with?"

"My grandma," he said resolutely. "She can come get me. Can I call her, Mama?"

Meekly nodding, she gave her permission. Within minutes, the grandmother came for the boy and the dog. She informed us that this kind of thing was a common occurrence between the couple and that she thought a stay in the pokey would be good for both of them. She assured the little boy that he had done the right thing, and told him she was proud of him. Before he left, the boy wrapped his bony little arms around my legs. I patted his head to reassure him. He looked up at me with big blue eyes and said, "Thank you, Officer Randel. I'm gonna be a policeman just like you, when I grow up."

Grumpy grabbed the BBQ fork, and retrieved the knife from the drawer to place into evidence. We transported mama and papa to be booked and informed child protective services. Afterward, Grumpy and I went to IHOP where Lisa had my iced tea ready. Sam had to wait for his drink, which as usual, made him even grumpier. We ordered and had our fill of bacon and eggs.

The *loving* family filed a complaint with IAB, Internal Affairs Bureau, over the bacon incident. No one could believe it, and they all chuckled about it. However, it was ruled unfounded due to the fact that there was no bacon for evidence. So, IAB dismissed the complaint. *Just goes to show you can't have your bacon and eat it too!*

JUDGE WHITE

The Las Vegas Club sits on the north corner of the junction of Fremont and Main Street. Main Street runs directly in front of Union Plaza, and Fremont ends toward the Plaza on Main Street. The front of the casino is wide open, with doors that roll down when they close. You could hear all the noise of the play with the hubbub of voices, the click of chips and the timbre of music. The change girls there were told to watch their change trays very carefully, and to always lookout for would-be assailants. As police officers, we ate there often and consequently, I knew all the girls.

My partner and I were walking on patrol at First and Fremont, when my attention was suddenly drawn to a black guy wearing hang-down shorts, like the ones that show the crack of the ass, a black T-shirt and white tennis shoes. There was a pillar in front of the casino blocking my view, but I observed him as he ran in and then quickly ran out, and I could see that he had a wad of money. The change girl that was at the front had screamed. I knew exactly what he had done; he had ripped off her tray. He ran out and across Fremont Street to the south side. He dashed in front of the Golden Nugget. I told my partner to find out what happened and to let me know, as I took off on foot after him.

I pursued him down to Third Street where he made a right turn and headed up that street. He looked back and saw me and then ran across Carson. When you run across Carson there is a big sidewalk that meets stairs that go to the courthouse. The fellow looked back again and saw me hot after him. He scrambled up the steps and I sprinted up them right behind him. He hurriedly bolted through the door where people where being cleared by the metal detector to enter the courtrooms. There were three U.S. Marshals that served at the detectors. The robber started to go first one way and then another and finally dodged through the passageway of one of the detectors, pushing a citizen to the floor. At this point he had a choice of going straight or upstairs. He chose the stairs.

Before the Marshals even had time to react, I charged in and crashed through the metal detectors. Of course, the alarms sounded as I had all kinds of metal on my body. I hollered, "Where did he go? Which way did he run?"

One of the marshals, Rocky, yelled back, "He took the stairs, Randel." He informed his comrades, "I'm following Randel." Rocky was a large black marshal, and he sped close behind me. As I topped the stairs, a girl that was standing on the landing, pointed toward the courtroom and tattled that he had gone in there.

I opened the door just in time to see the lawbreaker quickly take a seat about halfway down and in the center of the bench. There was a trial in progress, but for me, there was an escape in progress. I swiftly followed, and as the heavy door slammed shut, the bailiff called out, "What's going on here?"

The judge banged his gavel and hollered, "You can't do that in my courtroom!" I continued to the center of the bench directly behind the assailant, and grabbed him by his hair. As he yelped and raised his arm, he gripped my hand. *I'll make this bastard let go of my hand!* With a quick switch from his hair, I gave him a jab right to his throat, a perfect move for a head already leaning over the back of the bench. He let go of me and grabbed his throat, coughing, gagging and gasping for air. I shoved the man forward and then backward again as I clutched his arm and placed the cuffs on his wrist. Rocky was quickly behind me helping me to subdue him. The judge was standing, striking his gavel again and again, yelling, "Order in the

Frank-3 Enroute

court, order in the court. Damn it, I said order! Charge that man with contempt of court." I thought, *I hope he's not talking about me!* "Bailiff, what the hell's goin' on in my court?"

The criminal was gaining his voice and sputtering, "Asshole! Pig!" He was spitting all over the place as he continued to cough. Rocky held the other hand while I secured the handcuffs and locked them. "Agh, you pig," the perp offered again.

I snatched his hair and pulled his head back so that he had to look up at me as I hung menacingly over him. "Listen here, Asshole," I growled, "you have the right..." The judge continued to call out asking what was going on. After I finished the Miranda Rights, I told him, "You are under arrest for a felony, grand larceny or robbery. We're not sure yet, but we'll know in a few minutes."

The charge of grand larceny is made when someone takes something from someone else without the use of force and the amount is over one hundred dollars. If it is under one hundred dollars it is a petty larceny, which is a misdemeanor. A grand larceny is either a gross misdemeanor or a felony, a serious crime. This suspect had probably stolen several hundred dollars.

I looked up at the judge and offered, "I beg your pardon, Judge White. I'm sorry for interrupting your trial. But we just had this person rob a change girl at the Las Vegas Club, and he ran in here." Rocky validated my story telling the judge that I was right behind the man and that Rocky followed in pursuit directly following me.

More composed, the judge sat and struck his gavel once more. "We will take a fifteen minute recess." At that moment, the door swung open and who entered? Grumpy. I acknowledged him and turned the suspect over to him. The judge asked me if he could see me in his chambers. He wanted to know what was going on and I explained that the man was going to jail. I asked, "Your Honor, would you write out a witness statement for me, please."

"Sure, Officer Randel, I can do that." He wrote that 'the suspect, a black man, about twenty-three, wearing a black shirt, baggy shorts that almost fell off, black and white tennis shoes, and breathing heavily, ran into my courtroom. He had no more than sat down, when Officer Randel charged in behind him, grabbed him by the hair and gave him a chop to the throat. I thought that he had killed him.' He elaborated on how, 'Randel overpowered the culprit with the help of one of my US Marshals and Marandized him, then safely arrested him without harm or violence to any of the citizens in my courtroom.'

Because he gave me such a good statement, I told him that I would see that he did not have to come to the trial. "Officer Randel," he allowed, "I will be available if you need me and I will be proud to testify as to how well you conducted yourself, and how appropriately you handled that black bastard." Then he said, "If you have time, I'll call a break and by gosh, we can go have lunch." We headed back to the courtroom where he put everything and everyone on hold while we went to the Fremont for Chinese food.

My partner retrieved the money that the suspect had thrown away as I chased him. Other officers obtained statements from the young girl that stood at the stairway landing, and the four bailiffs, one that served in the courtroom, and the three from the entry to the courthouse. Rocky was especially good during the trial. He was an older, semi-retired police officer that continued to work, serving the people. Judge White did not have to appear. Oh, yes, I neglected to say that interestingly, Judge White was black.

RADIO 'N ANTS

"FRANK -3 COPY A CALL. WE just had a grand larceny, possible robbery on Fourth Street just north of Fremont, next to the Fremont Drug Store."

"**Frank-3 enroute**." When I arrived, Grumpy was already there. He was talking with a tiny, thin, gray-haired lady. She had told Grumpy that a white man with dark clothing had attacked her. He headed down the alley behind the drug store, close to Las Vegas Blvd. I jumped back into my vehicle, turned around and headed in that direction looking for him.

Grumpy called me with a further description of him. He said he was wearing a dark T-shirt, Levis®, tennis shoes, and he had a gold earring in his left ear. I spotted him about the same time that he saw me. He turned around and headed eastbound from Las Vegas Blvd. and Fremont.

I called, "Control, give me a Code Red, foot pursuit, eastbound." I jumped out of my patrol car and took out after him. I chased him about four blocks and I tell you what. It was hotter than hell, about 100 degrees, in broad daylight. I was becoming damned tired, and he was tiring too. He stopped abruptly when I used my ploy, "Stop or I'll turn the dog loose." He looked, then looked again, hunting the dog. When he did not see my invisible police dog, he took off running again. However, that little bit of time gave me the opportunity to gain on him. We were at about Ninth or Tenth Street where there are a lot of low-income houses. I knew that if he ran away from me in there I would lose him for sure. Usually, I do not carry my radio. However, this day, I had my big, brick-like radio not attached to my belt, as per regulations, but in my reinforced back pocket. It was one of the heavy items that was holding me back, along with my guns, knives, my PR-24, heavy boots, and a few extra pounds. I pulled out the radio and gave my position, "Frank-3, still in pursuit on foot at about Tenth and Fremont." I was breathing hard, puffin' like a son-of-a-gun, and he was starting to pull away from me. I was in a difficult position; I didn't want to lose him. Consequently, thinking fast, *like I always do*, I surmised that I had that damned heavy radio in my hand, and I would be lighter without it, and maybe, just maybe, I could run faster, so hell, why not just chuck it. Well, if I was gonna chuck it anyway, why not hurl it at the robber? So, I did! I shot put that heavy brick as hard as I could. He was running, and to this day, I don't know how I hit him, but the bottom of that damned radio caught him in the small of his back, directly on his spine. He fell against a small chain-link fence next to the sidewalk. I was on him in a flash, like greased lightening. I gripped his left arm and bent it as I grabbed his hair. He was trying to fight me. He tried to wiggle away from me, and I clutched his shirt, which tore away like rice paper. *Where the hell are the other units that are supposed to be here to help me?* I shoved his head down as hard as I could. He was trying to kick me so I shoved him again. He tried to get up on his knees so I kicked him behind his knees and again in his thigh. He went down again. He began screaming and fighting me. I yelled, "Hold still, you SOB, or I'm gonna hit you again." I whacked him in the back and I ran his face into the ground. Finally, I cuffed his first arm and still he continued to kick, to fight and to scream. I started giving him kidney punches, and swore that I would kill him if he did not lie still. He brought his other arm back to grab me and I grasped that arm and cuffed him. Then I snatched him by the hair and by the cuffs, forcing him to stand.

It was then that I saw why this sucker was squirming and screaming. He was covered with red ants and they were biting him everywhere. He had landed on top of their ant pile and they were hotter and angrier than I was. I turned him around and started brushing ants from his bare chest, his arms, his neck and his face. I didn't deal with his legs or his feet. He kept screaming and it turned into blaming me for hurting him, and he touted that it was my fault that he was stung.

I informed him quickly, "Listen up. You have a right to remain silent. Anything you say can and will be used against you in a court of law. You have a right to an attorney. If you cannot afford an attorney, one will be appointed for you at no cost to you. Anytime during questioning, you have the right to have an attorney present. Anytime during questioning that you refuse to answer a question, the questioning will cease. Do you understand your rights?"

He stated loudly and clearly, "F-U and your rights."

"Well," I stated unhurriedly, "I'll just put you back in the ant pile while I read them to you again, very slowly until you understand them." He was already showing lumps and bumps from the multitude of bites he had experienced. I jerked his cuffs and his hair to show that I meant business. I began deliberately, "Y.o.u. h.a.v.e…"

Instantly, he avowed. "Okay, okay, I understand my rights. You're an asshole!"

Just in time, to save his sorry ass from the ant pile again, here came my backup; it was Grumpy in his patrol car. "Sikes, what took you so long?" I was still huffing from our altercation and sweating like a mule.

"Sorry, Randel," he said looking over the situation. "I waited for the am-bo-lance and then I left my rookie taking notes and came as quick as I could. We're charging this little bastard with grand larceny. I think he broke that poor little old grandmother's hip when he tried to grab her purse off her shoulder. He knocked her down and dragged her down the street. She gave him quite a struggle though. She wasn't gonna let go of her purse." Grumpy glared at the robber, "I ought to take my knives and stake you out right here and let those damned ants eat you alive! Hee hee hee! I can just hear your mama cryin' over her baby boy's grave."

"Hell no, Sikes, we're gonna charge him with robbery." Grumpy and I loaded the suspect in my car and returned Grumpy's car to the site for his rookie. The ambulance crew was loading the sweet little lady's gurney.

She smiled bravely up at me, and uttered, "You got him, Officer Randel. Thank you. Oh, you poor thing, look at your uniform. It's all wet and dirty. I wish I could clean it for you. But I think I'll be out of commission for a few days. Thank you too, Officer Sikes."

We figured that with her age, she was 87, she would probably never heal properly. Together, we escorted the culprit to jail. We booked him and charged him with robbery and with the added senior citizen law that doubles the penalty. And substantial bodily harm made it a felony. "You're goin' away for a long time," I informed him. The robber stared stupidly at me, not understanding what I was saying. I think his brain was starting to absorb all that poison from the ant bites. Grumpy and I left him in the competent hands of the jailers after we told them what he had done. Most police officers don't like people that hurt little old ladies. *I wonder how long it will be before he receives medical attention? Wonder if he still has ants in his pants? Hmmm...*I thought maliciously.

I left the jail and went to UMC to see the little old lady. She had scratches and scrapes from being dragged, and her hip was indeed broken. I told the nurses at the desk that I would need pictures of Mrs. Mc Sorley's injuries, and April, a sweet, beautiful, tall, jet-black haired creature there told me not to worry, that I would have pictures of all the injuries as soon as she could acquire them. Incidentally, that turned out well for me as April and I became well acquainted during my frequent visits to Mrs. Mc Sorley, and we dated for a while after that.

I had all the information and photos that I needed when we went to court. During the trial, the robber kept making noises and calling attention to himself. Finally, the judge stopped the proceedings and asked the robber's attorney what the problem was. Immediately the accused yelled out, "That pig!" *He's pointing at me!* I grinned. "He kept lettin' the ants bite me, judge, the ants." *He's gonna get what he deserves.* I thought.

The judge reprimanded, "Counselor, we're not here to talk about ants, we're here to talk about what your client did to Mrs. Mc Sorley."

"But it's still not fair to have ants bitin' you while you're bein' 'rested. An' besides that pig shot me in the back!"

"Counselor, please control your client, or I will have him removed from the courtroom."

The judge asked me when I was on the stand if I had drawn my weapon at anytime during the arrest. I told her no. The perp continued to claim that I shot him, and the judge finally asked to see the wound. He stood and raised his ultra-clean, heavily starched and pressed white shirt to show her the location. "Sir, I do not see any evidence of a bullet wound, and there is no mention of it in your file. I will ask you, however, what that mark is on your lower back. It has a curved angle and reads US Patent. Where did you get that?"

"I think it's a tattoo or sumpin', judge. But, what about the ant bites. Don't he have to pay for my ant bites?"

"No, he does not. He did nothing wrong." The judge gave him twenty years and with the double senior citizen penalty he got forty years and for the first thirty, no parole or probation. However, even as he was leaving he was yelling, "That pig! He kept lettin' the ants bite me, judge. What about the ants?"

I did have some repercussions over the incident though. Lieutenant Dan (Benedict) Arnold, the asshole that was always trying to nail me, wrote me up for discipline because it is against department policy to throw or to launch your radio at any time. He insisted that I had to personally pay for the radio that was broken, which incidentally was lost after the incident. Of course, without the radio as evidence, he would have been hard pressed to make the action stick. My Lieutenant, (Mean) Gene Germain, strolled into Arnold's office and asked for the report. He looked at it and remarked, "Arnold, this is bull shit," and he summarily ripped to pieces the papers of the complaint Arnold had written. *I know that bastard was afraid of Mean Gene and I'd like to have watched him. He was probably still squirming as bad as that robber was with ants in his pants,* I thought, when Lt. Germain told me how he had saved my ass.

METER MOLLY

It was my day off and I was sleeping in real good, dreaming about a sexy, sultry, good-looking blond that was breathing heavily in my ear and whispering sweet nothings that were so inviting. The whispers started ringing in my ear. Not once, but twice, then three times. I answered my damned phone and said in a pist voice, "Hullo." It was Willy. "What the hell do you want? This is my day off!"

Willy explained defensively, "We have court. I called in and we have to be there at 9:30."

"Hell, Wells, if you're goin' then I don't have to be there."

"Randel, if you're not going, I'm not either."

So, I left the warmth of my dreams and jumped into a cold shower, dressed for court, adding a sport coat. I told Wells I would meet him at the courthouse, and he informed me that I would have to pick him up because his car was not working. I swung by in my 1980 souped-up Camero, silver in color. Willy was all wide-eyed, bushy-tailed, and ready to go. I was not! I, of all people, was kind of grumpy. I didn't want to go to court. It was my day off. My intention was to sleep late, have a leisurely breakfast, read my newspaper while talking with Jamie the nice little waitress, and to enjoy my day.

Anyway, we went to Municipal Court where I pulled into the

parking garage. To my appreciation, there was a vacant parking space just inside. I hung a left and turned deftly into the space. *At least I don't have to walk too far.* I relished my good luck. Of course, it was metered parking. I checked and the meter had about thirty minutes left so I fed it a couple more quarters, figuring we had an hour-and-a-half, plenty of time for one hearing. On the way we stepped into records for the reports relevant to our arrest case.

Cute, little Linda was behind the counter. She said pleasantly, "How are you today, Officer Randel?" As I replied that I was fine, she pointed toward Willy and queried, "And how is *he?*"

Willy spoke up briskly, "Oh, I'm just fine!"

Linda asked coyly, "What you doin' for lunch, Randel?"

I raised my arm over and behind Willy's head, pointed my finger down at him and responded, "He's buying lunch for us."

To which Willy rapidly responded, "But I didn't bring any money."

"Well, you'd better find some before we leave here, Wells," I instructed, "or you'll disappoint this nice young lady." I gave her one of my friendliest smiles and we headed for Judge Troy R. Randolph's Court One. As we passed through the metal detectors I hailed the bailiffs who all knew me. As we entered the courtroom, Bailiff Robinson acknowledged me and we took seats close to and watchful of the outer door. There were four or five cases before ours and I wondered, *why the hell did I have to get up when I was having such a good dream just to come down here to wait for all these dirt bags to be sentenced.* My patience was wearing thin when our case was finally heard. We dealt the case and the guy only got thirty days. Waving goodbye to the judge, I left in a sour mood. I pouted; we *had that scumbag dead to rights. What the hell's wrong with that judge today? He should have doubled his sentence.* Grouchily I stated, "Let's go get something to eat, Wells."

"What about Linda?" He asked hopefully.

"Take her out if you want to, she's not my type. But you'd better wait until you have a car and some real pocket money. She could have very expensive taste."

His glow gone, Wells lumbered after me to the parking garage. *What the hell is that,* I wondered? It was a meter cart stopped directly behind my Camero, blocking my way. There standing beside the cart was *'little miss'* Meter Molly, closing her ticket book after writing out a ticket because my meter had expired. I recognized this particular meter molly. She was about 5' 5"tall, her brown mousy hair, slicked tautly up in a pony tail that made her eyes look Asian it was so tight. Her wide squat-shape, her flat-footed, black, Nazi shoes, and her bitter-face did nothing to endear her to me. *Oh no way*! I knew this bovine was out to get me again. She hated me and she thoroughly disliked Willy. If she saw Willy's car extending past a touch of red, or even yellow on a curb, she ticketed his car. If she found my Camero touching anything or one inch too far into the street, she delighted in writing me a ticket. Hell, between us we probably had thirty or forty tickets just from her. *She is not my friend, believe me!* We called her Cobra One; she was so deadly in her intent to strike at us whenever she could.

    I walked politely toward her. She walked to my windshield and placed the ticket beneath my wiper blade. I spoke in my nicest *my day's already screwed up* voice, "Hi, I'm Officer Randel."

    Immediately she retorted, "I know who you are Randel, and you don't affect me at all. I'm not one of your cute little Meter Mollys. You may sweet talk and outsmart the other Mollys, but you don't sweet talk or fool me."

    I replied earnestly, "I'm not trying to." I retrieved the ticket from beneath the wiper blade and explained that Officer Wells and I had been in Department One and with my hand outstretched, politely asked if she would take care of the ticket for me. The norm was that if you received a ticket while in court, you could take it to the bailiff that would cancel it, or the meter molly could write Department One on it and it would be canceled. Well, this did not set well with Cobra One. She had an attitude.

    Haughtily and with a snide grin, she hissed, "I wrote it, you can take care of it! I am not one of your sweeties." *Cobra had struck!* She turned on her heel and quickly returned to her cart.

    Now as I said, I had already had a bad morning, so I followed her right to her little Molly Cart, placed my body about two feet in front of hers and seethed, "Look, this is what I think of you and your ticket." I proceeded to carefully, and ever so o o… slowly, fold that ticket again and again until it was about a one-inch square. As she watched, in wide-eyed wonder, her body starting to waver, I stuck out my tongue, placed the ticket on it, drew it gradually in and closed my mouth. I started casually chewing, deliberately moving my face closer and closer to hers, until our noses almost met. As I loudly swallowed the ticket, which incidentally tasted like crap smells, Cobra dropped her ticket book. She had to squat down to get it, and all but came up under my chin. Without another word and in great contempt mingled with fear, she launched her little cart and speedily made her departure. She was in such a hurry that she missed the turn at the end of the garage and hit the wall. She screamed as the cart teetered and almost toppled.

As it righted itself, Willy and I were climbing into my Camero to assure our imminent retreat. If I hadn't been in such a foul mood, I probably would have wondered, p*oor thing, was she hurt?* But I didn't. Vindicated and laughing, we headed for Coco's where we enjoyed a relaxed and delicious breakfast.

Just as I was indulging the last of my iced tea, my phone rang. It was the Commander. *Uh oh!* Commander Church! He asked Wells and me to stop by his office as soon as possible. Now when the commander said 'as soon as possible', I knew that something was up and interpreted that to mean, 'right now.' Willy looked at me with alarmed anticipation and admonished, "Uh oh, my career's over. Here we go, here we go again," he lamented. "This is sure to be the end of my career."

Unrattled, I soothed, "Ahh, don't worry, Willy. It's nothing."

We arrived at Commander Church's office where he directed his question straight to me. "Randel, did you tear up a meter molly's parking ticket?"

Well, I don't lie, so I replied, "No sir, I did not."

"Are you sure? A meter molly's supervisor called and said she had to send a certain meter molly home because she almost had a heart attack after you threatened her and tore up a ticket she had placed on your car. She was so upset that she wrecked her cart and is now in a terrible state. She told her supervisor that Officer Randel tore up a ticket and threw it on the ground right in front of her."

As I said, I was not going to lie so I told the commander, "No sir, I did not do that at all." I looked at Willy, whose eyes were about as wide as his wire rimmed glasses. I figured he was thinking, *what the hell are you saying, Randel.* My look cautioned him not to speak and I replied, "No Commander Church, I didn't rip anything up in front of her, no not at all."

The commander regarded me momentarily and remarked, "I'll check it out and get back with you after while."

"Thank you, sir," I uttered politely and Willy and I left the room. As we were walking down the hall, Wells was trying to say something. I held my hand out warning him to be quiet. About out of voice reach, I blurted out, "But I ate that son-of-a-bitch, sir!" I could tell Wells was thinking *Randel that is our commanding officer. He deserves our respect.* Pensively, I silently responded, *I gave him respect; I called him sir!*

There was no responding telephone call. However, when we came in for briefing on Thursday morning, Commander Church was sitting at the front desk. He looked at us and said, "Randel, Wells, I want to talk to you in the hallway." The lieutenant and others were probably wondering what the hell was going on, but the briefing continued. Commander Church informed Wells and me that we were to take care of our outstanding tickets and to be in his office promptly at 2:00 p.m. that afternoon to apologize to that meter molly and her supervisor.

"Sir," I complained, "It was not our fault. All she had to do was void the ticket and go on. Everything would have been over and done. I spoke very nicely to her even though I don't like Cobra One."

"Who?" The commander looked confused.

"Cobra One. I mean the meter molly."

"What's Cobra One?" he inquired.

"That's her nickname, sir."

He reiterated, "Two o'clock sharp. Don't be late."

The fact that I was actually going to have to apologize to that bitch stuck in my gut like gravel in a rooster's craw. As Willy and I left the briefing room, I was not my normal jovial self. I was outraged and provoked. I even gave a little old man hell for jaywalking from the Blvd. to the courthouse. I don't think I called him sir, either.

I was just about to step off the stair at the plaza when the movement of a tall, willowy, very buxom woman caught my eye. My demeanor changed immediately. *Ah ha!* I thought. I smiled warmly as this dark-haired, high-cheek-boned, chocolate-brown eyed beauty walked by. She graciously smiled at Willy and me. I turned my head as she passed by, taking in the full sensuality of her well-rounded buttocks, and her shapely, long legs. Turning back to Willy, I surmised, "Wow, I don't know her, but I'm gonna!"

"Ha," laughed Willy. "A hundred guys have tried, and failed, Randel; you don't stand a chance."

"Oh, do you know her?"

"No, but she's the niece of Bill Turner of Turner Enterprises and she works for Judge Dunn."

Smugly I reiterated, "Willy, watch and learn." She went into the record office of the Court. I followed her inside and stood a few minutes for someone to wait on me. After an adequate time, I asked, "Excuse me, are you going to help me or just let me stand here, ma'am?"

She responded, "I am not the clerk that works in this department, Officer Randel."

"You know who I am, but I don't know your name."

"Everyone knows who you are, Officer Randel. Let's keep it the way it is."

"Okay," I rejoined, "I'll pick you up for lunch at noon, my treat."

"Look," she haughtily replied, "I don't want to have you treat me for lunch or anything. Find someone else."

I sulked, "No one will go to lunch with me and I don't like to eat alone."

"Then take Wells to lunch with you."

"Oh, he's not hungry. I'll see you at noon, Cheyenne." *She's surprised that I know her name,* I guessed. Willy started to say that he was hungry, but I shoved him out the door before he could open his mouth. I told Wells, "Sorry, Willy, you'll have to find your own ride." I knew he was not a happy camper. *Hell, he's a police officer; he ought to be able to find a ride with someone.* I handed him a twenty. "Why don't you go ask that cute Linda to lunch?" His eyes lit up and he made a beeline back to the records office.

I showed up fifteen minutes before noon, just in case Cheyenne left early. I parked my Camero, which I had washed and cleaned in the meantime, right in front of the court. I checked my hair and breath and added a bit of Lagerfeld Men's cologne, a sure bet for catching girls. I exited the car and languished at the passenger-side door. My feet were crossed as I leaned against the body, and I had my arm resting on the top of the car when Cheyenne came out the courthouse door, just a minute or two past noon. I gave her my most enchanting smile as I told her I had been waiting.

"Look, Randel, I am not going with you. I don't go with smart-asses. Everyone knows you're incorrigible."

"I know what they say about me, that I am a one-way, egotistical, self-centered, conceited asshole. But, I'll be on my best behavior." I opened my car door for her as I pledged, "I promise!" Her eyes met mine and I said a thousand words to her without speaking.

"Well, you did open the door like a gentleman," she submitted. "I guess lunch won't hurt. But it will cost you!" She sat gracefully on the seat and swung those long, perfectly shaped, tanned legs lithely into the car. I helped her reach the seat belt, and our fingers touched ever so briefly. It was as if a shock of lightening went directly from her fingertips to my heart. I was awestruck. It seemed that we hardly spoke, and the trip went too quickly as we rode to the Peppermill on Las Vegas Blvd.

We were immediately seated as Joan, the pretty blond hostess, welcomed me with a big hug.

Snidely, Cheyenne commented, "I should have known, Randel, she's probably one of your bimbos."

"No, she's going to college and will have a degree in law next year. We're just friends." I subtly remarked, "Do you have any friends, I mean real friends?"

She smugly replied, "That's none of your business."

We ordered and Cheyenne chose a costly menu that included a virgin daiquiri, soup, salad, an entrée, side vegetables and even dessert. She seemed very satisfied with her choices, though she ate very little of each course.

We made small talk about ourselves. I learned that she was a

Native American and then we discussed what each of us liked to do on our days off. I discovered that she liked to play poker and thought she was pretty good at it. I mentioned that it was a bad habit, especially for Las Vegas. She assured me that she only played at home with people she knew. As we finished our lunch, the waitress brought the ticket, which I only signed, as the lunch was comped to me since they knew me. I figured that Cheyenne felt embarrassed because she had ordered so much. "I should have known, Randel. What else don't you pay for?"

"Folks around here think I keep them safe and that they can count on me when they need a police officer." I left a ten-dollar tip. I let things settle in her mind and as we approached the courthouse again, I chuckled, "All right, Cheyenne. That was a pretty lame trick. Let me make it up to you at dinner. I'll pay for sure this time. Lunch didn't hurt you, did it?" I gently touched her shoulder while I held the door for her as she exited the car. "So, dinner at 7:00 for the lady?"

Willy and I hit the streets until time for our meet, and were in the commander's office promptly on time. Already there was the supervisor, a stately woman about fifty with graying hair and a pinched, hawk-like nose. Raised straight-backed beside her, to her full height, and coiled ready to strike, sat the arrogant Cobra! Swaying vehemently in her seat, she would not look at me.

The commander asked, "Well," as he glanced straight at me.

I looked fearlessly into Cobra's spiteful, spinning, rounded eyes and apologized, "I'm sorry that you wrecked your cart, ma'am, and that you almost had a heart attack, but I'm not sorry I ate that ticket!"

Cobra's hawkish supervisor gawked at me in shock and looked imploringly at Commander Church, expecting him to order me to make a more sincere reply than my apathetic regrets.

Smiling agreeably at both the supervisor and Cobra, the commander praised, "Nice apology, Randel, you're free to go."

I could hear the *hissing* spi*t* across the room as both women's lips sputtered in disbelief. As Wells and I quickly exited, we heard the supervisor squawking, "That was not a very good apology, Commander. I would have expected more from you."

"I told Randel he had to apologize, period. I did not tell him how, or what to say. Good day ladies."

Wells and I went directly to take care of our tickets. As Willy stood at the courthouse counter paying about $150, I slipped into the judge's chambers and he withdrew all my tickets. *If Wells had only followed my lead*...Back in our patrol car, Wells allowed, "My career's still in tact and I've survived another day with you, Randel. Thanks for not getting me fired!"

Not wanting him to feel too gratified, I reminded him, "Hell, Willy, it only cost you one-hundred fifty bucks and the day's not over yet!"

BREAKFAST BURGLAR III

It was my day off and Grumpy called wanting me to meet him for lunch at El Michoacan, a great Mexican food restaurant. Still groggy with sleep, I told Grumpy that I'd be there in thirty minutes and informed him that he was buyin'. He agreed without an argument, unusual for Sikes.

Grumpy was seated and my tea was already waiting for me. The waiter was just bringing Sam's drink and the chips and salsa as I sat down. I quickly observed that something was really bothering Sikes. "Rod, we've got to do something."

"What do you mean, Grumpy?" He didn't even make a reference to pulling a knife on me or slicing me, so I knew he was preoccupied.

"We've gotta do something about that burglar, that damned Breakfast Burglar in our area before he hurts or kills one of our old people. Besides that, I have to find Tilly's ring for her."

"You know that's easier said than done, Sam. When we set out to capture him, we also have to learn who's fencing the stolen goods. I still feel the stuff will show up in a local pawnshop, unless this guy is smarter than I think. Finding the fence is the only way we're gonna get Tilly's ring back."

Grumpy let me know, "Randel, you and I gotta be up and hittin' the streets about four every morning. That's about the time he seems to be breakin' into the homes in our area."

"Okay. The first thing we have to do is obtain a printout of the area that shows where he's been hitting. We need to find his route on each one of the different sets of burglaries to see if we can establish a pattern. Then we can go after him, and maybe lay a trap."

We discussed some options as we ate our delicious food, and I was surprised when Grumpy reached for the check without hesitation. I understood then just how wrapped up he was with our senior citizens, especially Ms. Tilly and her Cracker Jack ring. As we were leaving El Michoacan, Grumpy stated, "I'll go get the stats and the printouts for us to look over, but you gotta go talk to the sergeant and convince him that we need to start at 04:00 hrs. every morning until we catch that bastard."

He was right; Metro was pressing its luck, waiting for old people to report after the burglaries. Someone was eventually going to be hurt at the rate things were being handled. Back at my house, I called Lieutenant Gene Germain and told him how concerned we were about the Breakfast Burglar. I explained that Grumpy and I wanted to be on the streets in the area so that we could possibly catch him in action. "Lieutenant, Grumpy and I will come in, off the clock and work the area until we have some success."

"No, Randel, you come in and start as early as you need to. You will be paid for your time, and I'll clear all of this with the sergeant. I want that bastard caught too. Do you need anyone else to work with you?"

"No sir, I think we can do better with just the two of us for now. We will still have the night shift for backup. Thanks, LT." I was back on the phone and I called Grumpy and announced, "See you at the station at 03:45 hrs in the morning, buddy, thanks to 'Mean' Gene. We'll be on the streets at 04:00 hrs. and by God, we're going to catch our Breakfast Burglar."

"Good, 'cause when we do, I'm gonna twist my knife into his gut until he tells me where Tilly's ring is, and then I'm gonna cut him long, hard and deep and finish the job so the government don't have to put him away."

"Well, Sam, don't let yourself become overwrought about this.

Frank-3 Enroute

We'll do our best if we're level headed and calmly do some good planning. We'll catch him." *I sure as hell hope so.*

Saturday morning Grumpy and I were on the streets as planned, expecting the burglar to strike somewhere between Maryland Parkway and Las Vegas Blvd., and between Charleston and Sahara. As it happened, we were looking at the area just west of Maryland Parkway and north of Oakey. We started walking the area, hoping to catch sight of our burglar. Just a little before 05:00 hrs. I spotted a black man coming out between two houses at 1002 and 1004 Griffith. When he saw me, he turned and sprinted back between the houses.

"Control, Frank-3. I am in a foot pursuit of a possible burglary suspect. I am in the back yards going from Maryland Parkway to Tenth Street." As I ran between the houses I saw the burglar with a white pillowcase in his hands. He jumped over the backyard fence. In hot pursuit, I ran and jumped the same fence just in time to see him climbing over the next fence. I jumped down into that yard, figuring I am in 1004 Griffith. As I climbed the brick fence between 1004 and 1006, I observed the suspect going over the next wall. I hollered, "Stop, you bastard!" Just as I dropped into 1006, the owner of the house opened the sliding glass door to the patio and allowed two black Doberman Pincers to run outside. Those two dogs came right toward me as the burglar leapt the other wall. I was instantly climbing back up the wall from which I had come, as the two Dobbies were snapping at my behind and legs. One of them grabbed my pant's leg and ripped it as I crested the wall and shook him off. I walked the wall toward the front of the house and called dispatch. "Control, Frank-3. I have stopped my pursuit because of dogs. The suspect is eastbound in the backyards on Griffith. He is a black man, wearing black pants, a muscleman black T-shirt, gloves, black rubber boots and is carrying a white pillowcase. The suspect has not crossed Maryland Parkway yet."

At this time the Frank graveyard units, Frank-23 and Frank-14 were in the area. Adam-4 and Adam-1 were also in the area. *We're gonna get this SOB this time,* I hoped. I continued to hurriedly walk the area checking between houses, down alleys and every nook and cranny I knew. After an hour and forty-five minutes, the graveyard patrols were leaving to end their shifts. I decided to stop my search, dejectedly knowing that the Breakfast Burglar had once again eluded capture.

I went back to the house at 1002 where I circled the house and found that the sliding glass door had been broken and someone had forced an entry. I contacted Adam-12, Grumpy, who immediately answered that he was enroute. I entered the home and proceeded cautiously to the bedroom after I checked the kitchen and living area. Not receiving a response when I called out, and not seeing anyone there, I walked into the bathroom where I found a little, old, white-haired, unconscious lady lying on the floor with a lamp cord wrapped around her neck. I quickly checked for a pulse and called control. "Control, Frank-3, roll an am-bo-lance and the FD to 1002 Griffith. I have an older female with a cord wrapped around her neck. Her condition is critical. Hurry!"

Grumpy charged through the sliding door and knelt in front of the little lady, checked her pulse and listened for her breathing. He stated that she was barely alive, and he cursed that damned Breakfast Burglar. "See, what did I tell you, Randel? Now he's gone too far. He's escalating his crimes. He almost killed this little woman."

"Sikes," I ordered, "don't let anyone else in here except the medics. Maybe we can get a print or some information on the burglar." About four minutes later, the ambulance arrived. I knew the para-medics and one of them was named Eric. He immediately went to work reviving the woman. I asked Eric to be extra careful with preserving the crime scene and his crew and he were meticulous and careful. They transferred our little lady to Sunrise Hospital. As we looked around, Grumpy spotted the woman's purse that still held her wallet with her money and her identification. By the looks of her bedroom and the bathroom, she had put up one hell of a fight, knocking things this way and that, trying to get into the bathroom with her purse. Unfortunately, the burglar had followed her there and had tried to choke her, but for some reason left without her valuables. Checking for her identification we found that her name was Gracie, Gracie Echstein. *Maybe, just maybe we'll get a break on this one.*

About fifteen minutes later, Maggie from Criminalistics arrived and began her systematic, fastidious investigation, checking for prints and clues in the bedroom and bathroom. We also noted that in the kitchen Gracie had made a fresh pot of chicken and dumplings and had left it cooling on the stove. It was apparent that someone had eaten from the pan with a large spoon that had been removed from a drawer that hung open. Of course, Maggie dusted for fingerprints and again commented that the burglar was wearing soft cloth gloves. We at least had a better feel for with whom we were dealing, a black man, approximately six-foot, wearing black gloves and he liked either black or yellow rubber boots. Not much to go on, but we would catch him.

Grumpy informed me that he was going to keep circling, looking for that Bastard Breakfast Burglar, as he now called him, and that he was not going to stop until he caught the SOB and did him in. He patrolled the area for another hour or so until I needed back up on another call.

Shortly after we were finished with that call, Cheri', who had come on duty at 07:00 hrs. gave me a call. Frank-3, switch to channel 5."

"What's up Cheri'," I questioned.

"I had a call from a medic named Eric who said that he had answered an emergency call at 1002 Griffith and that you were the officer on duty there. He wants you to call him. He thinks he may have some information for you." Cheri' gave me the number and I called Eric.

"Eric, this is Officer Randel, what can I do for you?"

"Officer Randel, that little lady, Gracie Echstein, is in serious condition, but she's going to be all right. She can't talk yet, but I found something that you might want. It is a gold looped earring that is still closed, has blood on it, and Mrs. Echstein had it clasped in the palm of her hand. I think she might have jerked it from the burglar's ear. You might be looking for a man with a torn ear lobe."

"Great, Eric. Let me call Maggie from Criminalistics and let her pick it up. Did you happen to bag it for us?"

"I sure did, Officer Randel. I know a little about protecting evidence, so I took it from her hand with a pen and placed it into a little bag and sealed it for you. I'll wait to hear from Ms. Maggie."

"Thanks a lot Eric. You've been a great help. Ever think about joining the police force? We can always use a good man."

"Actually, I have. I think the pay is better too. Maybe I'll look in to it, sir."

"You look me up when you're ready, Eric, and I'll give you a recommend. I'll let you know when we catch this bastard."

The Breakfast Burglar got away again, but maybe we have a blood sample. Not much to go on, but every little bit helps. We will catch him! And now we'll have him for attempted murder too. Maybe I'm on to another good man for the Metro Police Force too. You never know.

That afternoon, a tired, weary and unsuccessful Grumpy went to the home at 1006 Griffith and interviewed the people that had let their dogs out that morning. He explained that the burglar had outrun me because the dogs had interrupted my pursuit. The couple was very sorry, but said that they heard someone, and they had been frightened several times before and were accustomed to turning their dogs loose when they heard strange noises. Grumpy also informed them that their dogs had almost chewed me to pieces. They were very apologetic and felt terrible when they found out that their neighbor, Gracie Echstein, had been attacked. They asked how they could be of service, and Grumpy told the man that he might watch her house until someone came to replace her sliding glass door. He gladly accepted the responsibility and said that he and his wife would see to everything for Gracie.

A couple of days later, Grumpy and I visited Gracie when she could have visitors and could talk a little. Her voice was low and gravely, but she had a smile on her bruised little face. "Officer Randel. Thank you for saving me," she whispered. That man scared me half to death. He came into my bedroom and I knew he was going to rob me. I keep a baseball bat by my bed, but he knocked it out of my hand. I grabbed my purse because it has everything in it, and I tried to run into the bathroom and shut the door on him. He jerked the lamp cord from my floor lamp, and shoved the door open. I tried to fight him, but he turned me around, I'm not very big you see, and he wrapped that cord around my neck. I just knew I was a gonner, but I reached up to scratch him and to pull out some of his hair for evidence. My finger caught on his earring and I jerked it out of his ear. He screamed when I did that, and he dropped me to the floor. I guess that's what saved me because he left me alone.

"But it made me mad when my neighbors told me that he had eaten some of my chicken and mattzo balls. That's a Jewish dish; I cook kosher. But I thank the Lord that he was with me, and that he sent you, Officers Randel and Sikes. You will always be in my prayers. I know that God hears me, and I know that you will be led to that burglar in God's time. In the meantime, I'm buying a trained German Shepherd to live with me. I won't let him out though as the neighbors did if you come running by. But, Officer Randel, catch that Son-of-a-bitch for all us old people. We're counting on you!

Oh the heated words of truth that come from little, old lady's mouths. People never cease to amaze me!

MAC-ARONI

HELL, I THOUGHT, TODAY I HAVE to break in another rookie. Entering from the back I sauntered to the front of the briefing room. Sassily half-lowering my sunglasses, I turned, set a hard eye on the new officer that was about mid way from the front. Placing my right hand on my gun, I caustically remarked, "You're in my chair."

"Oh, I'm sorry," he excused himself.

"Move!" I scowled at him with narrowed eyes.

"Yes sir," he remarked as he quickly stood and looked around for another seat.

"Don't call me sir. If you have a need to speak to me, I am Randel or Officer Randel, not sir. Understood!"

"Yes.s.s... Officer Randel," he faltered as he took another chair, afraid to look at me.

I crossed my arms and assessed the rookies that would be assigned that morning. Glaring at each person, I almost dared anyone to stare me down. No one did. I thought there were several that would not make it through the week, especially if I had anything to say about it. Some people just are not fit to become police officers for a hundred different reasons. I could be objective and critical if I wanted to, especially if I didn't think they could make the grade. You have to make the grade! I repositioned my sunglasses as I slipped into the vacated seat, slid down in a relaxed fashion, crossed my legs at the ankles and crossed my arms, waiting to hear who my new partner would be.

Then my good friend, Grumpy, our fifteen-year veteran, entered noisily at the back. I heard the shuffling of feet as rookies squirmed in their seats after they turned to see who entered. *They've all heard about Sam Sikes and his reputation,* I thought. *They're probably all nervous as hell wondering which of us hard-nosed trainers they're gonna get.* Clearly, he was called Grumpy for a reason. Stomping his huge number 14's to the front, he shook a rookie's chair and growled, "Move." The rookie moved! Grumpy, now in place, pulled his smaller knife, a four-incher, from his right pant's pocket, arrogantly flipped it open and was feigning cleaning his nails as the captain walked briskly to the podium. The captain shook his head at Grumpy who took his seat and ignored him. He did not pocket his knife!

After greeting the rookies with a friendly, "Good morning," and introducing himself, the captain turned the podium over to the lieutenant who started making assignments. It took a while as each new person was teamed with a Field Training Officer (FTO). As the room became less and less crowded, there was audible clearing of throats and movement of chairs. I smiled inwardly knowing that everyone left was hoping above hope that they were not going to be assigned to that harsh, hard-to-please, hard-nosed Randel, or that gruff, contrary, unsympathetic Sikes they had heard so much about at the Police Academy. I never turned or looked around but kept my eyes straight ahead on the lieutenant. At last he looked at me, smiled and surmised, "Well, Randel, it looks like Rookie Marconi will be your new partner." I turned in my seat to see the same man that I had previously unseated. *Oh shit! Some new beginning!* "Officer Sikes, Gilmore will ride with you!"

The room was quiet, you could have heard a pin drop; then Grumpy loudly scraped his chair on the tile floor, sounding worse than chalk on a blackboard, heaved a grand sigh and stood to his full six-foot four inches. Slowly turning he snapped "Out of that chair *now,* boy, or I'll cut you long, hard and deep and watch you bleed to death right where you are. I ain't got all day." Gilmore paled, but was on his feet in a flash. Grumpy pocketed his knife, removed his sunglasses, glowered at Gilmore and winked at me on his way out.

By that time, Marconi had rallied and was waiting for instructions from me. I indifferently rose from my seat, smoothed my mustache, adjusted my sunglasses and removed a set of keys to the police car. I curled my top lip and scowled, "What the hell you lookin' at *MAC-aroni?*" With a snide snort, I haughtily tossed the keys to him. *That was a good crack,* I silently praised myself, *MAC-aroni, Ha!*

Wide eyed, the short, Italian-bred, New York trainee neither spoke nor moved. He was of slight build and did not look strong enough to tackle a gnat. *This is gonna be one tough first week for this rookie,* I reasoned. "Get out there and start my car," I ordered.

"Right away, Officer Randel," he gasped as he stumbled over the leg of his chair and hastily exited the room. *At least he learned about the 'sir' business.*

When I arrived at my patrol car, Marconi was standing at attention on the driver's side. "Do you want me to drive, Officer Randel?"

"Are you crazy, MAC-aroni? I don't let rookies drive. Is that clear? Get around there and get in." I watched as he slid into his seat and fastened his seat belt. "What the hell are you doin'? Do you think you're gonna have time to fiddle with your damned seat belt when we're on a call? Hell man, you could be dead or someone else could be by the time you unhook yourself."

I angled behind the wheel. "What the F... is wrong with this seat? My knees are clear up to my elbows. Do I look like my six-foot frame will fit where your short, skinny ass has been? Don't even bother to answer. Just remember to have it right next time." I adjusted the seat, turned and looked at the befuddled rookie and announced, "Marconi, you don't have to kiss me or hug me or even like me. You only have to learn from me so you can go home when your shift is done." With that I revved the engine and we left the station.

"Frank-3, copy a call?" Dispatch waited for an answer.

"Frank-3, go ahead."

"Adam-12 is downtown and cannot take a call. Can you proceed to a 416 at Jaycee Park, northeast corner?"

"Copy, **Frank-3 enroute.** Send Adam-12 for backup when he's free." To Marconi, "Why the hell didn't you pick up the mike? How do you expect us to take a call?" As we wheeled up to the park where three subjects were indeed involved in a fight, a 416, I barked at Marconi, "Arrive us!" Grinding the car into park, I bounded out my door, PR-24 in hand. "Marconi, nobody jumps me. You've got my back at all times." I shouted at the fighters, "On the ground!" I heard Marconi telling dispatch that Frank-3 had arrived.

It's amazing that when an officer of the law approaches some people, the officer is suddenly the bad guy. One of the subjects turned and angrily ran at me. Not waiting for his attack, I kicked him in the chest with my foot, and he went down. "MAC, hook him!" The second subject was now running at me. I swung my PR-24 left to right and caught him with an audible crack on the leg, splaying him to the ground like a goalie on ice. The third man halted, wavered, spun around and fled.

"Do you want me to chase him, Randel?"

"Nah, MAC, we'll catch him later." I proceeded to cuff my subject then turned to observe Marconi. He had only one cuff on his offender and they were both lying on the ground, rolling around. I feared that the subject might wrestle Marconi's gun out of its holster. I left my man and shoved my foot on the other offender's head, then slid my foot to his neck. "Do you want to end up in a wheelchair, Asswipe? You will if you don't quit strugglin'. Cuff him MAC," I ordered. "What took you so long?"

We each quickly frisked our culprits for weapons, and finding none, we were ready to put both men in the patrol car. Adam-12 arrived with Grumpy and Gilmore. "Gilmore and I'll take one of these sons-of-a-bitches off your hands, Randel," Grumpy tossed his head toward his partner whom he thought could use the experience.

"Sure thing," I said. "Fill Gilmore in, 'MAC'," I instructed. He had risen to more than MAC-aroni after his tussle.

"What you waitin' for, Gilmore, get over there and help that rookie." As Marconi handed one suspect over to Gilmore, Grumpy admonished, "What the hell is that, Gilmore, a beer-can opener? That looks like a weapon to me. Confiscate it."

When we were in the car, Marconi questioned, "Why didn't we search them both for drugs, Officer Randel? They're obviously high."

"We'll only arrest them for disturbing the peace. If you find dope, leave it there, don't take it. We always search for anything that can be considered a threat to your safety, but not the drugs."

"Why?" Marconi was confused. Did this go against what he had learned at the academy, or what he thought was right? I could tell the kid was mulling over my decision against what he thought he knew.

"Once we book them for disturbing the peace, the jail personnel will search them thoroughly and confiscate any drugs. Then, when they are convicted for disturbing the peace, they can be charged for possession, in a search incidental to a lawful arrest. Makes for an easy conviction.

"Now, Marconi," I used his given name, so he would understand that what I would tell him was to teach him, "I want you to use the radio. I want you to know your area and I want you to always, and I mean always be safe in what you do. You will be observant of everything that goes on around you both on and off duty. You are a police officer now and you will conduct yourself as such at all times. Understood! How long have you been on the street?"

"This is my first assignment," he replied.

No wonder, I rationalized. "Tomorrow I expect you to have a good knowledge of your area and I will really introduce you to the business." I believed, *you've got a lot to learn.*

"Yes, Officer Randel." He seemed to appreciate the gravity of what I told him, but I felt his hesitation, maybe because he was so fresh out of the academy.

As we arrived at the jail and exited the car I looked critically at Marconi. I waited until he removed our prisoner and asked, "'MAC-aroni', what the hell's wrong with your uniform? You look like you've been in a shit-fight. Square yourself away before we go inside. You're disgusting."

Marconi positioned his prisoner against the bumper of the car, brushed and straightened his uniform, slicked back his thick, black, Italian hair, looked in the side mirror and seemed pleased with himself. "Always look fresh when you enter the jail. You never want to look like you can't handle anyone or anything." Sarcastically I added, "Is that your best? I guess it'll have to do." We entered, placed our weapons in lock boxes and proceeded to the elevator. As I pressed the 'up' button I asked, "You hungry, MAC?"

"No, not really. Officer Randel, I don't know if police work is for me."

Poor kid, probably his first real scuffle. "This is real fun, inn'it?"

"No."

"Heck, it's only nine a.m. We've got all day to have fun." I looked at our arrestee and he did not look as if he were having fun either.

After we left the jail I swung into the nearby 7-11 at Oakey and Las Vegas Blvd. I notified dispatch that we would be out of the car. We went inside where Gail greeted me with a fresh iced tea. Marconi grabbed a Coke. As we were leaving, I looked sternly at MAC, "Did you pay for that drink?"

"But Gail said…"

"I don't care what Gail said. You go pay for it. You haven't earned shit yet. Believe me, you'll earn every drink someone wants to buy for you. But not yet."

"Frank-3, copy a call? A domestic disturbance at 309 West Chicago, down in the Naked City. Family fight. A son-in-law and a dad are sloppy drunk."

"**Frank-3 enroute.**" As we approached, I warned Marconi, "Watch everything, watch my back, until I say different." Upon entry, we observed that the son-in-law had a bloodied nose and the father had a raised, red bruise on his cheek.

I identified myself and the son-in-law came at me saying, "You're not so damned hot!" I popped him in the throat. He quickly put both hands to his throat and I slung the cuffs on his left arm and threw him to the floor.

The father raged, "What the hell's he doin' down there? You can't do that to *my* son-in-law." With that he lunged at me. I planted my foot in his crotch and he went down. But he wouldn't stay down so I kicked him in the head.

"Sir," I explained, "lie still." As I took the father down, Marconi was trying to hook the son-in-law who tried to get up. The younger man was close to me so I placed the heel of my boot on his hand. "Hell, MAC, finish hooking him up!"

The son-in-law had rolled over and had his right arm under his chest, holding it close so Marconi couldn't pry it out. The father was in frenzy, cussing us with every foul word that he knew. "I can't get his arm, Randel," complained Marconi. I took my PR-24 and wedged it under the man's arm at the elbow, twisted it and the arm came out. Marconi hooked his subject just as Adam-12, Grumpy and Gilmore, arrived for backup. We escorted the son-in-law outside to frisk him. Grumpy nudged the father outside with a swift kick in the butt, and was all business as he frisked him.

Grumpy and I studied Marconi. He was totally disheveled. His badge was torn off his shirt and barely dangling by a thread. "Damn, Randel," queried Grumpy, "can't MAC-aroni arrest a fellow without a fight?"

"Sam, I'm teaching him that when you're dealin' with ass holes, you always gotta do what you gotta do," I prodded.

Grumpy and Marconi shook their heads in disbelief as Grumpy ordered, "Okay, 'Gilly', put your man in the car." He addressed the dad, "Look, ass hole, I'm gonna cut you long and hard and deep if you give my rookie any trouble. Set your ass in the back seat, sir."

Gilmore, looking shocked asked, "Do I have to ride in back with him, Officer Sikes?"

"Hell yes, you do," Grumpy responded forcefully. "We have to transport him and book him, just like anyone else. If I have to, I'll shut his mouth for you." The father suddenly quit yelling and we watched the mollified woman looking out the door as we drove away to book in City Jail.

The next call came, "Frank-3 can you copy a call?"

Marconi took the mike, "Frank-3, copy."

"We have a 416 involving three Indians fighting at the Peace Pipe Bar on Eastern at Sahara Avenue."

Say **Frank-3 enroute,** I told Marconi. He did it right. Then, "Officer Randel, is this what we do everyday?"

"Yeah, Isn't it fun!"

"Well, not really. I thought police work would be more like being a park ranger."

In disbelief of his naiveté, I could not answer. What could I tell a young officer that was probably raised in the back woods in western New York and had never been exposed to the chaos of the big city? We proceeded to the Peace Pipe.

"Adam-12 can you back Frank-3?"

"Copy. Enroute." It was Rookie Gilmore's high, anxious voice.

We had no sooner arrived, when three large, drunken American Indians came barreling out the door, cussing and fighting each other. I threw the car into park, jumped out and the fight was on. When the Indians realized what was about to happen, they all came at us. As they haphazardly staggered toward me, Marconi covered my back. I punched the first one in the throat. He went down, grabbing his throat, gasping for air. Another came at me. I drew my PR-24, swung it like a polo stick and hit him behind the knee. He teetered like a frog with one leg and then, down he went.

Meanwhile, on the sidewalk at the parking lot, Marconi and the third Indian were scuffling around on the ground. The Indian probably outweighed Marconi by sixty pounds, but Marconi was giving him one hell of a time. "Who's winning?" I yelled.

Puffing hard, "Not... sure!" was all he could muster.

About that time, the Indian I had kicked was back up. He grabbed my shirt. I put him into a wrist hold, breaking his wrist as he dropped to the ground. The other one that I had hit with the baton moved. "Stay down," I ordered, "stay down, sir." And he did.

Irrespective of the situation, that soused culprit was yelling at me, slurring, "You broke my leg, damn you, you broke my leg."

Ultimately, Grumpy arrived with his trainee. "Who's winning between Marconi and the Indian?" he scornfully inquired. To Gilmore, he ordered, "Get your ass over there and help that little guy before that Indian scalps him." Grumpy hooked the Indian with the injured leg and warned, "Stay on the ground, you red-skinned bastard or I'll wound your other knee. Don't move, sir!"

I cuffed my man as Gilmore and Marconi were still struggling with the big buck. Gilmore finally grabbed the Indian's long, black hair, jerked his head back stomped his right eye, and then placed his heel firmly on his neck. The Indian still fought with Marconi, flailing his arms, until Sam came over and hooked him soundly. The Indian spit on Grumpy, who until now had been reserved. Grumpy socked the Indian's other eye; the man went out like a light. *He's going to be one helluva big fellow to get in the paddy wagon.* I looked over at the two rookies sitting a straddle the large, drunken Indian. Marconi looked as if he had been in a fight with a rabid badger, one of the meanest, orneriest mammals one would ever want to tackle, and I was sure he felt every lick his opponent gave him. Gilmore sat atop the Indian with a satisfied grin on his valiant and triumphant baby-face. I had a strong sense that Gilmore had what it took. Pathetically, Rookie Marconi, on the other hand, wore cuts, scratches and sidewalk burns on his face. His hands had abrasions, his knuckles were bleeding, and his PR-24 lay across the parking lot. His badge was hanging again, his nametag was missing, his gun belt was crooked, and one of his eyes was bloodshot and turning black.

"Good job, Marconi," I lauded. Marconi squinted up into the sunlight at me in pure wonder. "Okay, MAC, let's frisk, load and transport," I commanded.

As we followed the paddy wagon to jail, Marconi admitted, "This ain't fun, Randel."

"What do you mean?"

"I don't think police work's for me."

After we booked our unpeaceful Indians from the Peace Pipe, I told Marconi that we would see how the rest of the day went, and then we would talk about it. Actually the rest of the day was quiet and rather dull. Marconi kept editorializing that police work was not what he expected. "Don't you ever get scared?" he asked.

"If you're scared, then you shouldn't be in police work. You should quit. If you are scared, you can be hurt or get someone else hurt. You have to act now and be scared later. Otherwise you or your partner will end up being oil and dirt spots on the pavement. Remember though, all days are not like this." I smiled sardonically, "Some are worse." When we went to debriefing, I privately told the lieutenant that Marconi had doubts.

Marconi was sitting, with a downtrodden look as Grumpy came in. Grumpy slapped him fondly on the shoulder and chided, "Didn't you have fun today, boy?" Sam had one of his bigger knives in his hand as he spoke and Marconi just stared past him, dumbfounded.

The lieutenant came forward and invited Marconi into his office. He advised me that he had given Marconi the next two days off to think what his decision would be. On Monday morning he said the police department was not for him and he quit. He told the lieutenant, "Those 'guys' are crazy and they think this is fun."

I had heard that he became a cab driver and one-day Grumpy and I ran into him. I asked him how he liked that job and he told me he had not had any more fights. He acted as if he were anxious to drive away from us, as his glance shifted quickly between Grumpy, who had drawn one of his many knives, and mild mannered me. As I said, police work is not for everyone.

PUPPY LOVE

6:59.40 HRS. A.M., MONDAY MORNING. I was conducting myself in my normal, polite manner as I entered the briefing room and claimed my usual chair at the back, anticipating my next, newly assigned rookie. Sam Sikes and Gilmore were still paired and apparently surviving together. *Who the hell will I get this time? Some candy-ass ingrate probably. Oh well, it's more than halfway through the week for me. Maybe I can save the department from another mistake.* Surly tempered, I felt no need to greet anyone. I sat moodily facing the front as the lieutenant called out the partnerships. *Why does he always wait to assign me last? Hell, I have a lot of things I could be doing rather than sitting in here. I could go have an iced tea and argue at the office with Grumpy. I really don't care who the hell I get. It's always tough breakin' in a rookie. It takes more time and extra care for their safety. I'd rather be ridin' alone. But... somebody has to train these young people.*

"Officer Randel," the lieutenant drew me from my reverie, "you're the last man up today. Let me introduce you to your new rookie.

"Good luck, Officer Love!"

I almost sputtered aloud. *"I'll be damned,"* I thought as I gawked at the front where a young, black woman stood as her name was called. "Officer Love, meet Officer Randel. You'll ride along with him the next three weeks." The captain looked notably pleased with himself.

She was 5' 9" or 10", slender, neat and crisp, very attractive. Her uniform, hair and face were immaculate. She smiled readily, a big smile, revealing the biggest, whitest teeth I had ever seen, and I thought *the biggest mouth.*

As the other officers partnered and left, I stood and strode toward her, taking that one extreme step that invaded her personal space, and barked, "What's your name again?"

"Love, Kimmie Love," she replied boldly.

"Hell, that's no name for a police officer," I scowled. "What's your middle name?"

"LaRue."

"LaRue? That's no good either. Kimmie LaRue Love!" *That was sarcastic.* "No! Hell no!" Then thoughtfully, "From now on you're Rosco, Officer Rosco. Well, get your gear, Rosco. We're burnin' daylight," I ordered as I bulldozed past her. She immediately followed, keeping in close step behind me. We exited the station and I went to our patrol car and waited at the driver's door. She hesitated at the passenger door. "Get in," I cajoled, "I ain't comin' around there to open your door for you, Kimmie."

"The name is Officer Rosco," she replied snidely, "or did you forget, Randel? I didn't expect you to help me, I can take care of myself," she assured as she seated herself. "I am not a feminist, if that's what you think."

We'll see, I vainly thought to myself. "I don't care what you think, Rosco. There won't be any hugs or kisses and definitely no LOVE in this car. Here's the way it's gonna be. I expect you to only learn and to go home each night, *alive.* You do what I say, when I say, without any questions. You keep one ear on the radio, know your area, and be safe." I was silent then, wondering what she was thinking. I looked at her profile. *Strong, resolute, self-assured,* I surmised. *I'll see what I can make of her.* Then I noticed her long, painted fingernails. "What the hell are those? Claws? You know what regulations say about..."

"Frank-3, copy a call? A 425 at the Villa Motel, 225 Las Vegas

Blvd. South. A suspicious circumstance at one of the rooms toward the street.

Rosco did not delay. She immediately picked up the mike and answered, loud and clear, "**Frank-3, enroute.**" We were on our way.

"Did I tell you to answer that call?"

"No, but I expected you wanted me to take it. I didn't want to keep dispatch waiting."

I figured she was thinking, *Who does this ass hole think he is?* But I wanted to test her mettle. "Okay, Rosco, you handle the radio. It's yours---Don't mess it up."

"I know how to operate the radio, Officer Randel. And, I know how to drive, and I know how to do my job." I thought, *no you don't, but you will.* "I do not know, however," she chattered on, "what you expect of me, so that's what I am here to learn. I'm aware of your reputation and I'm willing to put up with that because I figure you're one of the best officers on the force, and I'm delighted to be riding with you."

She'll be delighted, HA! I rubbed my hand over my mouth and down my chin, hiding the smirk as I wiped it off. *Hmm,* I thought, *this is one spunky gal. Let's just see what she's got goin' for her. Maybe she'll stand up to the test.* I backed quickly out of the parking space and replied. "We don't lolly gag, Rosco, tell them Frank-3 is enroute."

"I already did, Randel."

"Oh, right." I was definitely feeling no love that day for my new rookie. *I think it's gonna be a long day.*

Day two. Roscoe was seated in the patrol car, ready to roll as soon as I came from talking with the lieutenant after briefing. "What you sitting there for, Roscoe?" I pursued, "This vehicle inn't ready yet."

"Yes, Officer Randel, it is. I've checked everything, mirrors, bumpers, radio, under the hood, brakes, lights, tires, the back and front seats, and the locks. All sides of the vehicle are cleared. Is there anything I've missed?"

"Did you check the shotgun?"

"Yes."

"How many rounds in the gun?"

"Four," she answered.

"Is there a round in the chamber?"

Roscoe hesitated and acknowledged, "I don't know."

"Well, find out," I advised, "always know your weapon." As she started to open her car door, I held up my hand and said, "Hold up, Roscoe. I never carry a round in the chamber. I like the brutal, powerful sound of metal to metal when I jack the round into the chamber; it's the somber sound of death. When bad guys hear it, they know without a doubt, I will ventilate them! Do you get what I'm talking about?"

"Yes, it sounds so final. It still startles me almost as much as the actual shot."

"Well, get our friend and put it here between us. You never know when we'll have to use it. Be sure the safety's on."

When Roscoe returned after checking the shotgun thoroughly, she reiterated, "Is there anything else that I missed, Officer Randel?"

"We'll see!" I was sullen. "If anything goes wrong with this damn car, you'll be responsible, Roscoe. Got it?"

"Anything other than mechanical, and I could probably take care of that too. I was brought up the hard way in the projects, Randel, and I had to learn from experience how to take care of everything I ever had. I know when an automobile is in good condition and when it needs servicing. I see by the logbook that it was given a complete overhaul three weeks ago, and that you have only driven 779 miles since that time. Is that correct? Oh yes, and I logged in our mileage last night when we finished."

Oh put a lid on it, Roscoe, I thought. *I'll find something to test you on soon. You're too good and sure of yourself. Yeah, but as a matter of fact, you did a damned good job checking out the car.*

We patrolled the streets for a while as I tested her knowledge of the area. Finally, at about 10:30 I pulled into an alley and drove midway to the next street. "Where are we, Roscoe?"

"We're between Third and Fourth Street just north of Charleston Blvd."

The girl knows where she is all right, I thought, almost proudly.

We proceeded to about a half block from the corner of Las Vegas

Blvd. and Charleston Blvd. "Okay, Roscoe, you're going to direct traffic for a while." *Let's see how she does in the blazing sun on that searing pavement. I'll bet her little tootsies will be burning and aching tonight.*

"Shall I turn the lights off, or direct with them as they are?"

"As they are." *That's hard enough because people are waiting and watching for the light to change, not for a policewoman standing in the middle directing.* "Direct with the lights, and don't allow anyone to make a left turn. I don't want you gettin' any of our good citizens killed. Clear?"

"All right, Randel." Roscoe merged carefully into the middle of the intersection with her white gloves sassily on and a whistle that I was surprised she had, and began to direct the traffic flow. There were a few screeching tires, horns honking, some men flashing big, friendly smiles, and irritated drivers screaming obscenities, but all in all, the woman did a good job. After about forty minutes with me watching in my air-conditioned car, and her standing in the steaming, torrid fray of downtown traffic, I thought she was probably about worn out. But, even though her arms had been swinging first left and then right, forward and then backward, she maintained a quick smile at the pedestrians and the drivers of the passing cars. Large beads of perspiration ran down her face beside her ears and her once crisp uniform showed wet lines down her back.

Leaving the patrol car for a few minutes, I sidled into the traffic, and stood behind Roscoe, "About ready to pack it in, officer?" I chided.

Stopping the traffic from all four directions, she retorted, "Certainly, now it's your turn to take over, Randel." She turned briskly and headed toward the car. I checked the lights to see which direction had the green and waved those folks forward. I was not going to stand out there with a perfectly good traffic signal and direct traffic. *Not on my life!*

Roscoe had removed her cover and her gloves and had wiped the perspiration from her face. She looked amazingly fresh and composed and rendered a generous smile as I slipped behind the wheel. She reached into a large red handbag and removed some hand lotion and started applying it to her hands. "Where the hell did that bag come from," I huffed. "You can't carry a suitcase around with you when you're on duty, woman. Everything has to be on you and ready to go. Get rid of that damned thing. Get a little ditty bag like mine here next to my seat."

"All right," she said respectfully. Fussing with her hair, she asked, "Does my wig look okay?"

"What wig?" I queried in astonishment.

"Oh, didn't I tell you, I always wear wigs!"

What the hell else is she going to tell me, I pondered? *Too late!*

Roscoe dumped her belongings out of the bag into her lap and tossed the red bag into the back seat. "I'll dispose of the bag at the first trash can, Randel. Will you kindly put my lipstick and my comb in *your* bag? Oh yes, and I may need these tampons today, too. Do you have a place to stick them?"

"What the hell...." I was beyond thinking.

She busily tucked a small bottle of cologne in her vest pocket, her tissues in her back pocket, her billfold into her bra, her personal car keys in her left pocket, her nail file and clippers and her bottle of nail polish into my ditty bag, and without looking at me, happily continued, "There, that should take care of everything."

Oh, crap! There is something definitely wrong with this girl, I surmised. Ducking my head toward my chest, I shook it sideways, "Roscoe, is everyday going to be like this?"

"Aren't you having fun yet, Officer Randel?" *She had no fear of me, I could tell. She's laughing like crazy behind that smug look she has on her face.* Coyly, she prodded, "What shall we try next?"

"Well, now we're going to stop a few cars, and you can issue tickets." We didn't have to wait long before a long black Cadillac breezed through the light.

"Let's go, Randel," she pressed, "go get her!"

I placed the car into gear and left our parking space, following a woman who was obviously not aware that we were behind her, even though I turned on the flashing lights. We followed her for a block and a half, and finally, I gave the siren one small blast. Startled, the lady abruptly stopped right in the middle of the street. "Get on the horn and tell her to move to the curb," I ordered. Roscoe quickly responded. The woman revved the engine and jerked the car onto the sidewalk, applied her brakes and jolted to a stop.

Roscoe was expeditiously out of the car, holster unbuckled, hand on gun. She advanced cautiously, and knocked on the raised window, her stance at a safe and correct distance. *Excellently maneuvered, good job, score one for safety,* I observed. I ran the license plate and checked the registration. In a moment Roscoe was back to her side of the car. "Well," I said, "what are you going to do?"

"I'm not going to give her a ticket, Randel. I told her to wait for a minute while I check her license and registration. Poor little thing, she's crying and I think she may have wet her pants."

"Poor little thing, hell, she could be a mass murderer, and you're going to let her go?"

"No, I'm going to check her out." Roscoe turned the M.D.T. screen toward her and typed in the information from Mrs. Kathleen Atherton-Smythe's driver's license. She started to enter the license tag but I told her I had already run it and that the car was registered to a Theodore Smythe. Roscoe haughtily turned the screen back to me and said, "See, no priors, no outstanding tickets and no arrest warrants. I'm going to let her go, with a word of caution. She said she was upset and crying because her dear Teddy passed away and she just left him at the crematorium. She's going to look for a special urn for him. Bless her heart, she didn't even see the light."

"Bless her heart! She or some other driver could be lying next to *dear Teddy,* if she's not careful. Get on with it, Roscoe. Do what you gotta do." She looked as if she were not sure what I expected her to do, ticket or not ticket. *I really don't care, lets get this over with.*

When Roscoe returned, she looked pleased with her decision to not ticket and to send Mrs. Atherton-Smythe on her way. "What time will we be through this evening, Randel?"

"Probably by 5:30, 6:00 o'clock," I surmised. "Why, you got a hot date?"

"That's none of your business, but yes, I am going to the cemetery with Mrs. Smythe at 6:30. She has no one here to be with her when they bury her husband. No one should be alone at a time like that. Why don't you come too, Randel? That would be a kind and generous thing for you to do, and," she said lightly, "that might even help you."

Help me what? That's not an invitation, I thought, *it sounds more like an ultimatum. She can damned well forget that!* My thoughts were emphatic; *I'm not into that touchy, feely crap!*

At six-fifteen, I dropped Kimmie LaRue Love at Mrs. Kathleen Atherton-Smythe's massive house in the Park Ranch Estates. I was not willing to attend the funeral but I waited until a gentleman came to the door. Kimmie was out the door waving at me before I could drive away. "Randel, it's not what I thought! Teddy is not her husband; he's her dog. She has a bigger than life-size painting of him in the foyer with his name engraved in gold. The butler thought I would like to see the black Scottie's picture and read his epitaph. Please stay with me, Randel; I can't do this by myself." I looked at her, shaking my head, negatively. "Well, will you, please?" she begged.

"The answer is NO! I never get involved." I was stern and direct. *She might as well learn that about me now...*

Together, Roscoe and I attended Teddy's pitiful, wee funeral at the Craig Road Pet Cemetery with Mrs. Theodore Atherton-Smythe. I drove since both women were weeping, emotional messes. *What else could I do?* Afterward, feeling somewhat humbled and a little down, I asked Roscoe if she would like to catch something to eat before she went home. She thanked me for staying with her but said she had other plans for the evening. I breezed through the drive-in, headed directly home and put on the movie, <u>Old Yellar.</u> *Everybody cries over that one! But I'm a tough guy and I could handle that, and thankfully, tomorrow was my day off.*

8:00 a.m. and I was burrowed into my pillow, blissfully sleeping in. Ring, ring, ring. *What now?* "Hello. Who? ... Roscoe?" The cobwebs were clearing. "But, it's my day off."

"Meet me at the station right away. How long will it take? I need you there ASAP!"

"What the hell for? Another one of your wild-child ideas?"

"Maybe. I'll tell you when you get there. Hurry!" Roscoe hung up the phone. It was not uncommon for a rookie to call me in a panic, even on my day off. Sometimes things happened that they did not know how to handle, or they were afraid they might get into trouble over something they had done the night before.

I dressed quickly and headed to the station. Roscoe was waiting with her car running. "Come on, Randel, jump in," she exclaimed excitedly.

"What's up, Roscoe?" I cautiously inquired as I approached her car. I opened the passenger door and noticed a little white ball of fluff in the seat. "Be careful, Randel, she might bite you," she said teasingly. "Pick up that sweet little thing and hold it."

"What the hell is it?" I asked, poking it with my finger. A tiny, downy-soft, white face with large black eyes and a shiny black nose looked up at me. *Lord have mercy,* I thought, *it's a puppy. What now?*

"Isn't she precious? I found her through a friend and we're going to take her to Ms. Kathleen. Won't she be surprised and happy? Come on, climb in."

I'm surprised, but I'm sure as hell not happy. This is my one day to myself. Well, let's get it over. I picked up the wiggly, little critter and slipped into the seat. I found myself stroking her soft fur, and the little pup licked my hand as we rode to Mrs. Smythe's estate. I even carried it to the door as Roscoe led the way. After we were issued inside, Kimmie took the *little darling* into her arms and presented it to Ms. Kathleen when she came to the sitting room. "Officer Randel thought you should have a new little friend, Ms. Kathleen." *Like hell,* I thought. There were tears a-plenty as the two women cooed and fussed over petite *Theo,* namesake for both Theodore and Teddy. When we were ready to leave, Ms. Kathleen kissed Kimmie and though I tried to only shake her hand, she gave me a big smooch on the cheek and thanked me endlessly, as she hugged me tightly. The women lovingly embraced again, and I thought we would never escape.

As Roscoe was ready to drop me at the station, she praised me, "That was a real nice thing you did, Randel. Thanks a lot. I know that woman will never forget two officers who cared enough to be with her and to bring something new and comforting into her life. Thanks again."

"Oh well, I didn't have anything better to do today, Roscoe." Pensively, I asked, "You hungry? Want to grab breakfast at the Omelet House?" *That <u>was</u> a nice thing we did! Maybe I'm not such a bad guy.* That morning was the first of many breakfasts that Roscoe and I would share on our days off.

GRAMMS

Gramms was harassing one of the street people that was working on her block. She did not want anyone that she did not choose to be there. She was cursing him viciously and threatening bodily harm. "Frank-3, copy a call. We have a black female that is drunk and disorderly at the 400 hundred block of Hoover. .

"**Frank-3 enroute**." I knew exactly who the drunk and disorderly person was. Gramms had not been functioning very well ever since some street punks had knifed and killed her street friend, Hugo, and she had held him as he died. She had started drinking more heavily than usual and had become quite nasty and abusive to people around her. Wells and I had been to her location several times and had told her we would arrest her if she did not behave. Gramms lived on the streets of downtown Las Vegas just like so many other ne'r-do-wells. Today, she was sloppy drunk, filthy and her behavior was lewd.

Willy pulled the patrol car to the curb and I exited the passenger side. I approached Gramms, who did not yet see me. She was swinging her fists at the beggar that was swaying almost as badly as she was. He had a brown-bagged bottle of alcohol and was trying to tipple it while he avoided Gramms punches. However, one thump caught him on the chin and he stumbled and sat down hard, crashing his bottle as he did so. Gramms laughed and exclaimed in her drunken slur, "That'll teach you to work on my block, you filthy bastard."

"Gramms," I interrupted. "What the hell do you think you're doing? Haven't I told you that you have to play nice or I'll run you in? Now get your ass over here and leave that poor man alone."

"He don't belong here, Offither Ranel," she accused. "I don't want him on my block."

"Come on, Gramms, you don't own the street. He has as much right as anyone to be here. I'm going to have to arrest you for disorderly conduct or a public nuisance." I looked at Willy who had been tending to the drunken man on the sidewalk. "Is he okay, Willy?" Wells gave me an affirmative and I told him to help me cuff Gramms.

Wells pulled his cheat-sheet from his shirt pocket and started reading verbatim, "You have the right…"

"Hell Willy," I chastised, "When are you gonna learn that we don't have to read the rights for a misdemeanor. You've been on the force long enough."

"I'm sorry, Randel, I just don't want to make a mistake during an arrest. It might make me lose a case or something." *Yeah, you're thinkin' again that you'll ruin your career,* I thought playfully. Other street people had gathered and were watching us closely as we handled Gramms. She was a tall, skinny woman, weighing about one hundred forty pounds. She reminded me of a black 'Olive Oil', Popeye's girlfriend. Her natty, short, gray-black hair was hidden under an open-topped sun visor cap. A pair of sunglasses was hung from a decorative cord around her neck. She wore a huge, bright, flowered dress that extended to her ankles, but hiked up in the back so that if she bent over, her backside would show. She wore knee-length bloomers to protect her modesty. Gramms donned white sports socks with shit-kicker, brown combat boots that she sometimes used for kicking those she considered ingrates.

Gramms must have decided that Willy was one of those ungrateful, unwelcome people just as he started reading her rights. She jerked her leg back, swung it forward and landed a healthy kick on poor Willy's shin. Willy hopped back, out of her reach as I tugged on her handcuffs. In pain, with his leg tucked behind his other knee, and through gritted teeth, he complained, "Oww! Randel, do something!"

Gramms was hollering obscenities at Willy as I moved her toward the back door of the vehicle.

I was ready to open the door and Wells was rubbing his shin, when I noticed a long, black Cadillac pull up behind my patrol car. Cautiously, I held Gramms tightly as I observed the driver. To my surprise, I saw that it was Mrs. Kathleen Atherton-Smythe. She waved happily at me as she exited her vehicle. "Hello, Officer Randel. I haven't seen you for such a long time. You should come by to see my little puppy, Theo. She's so sweet and is getting so big. I'm not interrupting anything, am I?"

"Yes ma'am. I'm arresting this lady. Please stand clear, ma'am. It's nice to see you too."

"Oh my, why are you arresting this poor, dear lady?" She could see that Gramms was inebriated as she swayed back and forth. However, Gramms had stopped cussing and was looking curiously at Mrs. Atherton-Smythe. Gramms immediately spotted the large diamond rings and expensive jewelry that she wore. She started smiling at Mrs. Smythe.

"Tell Offither Ranel not to arrest me, ma'am. I ain't doin' no body no harm."

"Officer Randel, if she is only drunk and disorderly, please let me take her to my home so that she can get some rest."

"Ma'am," I stated kindly, "Gramms lives on the streets and would not make a good guest in your home."

"Pshaah! That doesn't matter to me, Officer Randel. She won't have to live on the streets anymore. Please let me take her with me. I have a guesthouse at the back of my property. She can stay there as long as she likes and I will furnish everything she needs. She won't have to worry about food or clothing or anything."

Mrs. Atherton-Smythe's words were not wasted on Gramms. She saw an opportunity to avoid the city jail and she smiled woefully at me. "Come on, Offither Ranel, you're a nice guy. Let me go home with her, okay? Offither Willy, I'm sorry that I kicked the hell out of you. Please forgive me." Her words seemed sincere, and Willy assured her that he was all right.

"Gramms," I cautioned, "that gentleman that you socked in the jaw may want to press charges against you. Willy, will you ask him, please? If he does, Gramms, I will have to book you."

Willy checked. "Randel, that man is blissfully, sound asleep. I don't think he cares about anything right now."

I was considering Mrs. Smythe's offer as I looked at Gramms. *Maybe this street woman just needs a chance to make a better life. I know Mrs. Smythe has been awfully lonely since her husband died. Maybe she can do some good with Gramms.* "Okay, Gramms, here's the deal. You can go home with this nice lady. But you have to behave yourself and be polite and clean yourself up. Mrs. Smythe has a nice home and she will be very good to you. I'll drop by when I get off work tonight to see how you two are doing. Is that all right with you, Mrs. Smythe?"

"Yes, Officer Randel, that will be just lovely. Come on, Gramms. Goodness, I don't even know your Christian name. We have so much to learn about each other. Officer Randel, when you come by tonight, you must stay and have dinner with us. I will tell cook to plan for you. Little Theo will be so happy to see you too. By the way, how is Officer Roscoe?"

I uncuffed Gramms and led her to the black Cadillac. I politely opened the passenger door as Willy assisted Mrs. Atherton-Smythe on her side. The two ladies, *even Gramms is acting like a lady,* were already chatting joyfully about going to church together on Sunday. *I hope the roof doesn't fall in on them when Gramms enters. Ha!* I tucked Gramms dress into the seat, handed her the seatbelt and shut her door. The street people that had been watching yelled in approval, "Way to go Gramms. Good work Officer Randel. Come see us Gramms! Bye!" *I guess all's well that ends well. We'll see.*

About a month after Gramms had gone to live with Mrs. Smythe, I received a call from Mrs. Smythe inviting Wells and me to her Southern Baptist Church the next Sunday to hear Gramms sing. Evidently, Gramms, Ms. Elvira Livesay, was raised in the Baptist Church, was a card carrying Christian and could belt out 'Amazing Grace' and other hymns like nobody's business. She had been singing in the choir for three weeks, had been a regular at practice and this

Sunday evening she was going to solo. I told Willy that we were going to church that night and I thought he was going to go into shock.

"Randel, I don't think the Baptist Church is ready for you. I've never seen you in church before."

"Hell, Willy, I was raised an Episcopalian, down on my knees to pray and singin' in the choir when I was a kid. My mom said if I wanted to go out on Friday and Saturday, I would be in church on Sunday morning. I can't remember missing many Fridays or Saturdays with the guys or out with some pretty little girl from my hometown. Also, it's amazing what can go on in the choir loft when nobody's lookin'."

"I should have known, Randel. Please try to be respectful while we're there. Remember, it is the Lord's house." *I can be nice,* I thought, *but I sure as hell won't be a hypocrite.* "Randel, I'll pick you up at your house around 6:00. Wear a sport coat, okay?"

You don't have to tell me how to dress you wet-behind-the-ears, young scoundrel. I wasn't born yesterday! "Yeah, yeah, yeah. Be sure you're on time, and put some gas in that tin can of yours. I hate to be left on the side of the road when I'm expected in church."

I wore a subdued gray-blue, turtleneck sweater, a tan, tweed sport coat, my pressed and starched, blue jeans, my silver concho and leather belt, and my brown, cowboy boots. My dark brown hair was neatly combed, I had showered and shaved again, my mustache was perfect, my teeth were brilliant, and my fingernails were clipped and clean. I wore Drakkar Noir so the Lord would be pleased, and so would any lovely young ladies that might sit near me. As I looked at myself in the mirror, I observed, *Randel, you're one helluva good lookin' guy. It's a wonder you're still single. You'd better watch out for those cute, little, church-goin' babes.*

When we pulled into the parking lot of the church, Willy reminded me, "Randel, isn't this the church where you had trouble with that hooker?"

I remembered, all right. About a year ago I had a call to check out a tall, blond, blue-eyed hooker that was working across the street. I pulled up about a half a block from her in my patrol car and observed her talking through a car window with a John. She turned and saw me and waved the man away. When I drove up beside her, she swore he was only asking for directions. *Like I believe that one!* As I put my car in park and called control, she realized that I was going to arrest her. She turned and fled across the street, running directly into the church. I was hot on her heels and I ran into the building behind her. *Hell, how did I know there was a service in progress*? The minister looked toward the congregation as I entered. He watched as the hooker, dressed in sleazy clothing, took a seat in the second to the front pew. He was astonished when I sat beside her. He turned over the service to one of the deacons and walked calmly to see what was going on. "I am Officer Rod Randel, pastor, and I am going to arrest this woman for prostitution."

Little-miss-do-right looked pitifully at the minister and blinked her heavy false eyelashes at him. "Please, sir, can't I receive sanctuary in your church? I thought an officer could not arrest a person in church."

The pastor stood by, somewhat dumbfounded as I cuffed the blond, and led her from the church. He followed us outside and stated, "I will look into Nevada law, Officer Randel, and will be in touch with this young woman at the jail."

Young woman, I thought, *she's forty, forty-five if she's a day. It must be the lights in the church that are blinding you, pastor. Could be lust, too. What do I know?* "Sir," I related, "I believe I have the right to arrest a criminal anywhere I find one. You may call on this woman at the jail, but you should do it as soon as your service is over. She'll probably be bailed out by her pimp by the time you get there."

I left the hooker at the jail and went on with my duties. However, she went to trial over the incident and the judge ruled that I was wrong to arrest her inside the church. If I had waited until she came outside, he said it would have been a 'good arrest.' *The hell, you say!*

So little-miss-do-right, as I called her, thought she had put one over on the Las Vegas Metro Police. She informed her fellow workers that anytime a cop tried to arrest them, they should run into a church, and that they could not be touched. However, she did not relay the message that they could still be arrested once they left the premises.

It turned out that the hookers had quite a going business in that area, and when Wells, Sikes and I decided to break up the little operation they were in for a surprise. We posted an officer in the close area, and we would cruise in front of them, and they would walk across the street and into the church. That was all right with us. We posted uniformed officers at the door, and one at the back of the church and we watched and waited until the girls would leave. Then we made our arrests. This was slowing down their action, and their pimps were paying bail more often for their release. The girls were not happy either.

At first, the church folks were very supportive about protecting the prostitute's rights. But the interruptions that the hookers caused for the pious and righteous soon began to wear on the congregation. After about a month of street ladies mingling with church ladies, our captain received a call from the pastor. He said, "Captain, the deacons and the ladies have asked that I not grant sanctuary to any woman who is a repeat offender because it is ruining the reputation of the church and some of the wealthy members have threatened to move to another church. Can you please speak with Officers Randel, Wells and Sikes and ask them to help me rid our church of these wanton women?"

The captain laughed when he told me what he had said. "I'm sorry, pastor," commented the Captain, "my officers have been instructed by the judge that they may not enter your church for the purpose of arresting any prostitute, no matter how many times one comes for sanctuary. I suggest that you enlist the help of your congregation to rid your church of these unwanted ladies. They should be strong enough to ward off prostitution in the neighborhood."

I dropped by to see the minister on my day off, and suggested that maybe the ladies could organize a protest march with signs and singing on both sides of the street. The pastor was delighted and set about organizing the ladies and the teens of his congregation. For two days and nights they were there, peacefully marching about a three-block area, singing hymns and carrying signs of disapproval. My buddies and I made ourselves available on our off time to make sure that no one disturbed these nice folks. Two young women carried one sign that cracked us up. It was painted in bright red and said, 'Protestants against Prostitutes!' The group even held a candlelight service each night in front of the church.

The only real problem that we had was from Lieutenant Arnold. He came by to make sure that the group had permits for their rally. *That's just like you, asshole!* I thought. *Why aren't you out here checking the prostitutes for their permits, or arresting johns?* Man, I hated everything that bastard stood for.

It seemed that the prostitutes moved to another location and we did not hear anymore about local churches being inundated with hookers looking for sanctuary. Kind of made me think of Sodem and Gamorrah.

After remembering that, I enter the church in a reverent manner, and enjoyed listening to Gramms hymns of praise. *Thank you, Lord, for good people like Mrs. Kathleen Atherton-Smythe, who do your work.* I left fifty bucks in the collection plate, and hugged both ladies as we left. I watched as Willy slipped in a twenty, and was proud of him for doing his part too.

It was less than two months that Gramms had lived with Mrs. Smythe when I saw her on the street again. I stopped and spoke with her. She was in high spirits both mentally and physically speaking. She was tanked up and yelling at street people like she had before. However, she was kind to the passers-by. I asked her, "Gramms, what happened with you and Mrs. Smythe? Are you still living at her place?"

"Naw, Randel. I have to do my business here on the streets. Somebody's gotta keep all these panhandlers in line. They don't work for no union. I guess you didn't know that all these pan-handlers in the area work for me. I takes care of them an' they takes care of me. I charge them some, but I see that no body bothers them, and if they're sick, I takes 'em to the doc. It all works out. I can't handle livin' in all that house with all those fancy clothes. Don' get me wrong, Ms. Kathleen is one swell lady, an' I sees her at the church when I goes there. But we can't be too good a friends. She's way up there above you and me. The Lord knows her name for sure!"

I left Gramms to her work and her bottle and wondered at what makes some people the happiest. I think it was being with all her friends and taking care of them in her own way, just like Mrs. Smythe wanted to take care of Gramms. I was sure happy, too, when I saw Gramms walking along and belting out hymns with the Salvation Army when they worked the streets.

NO MIRANDA

"**Frank-3 enroute**."

The sun had changed mounts from the eastern prominence of the Sunrise Mountains to the western Podice peak. It bid farewell to the Las Vegas skyline as it rode ever westward, relinquishing its light to the luminescence of the full moon that waited to spiritedly shine in the eastern sky. The daystar's blanket, a flaming, hot orange and a molten, mandarin red caressed the pinnacle, as it blended into the cloudless skies over the Nevada desert. The full moon, as was its norm, shined its malice on the city's inhabitants, its gravitational pull instigating denizens toward improprieties that doubled the strain on the already pressured metro police force.

Wells and I were about ready to pack it in for the evening when we received a call, "Frank-3, copy a call. Randel, we have a 425 and a possible 419 at 1715 Hassett Ave. A neighbor heard the two male renters from next door loudly arguing and then shots were fired."

"**Frank-3 enroute**. Send back up." *Well, so much for finishing before nightfall. I'll have to call Cheyenne and cancel our dinner. I don't think she and I will ever get it together at this rate.* "Willy, I hope you didn't have any big plans for tonight. I think we're going to be busy for a while on this one."

"I was planning on going to a church social with my cousin, Ben. We were going to check out the chicks there. He'll be pist off for sure if I don't go. Oh well." Willy was resigned to a wasted evening.

"I'll try to make short work of this then, partner, so you can attend your little soiree." As we wheeled into the area, our reds flashing and our headlights beaming, a male, about twenty-five, a little heavy set, and with dark hair came running out of the house with a gun in one hand and a knife in the other. I slammed on the brakes, jumped out of the vehicle, behind the safety of the car door, shot gun in hand. I alerted Wells, "Call in a *Code Red*. We have a shooting." He was on the radio immediately. Then he was out on the passenger side his revolver aimed directly at the man.

I yelled, "Stop where you are and drop the gun and the knife, sucker, or I'll kill you." He heard the ominous sound as I jacked the shell into my shotgun. "If this shotgun doesn't kill you, I'll just run over you with this car. Drop them now!"

Stopping in the headlight's beam and dropping the gun and the knife, the man wailed, "I killed him, I killed him!" There was blood on his hands and blood on his shirt and khaki pants.

"Turn around, all the way around so I can see you." As he did so, Wells and I were checking his waistline and his pant's legs for additional weapons. Satisfied, I hollered, "All right, sir, turn so I can see your back. Lie down on your belly. Do it now damn it. Now turn your head to the right." I moved from the safety of the car to his left, away from his line of vision. "Stretch your arms away from your sides, palms up on you hands." He was compliant.

Still sobbing, the man kept saying, "I shot him. I killed him, I killed him!" It was obviously a crime of passion.

"Sir," I continued, "turn your head to the left, facing me. If you move, or do anything I don't want you to do, I will kill you." Wells proceeded to the prone man's blind side, taking his right hand and placing it into a wristlock. Then with one knee on his head and the other on his back, forcing the man's arm and wrist between Well's legs, he hooked that wrist good and tight. Continuing, he brought the other arm back, palm up, to the small of the man's back and hooked the other wrist, locking the cuffs into place. With his man cuffed, Willy checked his waist, the small of his back, his legs and gave him a complete pat down. There were no other weapons. Wells pulled a billfold from the back pocket.

"Okay, Wells," I instructed, "get him up and bring him to the hood of the vehicle. If he so much as moves, lift his arms; that'll stop him." Taking the billfold, I saw that he had a Nevada driver's license with his information.

Wells began, "You have the right to remain...."

"Stop there, Willy. Don't read him his rights. We haven't asked him anything, and we won't." At that time Grumpy arrived. "Wells, place him in the back of the car, and stick with him, but be damned sure you don't ask him any questions or let anyone else talk to him. No one, understand?"

I called dispatch. "Frank-3 suspect in custody, but have not cleared the house. Adam-12 has arrived, and so has Frank-24."

The Frank-24 officers went inside to see what had happened. Officer Jones came out to me and stated, "Officer Randel, you need to come in and see this." Adam-12 and I entered the house. In the living room, blasted against the banister of the stairs, his jaw hanging loose, his eyes open in an astonished glare, and his left arm caught around the railing, lay a dead man, about 28 years old. It appeared that he had been descending the stairs when he was shot in the face, the bullet breaking his jaw, and its trajectory spiraling into his brain, killing him instantly. Blood and gray matter were splattered on the carpet, the stairwell and the flocked wallpaper. The gun, a 357 Magnum, had done a mean job from a close range.

"Okay, Officer Jones, place an officer at the door and do not let anyone, and I mean anyone else in this room unless I say it's okay. I don't want this crime scene compromised."

As more backups arrived, Sikes called dispatch with a Code 4, which released the airwaves for other calls. He requested, "Send me Homicide and Criminology. We have a 419 and a 420. Aw crap, roll me a damn am-bo-lance and the FD too!"

When I returned to the patrol car, I noticed another officer standing next to Willy. Wells quickly questioned, "Aren't we gonna Mirandaize him, Randel?"

"Nope."

"Why not?"

"No need to." It was obvious that Willy, still a rookie, was not clear. "We don't need to read him his rights until we're going to question him, and we ain't gonna ask him a damned thing. We'll wait for Homicide and let them question him." Turning to the other officer, I queried, "Who are you?"

She replied, "Officer Amy Mills." *Yes, and you're a cute little blond, Officer Mills*, I silently observed.

At that moment Homicide's Hanks arrived. I advised him of the situation. Hanks asked, "Has the suspect been read his rights?"

"No. We've had no need to. We haven't asked him one question," chimed in Willy, sounding very experienced.

Hanks inquired, "Will you transport him to the homicide office?"

"Damned right we will." I jumped at the chance. It meant that we would not have to write the report, Homicide would do it, and Wells and I would be out of there early. "Load up Willy, we're transporting."

Hesitantly, Willy replied, "Give me a minute, Randel."

As I waited, Maggie from the crime lab arrived. "Hi, Randel, what we got?"

"It's a bad one, Maggie, kind of messy. Looks like a homicide with blood all over the house and on the suspect."

"I need photo's Randel."

"Fine. Get what ever you need. Want me to call for another criminologist for you? There's gonna be a lot to cover."

"Thanks, that'll be great."

I told Officer Jones to allow Hanks and Maggie into the house, and left Hanks in charge. I returned to the car where Wells, with Officer Mills as a witness, had read the suspect his rights and had him exit the vehicle so Maggie could take his picture, showing his bloodied body, clothes and hands. There was blood on the car seat and Maggie took pictures of that as a safety measure for us to show that it was there before we transported. Before she moved to the knife and the gun that were lying outside, I bade her goodbye and asked her to call me when she was finished. Smiling sweetly, she acknowledged, "I will be more than happy to call you, Rod."

Back in the car, Willy stated, "Looks like Ms. Maggie could be interested in you, Randel."

"No more than Officer Mills was intrigued with you, Wells. She is a looker. Did you ask her out?"

"No, she asked me. She'll be off as soon as she leaves here. We're gonna meet at the station and go for dinner."

"Ah, sorry, Willy. We'll be hours writing our reports. I don't think we'll be finished before 22:30 hrs. or so. Too bad." Wells looked dejected. "Oh forget it, kid. The evening isn't a total loss. All we have to do is drop off our suspect and log out. Homicide will take care of everything else."

"Randel, you're a dupster and a prevaricator, but you're still all right in my book." Satisfied that he had done me a great injustice, likable Willy Wells lay his head on the back of the seat, smiled smugly, shut his eyes and relaxed.

"Wells, take my advice." I looked over at him for his reaction, "you know that I am a good judge of character. When you date Officer Mills, watch out for her handcuffs. She might be pretty wicked."

His eyes flew open, and as if in shock, he replied, "Oh no, Randel, maybe I should stick with the more innocent girls at church. I'm not ready yet for an authorized woman with *real* handcuffs."

DEAD WRONG

"SIKES," I QUESTIONED EARNESTLY, "HAVE YOU seen the news?"
"No, why?"
"Someone stabbed a little kid in the eye and killed him, right in his own front yard!"
"The hell you say! Where?"
"Right here in our neighborhood, over on Cleveland. He was only six years old."
"How the hell did it happen? Where were his folks?"
"His mother was in the house baking his favorite cookies. The front door was open and she never heard a thing. She went to check on him and found him lying on the grass right by the sidewalk, already dead. She said she had checked him less than five minutes before. He was just playing with all his trucks and cars on the grass. The yard is fenced and the gate was locked, so someone had to jump it, stab him and jump out in a hurry."
"Did they catch the bastard that did it?"
I reported, "No, there are no witnesses and no clues."
"Damn it, Hawk, someone had to do it. Somebody knows who did it!"
"Homicide is handling it, Grumpy."

"Hell, this is our area, Randel. We'll do our own investigation. What you doin' for the next couple of hours?"

"Whatever you're doin', I guess. What do you intend to do first?"

"You bring us a vehicle and I'm goin' for the report. They'd better give it to me damned quick. You know the sooner we're out there, the sooner we'll solve this. Come on, Hawk, I need those sharp eyes and ears of yours."

We cleared with the sergeant, called control and told the new dispatcher, Sharla, that we would be at the address on Cleveland, and headed straight there. What we found was a tragic situation and a very tormented mother and father. The father answered the door and after we identified ourselves, Mario Chavez asked us in and introduced us to his distraught wife, Paulina. He begged me, "Por que', señor? Por que'? Mi hijo tiene solo seis anos. Who could do a thing like this to my baby? Juanito is our only child. We waited so long for him, and we cannot have more bambinos. No, señor. He is our life. Pobrecito, mi jito; he is no more."

The Chavezes were a man and woman in their mid-thirties. Their house was immaculate. The little boy's toys were laying in the front yard where he had been playing and his stuffed teddy bear was held tightly in the arms of his mother who rocked back and forth, unable to say anything to us. She had obviously been given a sedative. A friend came from the kitchen and sat beside Paulina, placing her arm around her shoulder. "Officers," she said, "Mario and Paulina are the best parents I have ever known. Juanito was such a dear and good little boy. Never a minute's trouble. What are you going to do about this? Somebody has to pay."

"Yes, ma'am, and somebody will," insured Sam Sikes, all business. "The bastard that did this deserves to die. Officer Randel and I and our partners are running our own investigation. We will be on the streets as soon as we leave here. We will canvass the whole neighborhood, and we will find some clues. Someone had to see or to know something about this."

"Mr. Chavez," I queried, "do you belong to any special groups that might be targeted by another gang? I have to ask, are you involved in anything like drugs or scams of any kind?"

"No, no, señor. The only group is our church. We are Catholic. We don't go to clubs like when we were joven, young, before we had our Juanito. No, we don't even drink cervesa o' vino. I work for the city in maintenance and my Paulina is home all day with Juan. We have no familia aqui', and we do not know very many people, solo la gente de la Iglesia."

"Do you or your wife have any enemies? Anyone with whom you may have had a confrontation or a disagreement?"

"No, señor, nothing."

"Thank you, sir, ma'am. If you think of anything that you can tell us, please call either of us, day or night." I gave Mario my card with my office and my cell number. "I am so sorry about your son, Mr. and Mrs. Chavez. We will go now and start our investigation."

"Señor, Officer Randel, one thing was strange to the homicide detective. He said that whoever killed my Juanito wiped his bloody knife on Juanito's shirt. He meant to do it, didn't he? It was not an accident. I must pray for Juanito's murderer, señor, but I can only pray that he rots in hell for eternity. Dios, I am sorry, but that is the best I can do."

"It's okay. It's okay, Mr. Chavez," consoled Grumpy, "and Officer Randel and I will try our damnedest to put him there. Beg your pardon, ma'am for my language."

"No, no," Paulina replied faintly, "keel heem, for me. Keel heem for Juanito. He belongs in hell. Via con Dios, señores." She began to sob and her friend and her husband went to her as we took our leave.

Grumpy and I canvassed the area, offering money to anyone who had any information about the death. No one knew anything. I wondered, *could that little boy have been somewhere and seen something that he was not supposed to see. Maybe whoever killed him thought he knew something and would tell. So many Cubans live in this area. Could it have been a drug deal killing?*

"I know what you're thinkin' Randel," said Grumpy. "When the hell are they gonna let us clean up this town. I'm sick to death of all that's goin' on down here that we aren't allowed to do anything about."

"I hear you, and it makes me sick to see nice, hardworking people like the Chavez family torn apart by the ugliness that goes on in the Naked City. But you're wrong Sam, dead wrong. Someday, someday soon. We're gonna make a difference. This is our town, and damn it, I want it back."

Emphatically, Sikes replied, "Randel, it's up to you and me; we've gotta take it back!"

THE COMPLAINT

It was Lieutenant Arnold's turn to conduct our early morning briefing. He strode to the front in his usual, contentious manner, turned and sat his left hip on the desk with his left leg dangling, his right foot firmly on the floor, and his left hand on a stack of papers. "Good morning, Officers," he began, looking at his top sheet. He made a few cursory comments and tried to raise his left hand to turn his page. His hand rose but with it rose a white paper from the stack; it was stuck to his hand. He looked quizzically at the paper, laid down his other papers and tried to free his left hand of the page that was stuck to it with super glue. "What's going on? Who did this?" he yelled out as he tore at the paper.

There was not a sound to be heard, not a snicker, not a cough, not scuffling of feet. There was only silence. Arnold tried to raise his body from the table but found that the table moved with him, and that he could not straighten or place his left foot on the floor. The left side of his butt was likewise stuck to the desk. "I want to know who's responsible for this!" he exclaimed vehemently. "Sergeant!" he called loudly. "Somebody help me!" Two officers that were in the front of the briefing room calmly rose to assist Arnold. The sergeant entered the room and snickered when he saw Arnold's predicament.

Frank-3 Enroute

"Sarge, can you take over. Get everybody out of here. I can't move or I'll rip my pants, and my hand is stuck to this paper. Damn it to hell, who did this?"

The sergeant ordered everyone into the auxiliary room down the hall as the two officers continued to help Arnold.

Arnold was furious. "I want to know who would do such a thing. Help me out of my pants, men." He unbuckled his belt and tried to wiggle out of the trousers. They were so glued to the table that two other officers had to come in, climb onto the table and physically lift him from his pants as the first two officers removed his shoes and held each pant's leg. Unfortunately, the glue had also soaked into his undershorts and Arnold had to shed them, leaving him covered only by his shirt and his socks. The attending officers did not say a word about what had happened, that was, of course, until they were at their lockers and had a complete, howling audience. The last thing that I heard from Arnold was, "I know who did this; it was Randel and Sikes. I just know it! I intend to get to the bottom this and won't give up until every man that is involved is fired!"

I don't know who actually pulled that trick, but I wish I had thought of it. I figured that Arnold had already gotten to the bottom of things, so to speak. Somebody was really out to get the lieutenant.

However, I heard that when Arnold returned to his office, he could not enter because there was a 'Wet Paint' sign taped across his door. Fuming, he went to the Captain's office and lodged a complaint, and wanted to know who had authorized anyone to paint his office when he had not had time to remove anything. The Captain had no information to offer Arnold and told him he could occupy the desk at the front of the station until his office was finished. (Benedict) Arnold left more disgruntled than he came.

Arnold took it upon himself to look into things on his own. I walked into my office just in time to see Arnold messing with my desk. He was rifling through my center desk drawer. One quick step and I was behind my desk, my foot swiftly slamming the drawer shut on Arnold's hand. "Oww, why the hell did you do that, Randel?" Arnold pulled his hand back and held it as it throbbed mightily.

"What the hell are you doing in my office with your hand in my desk drawer, sir?" I asked in contempt.

"I'm looking for something and I know that it's here or in Sikes room."

"LT., you have no right to enter my office and to go through my things. If I ever catch you in here again, sir, I'll beat the shit out of you."

"You can't talk to me like that, Randel. You don't own this room or anything in it, and I have the right to go through any employee's desk if I choose to."

"And I have a right to my own privacy! Get the hell out of here before I shoot you, sir. By the way," I asked as I gave him room to pass, "what are you looking for?"

"Super glue! I know it's here somewhere, and I know that you and Sikes are responsible for today's little fracas. Just look at my hand; it's on fire from the shit I had to use to unglue that damned paper. Now, you've probably broken my right hand. I've already gone through Sikes' and your lockers. What a mess! Grumpy should be written up for the condition of his locker. You both try to irritate me every chance you get, and I am sick and tired of your pranks and your follies. I *will* find out who did this," he stated as he swept past me.

Unfortunately, he almost ran head long into Grumpy who was walking to his office. "Lt. Arnold," I warned, "I wouldn't go into Sikes office either if I were you. You know how crazy he can be. I wouldn't trust him not to hurt you real bad, sir."

Grumpy reiterated, "Don't come into my office for anything, Lt. Arnold, unless you have an engraved invite. I don't give invites to anyone except my friends, and you are not one of them, sir. If you need to see me, you talk with Ms. Tootie and make an appointment. Better still, go through Lt. Germain first. What the hell is he doin' here anyway, Randel?"

"Goin' through my desk, lookin' for super glue."

Grumpy laughed aloud. "Haw! That's a good one. Did you glue him to the desk, Hawk?"

"Hell no, but now I wish I had." Arnold skirted past Grumpy who lifted his number 14 shoe and gave him a swift kick in the seat of his clean trousers.

"This is not the end of this, you two. There will be punishment, and soon!" He went directly to the captain's office to complain and then took up his spot at the entrance to the station. As he was sitting where he could watch the door, and was responsible for speaking to anyone who entered, who should enter but dear, little Mrs. Jenkins from the Cincinnati Arms. She brought homemade Christmas cookies for Wells and me. When she sweetly asked specifically for 'Officer Randel,' other officers told me that Arnold almost keeled over with anger. Roughly, he asked, "What do you need to see Randel about, ma'am?"

"He and that nice officer Wells were so good to me, and my Blue Cadillac has been safe and so have I since they came to my home. I brought some cookies and want to tell them Merry Christmas, and I want to thank Officer Randel for my new screen door. It is lovely and it has a good lock and I feel safe now. Will you please see that Officer Randel and Officer Wells get these?" she asked as she handed a large plate of decorated cookies to Arnold. "No cheating, now, sir. They are for Officers Randel and Wells," she cautioned, shaking her small index finger at him in warning. Arnold accepted the cookies and set them on the counter behind him as Mrs. Jenkins left. "Merry Christmas to you too, Officer," Mrs. Jenkins called out as she went through the door.

"Harrumph! Merry Christmas? Bah, humbug!" Arnold was apparently sullen the rest of the day.

However, Sikes and I were called into the captain's office, *again*.

"Do either one of you want to tell me what is going on between you and Lieutenant Arnold?"

"Nothing, sir." I stated. "That is with the exception that I threatened him this morning when he was rifling through my desk. I threw him out of my office and Sikes told him not to come into his office."

"What about the super glue incident?"

Grumpy replied with almost a smile. "Sir, we had nothing to do with that, even though the LT. thinks we're responsible. We have no idea who has it in for him, sir, but it was pretty funny."

"He wants me go to IAB to bring you both up on charges for threatening him, but if he was in your office going through your things, Rod, I don't feel he has a leg to stand on."

"He didn't have one this morning either, sir," I laughed. "Seriously though, sir, we appreciate your help."

"Is there anything that I can help you fellows with while you're here, Randel? Sikes?"

Sikes spoke up, his voice changing to a serious note. "Yes, Captain, there is. Tell him, Rod."

I contemplated for a moment, then let loose. I knew that Grumpy and I were chomping at the bit about the Naked City. "Captain, when the hell are they gonna let us clean up this town? Sikes and I are sick of all that's goin' on in our town that we aren't allowed to do anything about. Somebody needs to get ugly and real mean and toss every rock and mattress until we find out who the real bastards are that kill little children, sell drugs, pimp whores and steal and rob from our seniors. We can't do it alone, sir, but we could do a lot more than we're allowed to now. Give someone the go ahead, Cap., and some leeway and let's clean up the Naked City while we still can."

"Officers Randel and Sikes, I appreciate your thoughts and concerns and I am taking it under advisement. I too am shocked with the murder of the little Chavez boy. I don't know how you do it, men, but you are always at the wrong place at the right time and are involved in more tragic cases in the city than any other officers. I do appreciate your work and dedication, especially what you're doing about the breakfast burglaries and helping our seniors. I know you are both putting in a lot of extra hours and you have almost caught him. Good work!"

"Thank you, sir, but that's just the point. We can be at the right spot at strategic times but our hands are tied because of protocol. We need to have the opportunity to be unorthodox in our methods in order to accomplish the changes we want."

"Unorthodox? Are you trying to tell me that you want to be able to be as bad as the bad guys are? How would that make you any less a criminal than they are, Officer Randel? By the way, what has happened to your faith in the system and justice?"

"I left my faith with little Juanito Chavez's mother and father, and I'm still waitin' for justice for our seniors and for the children that live on the streets because their folks have to pay for their own alcohol and drugs."

"Officer Randel, I think you need to step back and take a serious look at what you're proposing."

"I hear what you're saying, Cap., but you know that Sikes and I are 100% policemen. We've never been on the take, and all the pieces of shit out there know it. We would never think of taking a bribe or selling dope, or fencing anything, unlike some others we know about. Sir, we're clean. Give us a chance to make a difference."

"Randel, I think you need a couple of days off work, with pay mind you, to regroup your feelings and to get your act back together. You and Sikes were too close to the seniors and that little boy just about got to all of us. You are on leave with pay as of now. Both of you."

"Hell, Captain," voiced Grumpy. What do you expect us to do without workin' our beat. Randel and I have neither one had a vacation in years. Rod doesn't even know what sick days are for either. We'll go stark ravin' mad!"

"Well, Officers, I can arrange a couple of days of intense psychological assessment if you would like, but you are not to be on the clock for two days."

"No, Captain, hell no. Sam and I don't need to see a shrink. We're too crazy for them. We'll take the time, but maybe we can work on a plan for the city. What do you think, Grumpy?"

"Plan? Hell's fire, Rod, lets just go out there and shoot all the sons-of-bitches that we already know are rotten to the core. I have all my guns and knives ready, and I know you do too." Grumpy was working himself into a lather. "Ok, Captain," he continued calmly. "We'll see you at briefing three days from now, sir."

"You officers have a good day. And, Sikes, don't do anything I wouldn't do," he laughed as he shook our hands. "You two are some of the best officers I have ever known and I am proud to have you here. Thank you both!"

As we left the Captain's office, Grumpy stated, "Hell, Randel, I think that the Cap loves us. What the hell you gonna do with two days off. I know that Kate will think up something for me to do, but I won't like it."

"Let me think about it for a while, and I'll let you know. Be ready to work though, buddy. I really think the captain cares about our city too. We have to figure out what to do and how to do it on our own. Maybe we can become mercenaries or vigilantes, or silent warriors." *Hmm. What goes around comes around.* The wheels were already turning as we parted. On the way out of the station, I stopped at the front desk and picked up the Christmas cookies from Lt. Arnold. *Yeah, what goes around, comes around, asshole.*

STOOLIE

I WAS SITTING IN MY OFFICE contemplating what else to buy for Cheyenne for Christmas. Considering returning to Christiansen's Jewelry to look for something special like an extraordinary, silver, turquoise and red coral bracelet I had seen, I was half-heartedly working on a report.

"Officer Randel," Tootie interrupted my reverie, "there is a call on line one from Jasper Murdock. Isn't he your little buddy from the penitentiary?"

"Yeah, what the hell does he want? Never mind, Tootie, I've got it. This is Officer Randel," I spoke gruffly for effect. "What can I do for you, Murdock?" *You little weasel!*

"Officer Randel, I need your help to get my mother up here to see me before Christmas. She don't have the money for gas and I was wonderin' if you could loan me some dough so's I can buy her some. I sure would like to see her and the little kids, and I would make it worth your while."

Sure you would, Boy, I thought. *What the hell could you do for me?* "Jasper, there is a bus that runs up there every Thursday and your mother can make arrangements to ride up and back. I can't do any more than that, guy. I'm not allowed to give you anything."

"Not even if I give you some information, like who's killin' those women and dumpin' them all over Las Vegas. Come on, Randel, you know you could use some good info."

"And all you want is to see your mom and the family? Jasper, what the hell do you think I am, some kind of fool? I can't believe a single word you say. You've been a liar since you were a little kid."

"Honest, Randel, I know who's doin' it, but I'm not gonna tell for nothin'. Maybe you could bring my mom up and I could tell you who's doin' the women and I can shed some light on that little Chavez boy's murder. You're dealin' with some bad men. I know, 'cause I hear all the scuttlebutt up here."

"I understand that every stoolie has a story to tell to try to get early parole, but I can't promise you anything. You have a nice day, and I'll see what I can do for you. I'll make some calls and see if I can arrange transportation for your mother."

"Thanks, Officer Randel. You're a great guy. I knew I could count on you. Merry Christmas! Tell Officer Wells hello for me too."

That little bastard is going to be a lifer, I just know it. He's never going to stop trying to take the easy way out. Oh well, I'll see what I can do for him, maybe tomorrow.

BREAKFAST BURGLAR IV

"CONTROL, FRANK-3, BE ADVISED THAT I am enroute to check the welfare of an older man."

It was a Sunday morning about 09:30 hrs. and I was eastbound on Oakey about the 1500-1600 block. An elderly man waved me down, and I pulled to a stop just past him. He came to the passenger side of my patrol car and I asked if he were all right. "Yes, Officer Randel, I'm okay, but I'm worried about my friend. Warner and I meet for coffee every Sunday morning at Charleston and Eastern at Mc Donald's. Today he didn't come, and I'm concerned for him."

"Oh, really. What time do you meet?"

"About 8:30; never later than 9:00 o'clock, but this morning he wasn't there."

"Where does this friend live, and what's his name?"

"He lives in the seventeen hundred block of East Bracken. It's the white stucco house with red trim." I asked him his name so that I could get back in touch with him, and he gave me a card with his name and phone number. "Warner and I have cards that we give to ladies that appear interested in meeting us. You never know what some of these old broads might be interested in. You tell Warner to call me."

"**Frank-3 enroute**. Control, go ahead and arrive me; I am only a couple of minutes away. It's in the 1700 block of East Bracken. *Ah, yes, there's the white, stucco house with the red door.* It is at 1712, Cheri'." Grumpy called in saying that he was on his way to assist me.

I arrived at the house and the front door was locked and everything looked good and tight. Proceeding to the Eastside gate, I entered and noticed a back window broken, raised and blocked with a stick. I advised Adam-12 to meet me on the Eastside and we would enter. Looking at Sikes, I knew he would never make it through the window; he was a little too rotund in the girth. Grumpy reflected, "You don't think we could get lucky and this might be the breakfast burglar, do you?"

"I don't think so, because all the doors are locked and that's his standard MO, usually going through a back, kitchen door. Then, he usually fixes something to eat and leaves through that door, leaving it open. No doors are unlocked."

"Randel," he asked, lowering his voice, "do you suppose he's still in there?"

"We'll see. Help me shimmy into this window and keep an eye on me until I can open the door." *Hell, I don't know if I can climb through that window either. It looks even smaller from up here.* "Give me a leg up, Sam, so I can swing the other one over the sill." Slipping over the sill, I somersaulted onto a double bed. I rolled off the bed and took my gun from its holster, went into a guarded mode and checked the room clearing it. I proceeded down the hall toward the front door. However, as I approached the living area, I detected a man about eighty years old lying on the floor. Approaching him as I cleared the room, I noticed that he was still breathing. Quickly running to the front door, I yelled at Grumpy, "Kick in the door. There's no key and it's double locked. Call us a Code-Red and roll us an amb-o-lance; send Mercy and FD."

After control responded, Grumpy kicked in the door and entered. "Have you cleared the rest of the house?" Grumpy queried. I shook my head negatively. We carefully cleared the rest of the home and found no one else there. There had obviously been a struggle in the main bedroom as the mattress was half off the bed. We heard the sirens as the ambulance approached. I went back to the gentleman on the floor and saw that he had a black sock wrapped around his neck where the burglar had tried to strangle him. It was not just wrapped around his neck; in that sock was a pencil twisted several times like a tourniquet. Mr. Warner was breathing so I left the sock in place so I wouldn't damage anything. As the ambulance arrived, Mr. Warner was returning to consciousness. Realizing that the police were with him, he croaked, "Officer, it was a black man with black clothes that attacked me. I fought him as hard as I could. His left ear looked like somebody had bitten it or something."

"You did good, sir. You did a good job." I called in a Code-4, clearing the radio of the Code Red.

To my surprise, Grumpy knelt beside the man and growled, "Mr. Warner, I'm gonna get this Son-of-a-bitch if it's the last thing I do. If I get a chance, I'm gonna kill him, cut him so bad there won't be anything left of him. That's a promise!"

"Thank you, officer, what's your name?"

"Officer Sam Sikes, sir. You just lie still now; help has arrived." Grumpy rose and met the EMTs at the door, pointing to Mr. Warner and warning them to protect the crime scene.

As they were tending to Mr. Warner, I instructed, "Cut that sock from his neck and leave the twisted pencil in it for Criminalistics to note, fellows. Thanks."

Grumpy said, "Hawk, I'm gonna follow Mr. Warner to the hospital and see that he's cared for." I could tell that Sikes was angry, but I did not understand just how upset he was until later. We had not found Mr. Warner's billfold so he was without his identification and insurance card. We assured him that he would be well cared for without them. He left and I watched as Grumpy pulled out behind the ambulance.

I waited impatiently for Maggie to arrive and she began her investigation. I had already noticed that the burglar had not taken time to eat at this house, so I was wondering if it was our Breakfast Burglar, especially because he came in through the window. However, the doors were double locked and required a key to open, so he had been stuck inside and was only able to enter and to leave through the window. I watched as Maggie did her usual excellent job of investigation, and was becoming more and more discouraged as she found not one trace of evidence. Suddenly, Maggie called from the kitchen, "Randel, can you come in here?"

"What you got, Maggie?"

"Does Mr. Warner own a rifle, and if so, is this where he keeps it?"

"Let me make a call and find out." I called Adam-12 at Sunrise Hospital. "Buddy, ask Mr. Warner if he owns a rifle and if so, where does he keep it."

Grumpy called back within a few minutes. "He does have a gun, only one rifle and he keeps it in his closet. He has not had it out for years."

Looking into the closet, I found clothes tossed onto the floor and boxes that had been displaced and rummaged. I did not find a rifle there. About that time, Grumpy came back on the radio and advised me, "Randel, the rifle is a 30.06 bolt action and it was definitely in the closet when Mr. Warner went to bed."

Maggie questioned, "Why do you suppose it was here behind the kitchen door?"

"That's easy; he was planning to leave through that door, but couldn't open it, and probably forgot it when the old man surprised him. Either that or he found it after he thought Mr. Warner was dead and rummaged around freely. Either way, that SOB is going down for attempted murder."

"Well, Rod, we're gonna get lucky this time."

"Whatever! Yeah, just like we've been lucky the other times."

She began dusting the trigger guard and trigger area. Nothing! I had returned to the living area when Maggie called, "Randel, come here. Did you handle this gun?"

"No."

"Did Sikes handle this rifle?"

"Not that I know of. We didn't even see it."

Elated, Maggie stated, "Rod, I got one thumb print off the rifle"

"Maggie, I owe you dinner and I could kiss you if you can make this guy!"

"It's that important, huh?"

"Yeah, it is."

"Let me finish up here, and I'll catch up with you."

"Go ahead. I know that you're busy, but as soon as you finish here and go back to the office, could you run it on AFIS for me and let me know what you find?"

"Sure thing, Randel. I know how much you and Sikes want to catch this guy. This Breakfast Burglar is becoming more brazen with each breakin and he's going to kill someone if we don't catch him. He has been giving you trouble for about six months. By the way, Rod," she smiled coquetteishly, "dinner and a kiss are always welcome."

Damn and we're both on duty. I never fish off my own dock or I'd go give her a big hug and a kiss right now. "I'll talk with you later, Maggie. Thanks for everything," I said professionally. *And I mean the invitation too. We'll get together someday.*

I went to Sunrise Hospital to look in on Mr. Warner after I had contacted his friend and told him where he was. Mr. Warner confirmed that the rifle was indeed a 30.06 bolt action and that it had not been removed from the closet for years. I took Sikes outside the room and told him, "We may, we just may get lucky."

"What do you mean, Randel, what do you mean?"

"Maggie took a single print off the barrel of the rifle and is running it through AFIS now."

Grumpy, being the very religious man that we all know him to be, looked heavenward and entreated, "Lord, let us get this print and I won't cut anybody for a whole week." That was the end of his prayer.

I walked away shaking my head, but realizing how much this meant to him, especially all the elder citizens coming under the danger that the Breakfast Burglar rendered. Sikes followed me and we walked outside from the emergency room. Grumpy lit a cigarette, took a deep satisfying puff and commented, "Randel, if this is the son-of-a-bitch we've been chasin' this could mean that we might get Ms. Tilly's ring back for her, huh?"

"Let's hope it is, Sam."

About three hours later after Sikes and I had lunch at Macayo's and were returning to our patrol cars, I heard a voice on the radio that I recognized. My heart jumped into my throat as I answered, "Frank-3, go ahead."

"The voice said, "Go to five."

I switched to five and responded to Maggie's voice. "What you got, Mag?"

"We have over seven points on the thumb print. I ran it through AFIS. Your Breakfast Burglar is Henry Erwin Pike, ID number 162991, just released from Indian Springs six months ago."

"Frank-3, Copy," I sang out eagerly, "We'll be enroute to Criminalistics. We need pictures; anything you have, Maggie."

"You've got them. See you in just a few, Randel."

I went back to the regular channel. Grumpy was calling; "Do we know anything, Randel, do we know anything yet?"

"Yep, we do, Sam, and when we catch him, you get to cut him," I laughed."

"Who is it Randel, do we know him?"

"Sure do! His name is Henry Erwin Pike. He just got out of Indian Springs six months ago. He has a two-page rap sheet for burglaries, assaults and batteries. He's already a two time loser."

"Really! Good! I'm gonna go down and see if I can get a picture of him right away. I want to catch that bastard so bad that I can taste it."

"I'm already ahead of you; Maggie is gathering pictures, and everything she has on him will be ready when we arrive there."

"Son-of-a-bitch, Randel. I'm excited. When I catch him, I'm gonna find out where Tilly's ring is. If he has it on, I'll cut his finger off to take it before I kill him. Don't you go tellin' me nothin' about his rights, either."

"But we've gotta catch him first, Sikes."

"I'll catch him if I have to stay out here the rest of the week without no sleep."

"Okay, buddy. We're gonna catch him."

Maggie had pictures of Henry Erwin Pike, ID number 162991, a two page rap sheet, and his convictions; a really bad guy. He was wanted not only in Nevada but in California too. Now we had everything we needed to identify him, pictures, his vitals, his social security, and his date of birth. We put out an APB, "Pike is black, approximately 5' 10", short black hair, muscular, tends to wear dark clothing, preferably dark jeans, dark tank tops, and has been identified as wearing rubber boots, what we refer to as fireman's boots, either black or yellow, during his burglaries. Update--He is known to have a left ear that will show a tear or a deformity from an earring being torn from its place by a victim. Henry Erwin Pike should be considered armed and dangerous. He can be violent. He has already seriously injured two senior citizens." *God, it feels so good to finally have a description of this guy. I promise to try to keep Grumpy from killing this bastard. Give me strength. While you're at it, help us catch him soon. If possible, let us find Tilly's ring, too. That would make Sikes so happy. Thank you, Lord.*

THE CHRISTMAS PARTY

CHRISTMAS TIME AND NEW YEARS WAS in full swing. Our annual Departmental Christmas party was scheduled for Saturday, December 17th. On Tuesday before our party, I was informed that we were making one hundred fifty gift baskets of food we had collected for the needy, to be delivered on Christmas Eve. "Rod," I was told by Sheriff Morgan, "I want you to be in charge of this. Round up enough help to get the job done."

"Okay sir, but where will we assemble these baskets, and how do we arrange for delivery?"

"Well, the food drive drop site has been at the recreation center. They will probably let you assemble and disburse from there. I know you can handle it, Rod. Thanks, it's a load off my shoulders."

Yeah, and right on to mine! I thought. "Sir, may I offer an incentive to anyone who helps, like maybe and afternoon off, or something?"

"Well, sure, if they put in enough time to really help. But, I want every officer here at 16:30 hr. on Christmas Eve, in uniform, to deliver at least ten baskets each, no questions asked. This is an executive order. It'll only take an hour out of their day, and they should feel proud of Metro for doing something special."

We had a sign up sheet on the bulletin board for all the squads within thirty minutes. We would meet on Friday, the 16th, starting at 13:00 hrs. and go as long as it took to finish the baskets. By shift change that day, we had two officers that had signed up to help; one was Jeff Riley, a real nice officer from Dan Arnold's squad. Apparently, volunteering was not gonna work! Okay, so I wrote on the sheet, *Free Pizza and beer will be served. Bring your family and have a good time.* By morning, I had ten definite takers, and a couple of maybes. I enlisted the help of one of my favorites, Jeff Riley, one of the first to sign the sheet. He's a real first-rate young officer, about twenty-five years old, clean cut and very sharp. He said that he and his wife, Carrie, and their new four-month-old baby would be more than happy to help. I cautioned him not to let that little guy of theirs to be carried off in one of those baskets. Anyone would be more than happy to have him in a Christmas stocking.

Most of the officers, except those on duty, came forward and several from the other squads joined us. My lieutenant, Gene Germain, was there, but Lieutenant Arnold professed to have too much work to do. *I'm glad that SOB isn't here. He would just mess up the spirit of the whole thing with his negative attitude,* I believed. We all worked hard, placing bright paper on the outsides of the boxes and red and green tissue paper inside with the groceries. There was a large red or green bow for each box that had been donated by a local business. We were to leave room for a turkey or a ham to go with the box, last minute. There was a bag of hard candy, peppermint sticks and plenty of healthy food to make a good Christmas feast. These baskets would go to identified, needy homes, some for the elderly, some for families without enough money to go around. The homeless would be fed at the shelters on Christmas Day, and some of us volunteered to help serve there.

We finished about 7:30 p.m., a great time to enjoy the pizza and beer, and orange aid from Mc Donalds®. We sat around admiring our work and looking forward to our party the next night. I informed every person who attended that they could take a paid afternoon of their choice, between now and the end of the year. We left feeling the true spirit of Christmas. That feeling was not, however, to last long.

Saturday the 17th rolled around, and I decked out in dress trousers and a sports coat, as much as I ever dressed. My friend, Cheyenne, looked exquisite in her evening gown, with an open V down her back that ended at her narrow waistline. When we entered, I introduced my date and myself to our waiter. "Hi, how you doin' tonight, Randy? I'm Officer Rod Randel and this is Cheyenne. We're glad you'll be waiting on us. By the way, call me Rod." I shook his hand and slipped him a twenty to insure good service. We had wonderful, cheerful, spirited service. We ate with everyone talking across tables and admiring all whom entered. It was after nine and the band had started playing. I'm not much of a dancer, but I was doing my best with Cheyenne on a slow fox trot. Our waiter, Randy, approached me as the music stopped and told me I had a phone call that I could take in the office.

"This is Officer Randel."

"Rod, this is Jeff Riley…"

"Jeff, buddy, where are you and Carrie? The dance has already started, man."

"Rod," his voice was shaking and I could discern a sob in his throat. "Carrie's missing. I can't find her anywhere."

"Where are you buddy, I'll be right there." He told me that he was at the grocery store where she had gone for diapers and formula for the baby before they left him with the baby sitter.

"She just didn't come back, Rod. Her car's in the parking lot with her purse, the diapers and some other things, but she's missing. Rod, you're the first one I thought of calling. Hurry. I'm going crazy."

I motioned to Randy as I scribbled a quick note to Cheyenne and one to Grumpy about Carrie. I left within minutes of the call. I placed the red light on top of my sedan and rushed out of the parking lot, hell bent for leather. I was on the scene in minutes. "Have you alerted the police yet, Jeff."

"They'll be here in a minute. This lady and gentleman, he pointed to an elderly couple, said they saw her leave the store as they were going in. She was happy and wished them a Merry Christmas."

"She was so beautiful, like a Christmas angel, with her blonde hair, big blue eyes and her white sequined dress," elaborated the elderly lady. "We're parked next to her car. That's what my husband says."

The older gentleman stated, "There was a light tan colored van parked next to her car when we parked. I always tell my wife never park next to a van."

"Did you see any of the occupants of the van, sir?"

"Nope. Wasn't anyone there that we saw, right Mama?" She shook her head in affirmation. "But we sure saw that pretty little wife of yours, Mr. Riley. Prettiest woman I've seen in years. Just beautiful."

The police cars started arriving, sectioning off the area. We took the couples names and address and phone number and allowed them to leave, relying on them to contact us if they thought of anything that might help us.

I took advantage of one of the radios and called the crime lab and asked them to dust for fingerprints. I observed no signs of a struggle. I had control check all taxis and limousines in the area for a pickup at this address. None was documented. Once the men had dusted the car, I had Jeff start it to make sure it worked. It did. In the meantime, Jeff was checking with everyone that they knew, including her parents and her brother. No one had seen or heard from her. Carrie's parents were on the way to Jeff's home to take care of the baby. Jeff's folks were on the way to the grocery store to be with Jeff. Jeff was a wreck of nerves and anxiety.

"Do you have a picture of her in your wallet, Jeff?" He took it out and handed it to me. I gave it to another officer and said, "I want this on the ten o'clock news. See that it gets there pronto. And thanks. Call Crystal Li at KTLV and tell her I have a breaking story for her. She'll send their news cameras around. I'm not going to wait the customary 24-48 hours before we start looking for her."

Lieutenant Arnold arrived and informed me that he would take over since I was not on duty and this was not my area. All the officers looked at me, wondering what I was going to say. I affirmed, "Thanks, Lieutenant, you go right ahead with the investigation. I'll be here with my friend and you can call the FBI, and get them started with their investigation too."

"It's too early to call anyone else in, Randel. You're just trying to make a big deal out of this because Riley's your buddy."

"You damned right he's my buddy, and he's one of Metro's own.

Hell, he works for you, or didn't you realize that, sir?" I nodded to an officer that was standing at the ready for instructions and reiterated, "We'll call in every policeman and the FBI, and anyone else we can think of to help us."

Jeff squatted next to Carrie's car door and started to sob. I couldn't even begin to know what he was suffering, but I squatted there with him and supported him as he shuddered and sobbed. "She looked so beautiful tonight, like a doll. She was ready when I came home and she needed to run for a couple of things. When she didn't come by the time the sitter arrived, I was nervous because we would be late. I thought I would bawl her out for staying too long at the store. Now, I feel so sorry that I was angry with her. Rod, what can I do? What?"

"We need to return to your house, Jeff. We'll let Lieutenant Arnold handle everything else. He goes by the book, so the investigation will be good. The police will impound Carrie's vehicle until they have made a thorough search throughout. They'll catch the tire tracks next to her car, if there are any, and we'll go from there. They'll put out an alert for a tan van, too. Pray that someone came to help her, Jeff, and that she will be home soon." I didn't believe a word I said, but I wanted to comfort Jeff. I didn't have enough confidence in Arnold either, so I called Lieutenant Germain and informed him of the situation.

When we arrived at Jeff's home, a KTLV van was parked at the curb. "Mr. Riley, is there any news yet?" The friendly, compassionate face of Crystal Li was in front of us. "Sir, we want this live on the ten o'clock news. Can you give a brief statement telling us about your wife, what she looks like, how tall, her weight, and things like that? If you have a bigger photo it would be best."

Jeff allowed her to follow into his home, where he mechanically looked for a large photo of Carrie. There was one of her and the baby, Christopher Allen Riley, that Crystal chose to use. Then, not knowing what to do, and appearing numb, Jeff told Crystal all he could about his precious Carrie.

Half the people that attended the Christmas party were outside Jeff's house, waiting for news and wanting to help. The others were glued to the television at the party location, waiting for the breaking story. Cheyenne came with Grumpy and his wife, Kate, and made herself useful in the kitchen preparing coffee and tea. We sat around, dumbfounded, waiting for something, we did not know what.

At 2:00 a.m. the FBI was on the scene. They questioned Jeff, the baby sitter and the parents. There simply were no clues. They would do their best in their investigation and they knew that every policeman in the state would be looking for Carrie. How did a woman disappear from the parking lot of a grocery store in broad daylight, without leaving a clue? Would we ever know?

DEAF BUT NOT DUMB

Wells and I were working swing shift again, riding together and patrolling the area around Union Station. Looking both ways as I crossed the tracks, I spotted someone sitting on the tracks to the left of me, and a train coming at him from my right. We were several blocks away from him, but the warning signals were already blinking to stop traffic for the train to pass. The train was not going to stop until it reached the station and the man was directly in its path. I laid on the horn; no response. *Can't that idiot hear me or feel the vibration from the train? Is he asleep? Is he dead and just hasn't fallen over yet?* "Wells, buckle up, we're going to be riding the track," I instructed as I whipped the patrol car along side the tracks, floored the gas pedal and flew in the direction of the man that still gave no sign of recognition. My lights were flashing, the siren was blaring, and the train was bearing down on him. The train's whistle blew as the engine approached the street we had just left. Our speedometer hit sixty as I thundered toward the man, trying to reach him before the locomotive destroyed him. The train's engineer began braking the train. Without acknowledging my efforts, the man rose and started walking not toward me and not toward the oncoming freight train, but straight up the tracks, away from our car and the rushing train.

Wells and I were bouncing over rough, uneven ground, the vehicle was tilting sideways along the dangerous grade of the track, and then lurching forward after we hit deep ruts and grazed edges of railroad ties.

Willy had his window down and was waving his arm and hollering at the top of his lungs, "Get off the tracks, get off the tracks. You stupid idiot, get the hell off the tracks!" Still, no response from the man.

I flew along side of him and hit the brakes, spinning my car sideways. He must have seen us from the side, because he turned and looked at me. In fear and agitation, I was screaming through the windshield, my face very animated, "Get the f...of the tracks." He smiled at me and waved all friendly-like. Wells pointed behind him on the track as the train bore close. The man waved at us, stepped off the track and the train, with its brakes still applied, went speeding past. I thought Wells and I were going to piss our pants it was such a close call. Before I even realized it, I was out of the patrol car and in the man's face, yelling at him till my throat hurt, "You stupid idiot, you were almost hit by a speeding train. What do you have to say for yourself?" He smiled and shook his head affirmatively. *He doesn't understand a word I'm saying,* I thought. As the rest of the train passed, Wells was right there too. He was still flailing his arms and motioning at the train, screeching obscenities you would not believe would ever come from little Willy's mouth.

The man adjusted his backpack and held his hand forward in a halting movement. With the other hand, he reached into his vest pocket and withdrew a pad and pencil. He had our undivided attention as he wrote *'I am deaf and dumb!'* He pointed toward his ears and then at his mouth. Then he continued to write, *'No, I am deaf, but I am not dumb. I am mute.'*

"Oh, dear Lord," I mouthed with my hands together as if in prayer, "I was scared for you! I thought you were a dead man for sure."

The vagabond held up his one hand and with his fingers from his other hand made motions that I thought were like signing of some kind, which, I definitely did not understand. He recognized the look of confusion that I am sure he received from many people, and smiling, drew out his pad and pencil once more. He scribbled quickly, and I read, 'I guess it was a cluster f..., huh?'

With my head tilted back and my mouth wide open I laughed heartily, and patted the wanderer on the shoulder. Then I made the same finger movements, garbled actions that meant nothing I am sure, and shook my head affirmatively, pointing at his last message. His shoulders shook with mirth and he made a happy, laughing face, but no noise resounded. "This poor guy is deaf," I told Willy. He never heard anything. He must have a guardian angel!"

The mute smiled at us both and thanked us by writing, '*TX U.* ♥ *you guys!*' I didn't have the heart to tell him to stay off the tracks. He wasn't hurting anyone or anything, so I only watched as he waved and continued walking the tracks. When Willy and I were back in our suspension damaged, dust and weed covered car, Wells, who since his verbal tirade, had become as if speechless with the man, started talking. "Randel, I can't believe that we just saved that guys life. You were great, man! The way you handled this car, and the emotion you showed that poor g..."

"Just shut up, Willy," I interrupted. "Don't you realize that we just got cluster f...ed!"

"Yah, but I saw a dough ball side of you that I've never seen before. You were really concerned and nice to that guy."

I gritted my teeth and talked out of the side of my mouth to show I was tough. "Don't say a word about me being nice to anyone, Wells. I'll beat you within an inch of your life if you do!" Then in retrospect, I commented, "Willy, we just saved a guy that was deaf and dumb, didn't we. It's all right if we're a little bit proud, huh? I really hate the phrase deaf and dumb. Don't you? Deaf and mute is so much better. That fellow definitely was not dumb. Did you see how fast he could do sign language?"

"Sure did, Randel. I can sign fast too. Read this, he dared as he held up only one straight, middle finger.

COBRA ONE STRIKES

Tuesday morning about ten o'clock, I was patrolling by myself, westbound on one-way Fremont. "Frank-3, Copy a call. I have a 407 in progress at 300 South Fourth, the Bank of America."

"Arrive me, I am right there." The Bank of America in downtown Las Vegas is one block over from Fremont. The casinos, local businesses and many employees all banked there. I quickly turned onto Third, stopping my black and white in the traffic lane and turned on my flashers. I walked to the intersection of Third and Carson near the back of the Four Queens. I stepped into a protective alcove that afforded me a good spot to watch for the bank robbers to come out. Dispatch advised me that a man and a woman had held up the bank, taken the money and told everyone that they had a bomb and would blow them up if they moved. At that time, a man and a woman came out the door.

Sure enough, here came a tall young woman in black pants and a white and blue blouse. She carried a flashy gold-vinyl purse over her shoulder. The man, 40ish, short-build and heavy-set wore jeans and a white T-shirt, and carried a bag. I waited as they walked to the stoplight and halted, tarrying calmly as the light changed. They crossed, hurriedly rushing, and headed north, right toward me. As they were even with me, I stepped out and knocked the man down. The girl screamed, and reached into her purse. I kicked her legs from under her, and as she sprawled to the sidewalk, her open purse fell, filtering out stolen money. The man got up and started running down Carson, crossing Third Street and into the parking lot of the Four Queens. Other officers arrived and chased and caught the man. The girl, in her late twenties, was scratching, biting and kicking me. I turned her over, placed my knee into her back and was cuffing her.

Jasmine, a casino worker, from the Four Queens, came up behind me and alerted me, "Officer Randel, somebody is messing with your police car." With my suspect secure, I turned and looked at my black and white police car. There, writing a ticket was the infamous meter molly, Cobra One. *Doesn't she have a brain? Who tickets a police car in the middle of a robbery? She must have the brain of a piss-ant.*

I did a handoff to one of the other officers. I walked back to my police car and yelled at Cobra One, "What in the hell are you doing? Are you an idiot? Can't you see I'm in the middle of an arrest?"

Insolently, she replied, "I was told to ticket any vehicle that is double parked!"

"What the hell is wrong with you?"

She hastily placed the ticket under my windshield wiper. As she did so, an unmarked police car stopped. It was Undersheriff Collins, who runs the police department! He proceeded to speak with the officers that held the man and the woman. They explained what had happened. When he was satisfied, he walked back to me.

"Good job, Randel. Always at the right place at the right time." Looking at my distorted, angry face as I was reaching for my ticket, he queried, "What is that?"

"Ah hell, Sheriff, that idiot over there ticketed me for double-parking." Cobra One was busily ticketing the sheriff's car that was double-parked behind mine.

"Is she stupid or on drugs?" he shouted so she could hear him. "Don't worry, Randel, let me handle this," he said, taking the ticket. He strode back to his car where he confronted Cobra One, *little miss Meter Molly.*

About that time, Grumpy was advancing with some of the witnesses so they could identify the robbers. Grumpy shook his head at me in wonder when he saw Cobra One, a name we had vengefully given her.

After the entire hubbub was over, I went to the Blue Onion for lunch. Grumpy calmly joined me about forty-five minutes later. I was dictating my report over the phone. I seldom had to write my own because certain very nice people would do it for me because they knew I hated the paperwork. Grumpy interrupted, "Rod, you really gave that female suspect a bloody nose!"

"Oh, really! I didn't even notice. She sure fought like a wild cat."

We never had to go to court on that case. As far as I knew, I was the only officer whose police car was ever ticketed for double-parking during a robbery.

However, a couple of days later, I found out a little secret from Willy. Just around the corner on Carson, while we were finishing up with the robbery, *little miss* Meter Molly, who had already been talked to by Undersheriff Collins, placed a sweet little tan ticket for double parking under Adam-12's windshield wiper. *What the hell? Was Cobra One brain dead? Was Grumpy too proud to say anything, or did he want me to feel independently distinguished? Maybe that's what took him so long to meet me at the Blue Onion. Either way, we're going to get back at Cobra One! And, revenge is sweet!*

BLUE MULE

23:50 HRS. TUESDAY NIGHT. WILLY AND I had pulled a double shift each week for about a month. This was not our last, as the Christmas rush was not over. It would be a full moon at 2:01 a.m., and our shift had been 'one helluva week', all night long. You encounter and combat a lot more on nights like this. People go batty. It has to do with gravity's pull from the gigantic orb, so they say.

Well, vampires, were-wolfs, monsters or not, I believe that the evil in folks sneaks out of their bodies and minds and they act without considering the consequences. There are more fights, robberies, rapes, automobile wrecks and vandalism during the fullest luminescence of that terrestrial globe than any other nights of the month. Lord, protect us all from a major event during that time. Win or lose, idiots celebrate, cause fights and otherwise disturb the peace.

As our shift wound down and we cleared our paper work and reports, the lieutenant came by our office and remarked, "Let's all adjourn to the Blue Mule." Wells looked at me as if to say, 'Oh damn, Randel, don't say yes!' But, I did. I could hear him thinking, '*What else tonight?*' Giving him no out, I assured him that we would only have one nightcap because we were off duty the next day. After all, we couldn't say 'no' to the lieutenant. Of course, I only *planned* to drink iced tea.

I parked my Camero midway from the corner of Las Vegas Blvd. on Pecos, and waited for Willy. Parking ever so carefully behind me, Wells checked carefully to see that he had not parked in any yellow or red zone. *Who the hell cares,* I thought, *It's midnight. No Meter Mollys are out now.* But, I checked again just to make certain. I sure as hell didn't want my Camero towed, and that damned Cobra was spiteful enough to do it.

We joined the lieutenant at a small table amongst the boisterous din of music and laughter. I was pleasantly surprised to see our Coroner, Doli Leija, there with some of her crew. I hailed her and she remarked, "Randel, remember, you still owe me a pizza."

You are a real sweetheart, girl, I thought. "How about tomorrow for lunch Doli? We can bring our secretary and Grumpy, and go to Pizza Hut."

"Great, I'll bring a bib for Grumpy!"

We had just placed our orders with a sexy, long-legged waitress, Roxie, when the heavy door to the Blue Mule crashed open. Since the bartender had an outside camera and a button that he could use to open or to lock the door, we were alerted and all turned toward the clamorous intrusion. Obviously, Ben had forgotten the lock after we entered. A big, burly black man rushed through the opening brandishing a small revolver. Placing two feet in a balanced stance, he shouted over the commotion of the night, "This is a stick up!"

A thunderous, dead silence followed. Then as if in unison, multitudinous guns came from holsters, all pointed at him. That was the wrong thing to say in an establishment full of freshly off-duty cops, all still wearing their guns. The bartender ducked behind the bar, some cocktail waitresses stood frozen in utter shock and others ducked behind chairs. Roxie, tray in hand, squatted beside me, her hand on my knee for balance. "Asshole," one officer shouted. "Kill him," barked another. "Somebody shoot the son-of-a-bitch," echoed voices from every direction. "Get him, Rod," yelled Doli, her weapon drawn.

"Freeze, dirtbag," I instructed. The robber, eyes wide in fear and wonder, threw up his quivering hands, dropped his revolver, and caused his weak knees to stop vibrating as he spun around and turned to run out the door. Unfortunately for him, Ben had pressed the lock and the bandit hit the door soundly and was thrown backward, landing on his butt.

A huge guffaw roared from the crowd. He scrambled to his feet, as someone in the back hollered, "Open the door, Ben, let the asshole out." That idiot exited so fast that he left his revolver on the floor and definitely some shit and piss. I sent Wells to retrieve the gun, which turned out to be stolen, and we resumed our revelry. I asked Roxie what time she finished work. Nobody seemed interested in chasing the robber. Doli ordered hot wings for her table and mine. I sported for a round for all the officers forgetting that I was only having iced tea.

About ten minutes later, Grumpy entered. "Hell, Randel," he called out, "you gonna just sit in here and let some SOB mess with your car?"

"What the hell," I exclaimed, as I jumped up and hurried to the door. *Meter Molly!*

"Don't worry, Randel, I stopped the jerk and told him that Camero was my buddy's car and that if he ever had thoughts of stealin' anything of yours I would cut him long, hard and deep, and watch him die. He took off like a bat out of hell. You won't see him around here again."

"Thanks, Grumpy, but can't you ever arrive on time?" As I explained what had happened inside, Grumpy put the same description to our black bandit, and I wondered just how gutsy that inept black man was after all. *The nerve of that guy, after losing his revolver, fouling up his own robbery, and then having the gall to try to break into my Camero.* I had forgotten about the idiotic behavior caused by the full moon. *If that would-be robber had only known that my buddy, Grumpy, always comes right at the end of every incident, he would never have dreamed of trying anything else, especially since Grumpy is always worse than bad during the full moon too.*

BREAKFAST BURGLAR V

My cell phone rang. "Randel, whatcha doin'?"

"Hey, Sikes, I just finished a case in court. Why?"

"I'm hungry enough to eat the south bound end of a north bound skunk. Meet me at Denny's at Charleston and Fremont Street."

"You buyin'?"

"You on drugs? Hell, no I ain't buyin'. How long 'til you get your ass over there?"

"Give me ten, fifteen minutes. See you there." Grumpy and I arrived simultaneously at Denny's, entered and greeted the crew. Jade, the cute little hazel-eyed, brown, sun-streaked haired waitress that was earning her way through dental school, acknowledged us. She gave me a caring hug, ignored Grumpy, and quickly filled a glass of iced tea for me. Then, with menus tucked under her arm, she brought us to a half-circle table with cushioned seats at the back of the smoking section. It was the seat facing the door and giving us a view of the complete smoking section, the outside windows and the twenty or so customers. The waiting staff knew that we liked to have that advantage, with our backs to the wall, and the straight access to the doors. Also, they all felt comfortable when they knew that Metro's finest was seated close to their waiting station, even though Grumpy and I were dressed in civilian clothes. I wore a sport's jacket with a turtleneck shirt, dress jeans, and cowboy boots. I always dressed appropriately for court, but seldom wore neckties, never a bow tie. The jacket helped conceal the shoulder holster and gun that I always wore. Grumpy was more casually dressed because he had come from home and we were both on our day off. However, he too was always armed.

Jade brought the morning paper and laid it in front of me after she took our orders. Grumpy, in a sour mood, ordered a Coke and made a comment that I was always served first, and got the hugs and the paper. "What the hell am I, Hawk, chopped liver?"

"Grumpy, you need to try a little harder. The ladies like you too, but you never smile or say hello or even leave good tips. What do you expect?"

"Oh well, it doesn't make any difference. I never get my meals 'comped' either and you always do. They all think you're something special. Hah!"

"Oh, didn't I tell you, I am special!"

"Shut the hell up, Rod, and drink your tea, or I'll take out my knife right here. I have things on my mind."

"Well, you'd better keep that knife in your pocket as first priority, 'cause you know I can draw one of my guns before you can unsheath any one of your knives. Anyway, Sam, what's bothering you on your day off? Can't we just have a relaxing meal and shoot the shit for a while? You want the comic section of the paper?"

"No, I'm not in a funny mood, Rod. We've got to do something about the Breakfast Burglar and all the other shit that's happening in our area. I think we need to talk with the lieutenant and have him give us some more men early in the mornings to patrol our seniors better."

"You know they would, Grumpy, but we're already short handed. And you and I are putting in four or five extra hours a day to be on the streets at four a.m."

Dejectedly, Grumpy accepted his soup and salad. He loudly slurped his soup and his Coke and picked at his salad, spilling salad dressing down his shirt and on his pants. He didn't seem to care.

"What else can we do? That bastard is gonna kill somebody soon. We've got to stop him. And, I have to get Ms. Tilly her ring back."

"I know Grumpy. But that may never happen."

"I made a promise to that sweet little lady and with God's help, and my knife, Hawk, I'm gonna keep it."

"All we can do is to keep our eyes and ears open, Sam. He'll turn up. I believe he's still in the area, even with all the notoriety and someone will spot him, and turn him in. He's not going to leave such easy pickin's for stuff he likes to steal. And, I think he has someone fencing the goods for him somewhere on Las Vegas Blvd. or right downtown. Try to be patient. Do you want catsup or mustard with your cheeseburger and fries, buddy?"

We sat quietly, eating our meal, Grumpy deep in thought and me absent-mindedly reading the newspaper. I took a bite of my hamburger and was mixing my catsup and mustard together with a French fry as I casually looked toward the door. I noticed that the hostess, Mardy, was leading a black man to a table. His booth was two down from ours. *Damn. That guy is 5' 10", in blue jeans, a dark muscle shirt and tennis shoes. I can't see his hair for his cap, but he fits the description of our Breakfast Burglar. I'll be a son-of-a-gun; he has a mutilated left ear too. Oh shit! I've got to warn Grumpy, but I don't want him to screw this up because he's so mad.*

I nudged Sikes under the table with my knee, kept my head down and whispered to him, "Look two booths over, but don't say a thing. We're gonna do something right."

Grumpy looked, swallowed his bite of hamburger whole and choked on it, coughing hard and turning red for several minutes. I thought I might have to do the Hemleich maneuver right there. When he had finished and cleared his throat, he said hoarsely, "Randel, that's him; look at his ear! Let's go get him!"

"Just wait. We have to…just wait. Let him start eating his food and get relaxed. Then we'll act like we're gonna leave. I'll grab his left arm and grab him by his hair. You're to grab his right arm and bend it behind him."

"I hope he fights real hard, Randel, real hard. I really want to hurt him."

"This is a good day, Grumpy, a good day. I'm gonna enjoy the rest of my burger and we're gonna have Pike for dessert." It was hard for Grumpy, but we began eating our lunch again, trying to be casual. Jade came to fill my glass with tea, and I spoke softly, "Jade, honey, we're going to make an arrest. Without startling that man in the second booth, take all the waitresses and busboys behind the waitress station where you can all be safe. Go ahead like you are just conducting business as usual. Make salads and clank dishes or something. When I see that you are all safe, we're gonna take him down. He is considered armed and dangerous, so you duck down and don't watch."

I have to give Jade a lot of credit. She didn't flinch or look over at Henry Erwin Pike. She smiled and laughed lightly, "Okay, you've got it." *Thanks for not using my name, Jade,* I reasoned. She returned to the station and went into the kitchen. Within a couple of minutes the manager, Ryan, had all his staff doing other things than waiting tables. The manager went from table to table apparently asking how their meals were. However, the patrons in the nearby booths were carefully being cleared from the area a few at a time.

Finally, Grumpy rose and laid a $5 tip on the table. I was right behind him when we casually ambled past Pike. As Grumpy passed him, I slid into the booth beside Pike, grabbed his head and smashed it hard into his plate. Grabbing his left arm, I twisted it behind his back just as Grumpy did the same to his right. He was so stunned that he did not move for a second. Then he started fighting and struggling to free himself. He was kicking, twisting and trying to bite us. Grumpy was trying hard to control him and told me, "Smash this son-of-a-bitch's face into that plate again, Randel." I was happy to oblige him and once again smushed his mug into his mashed potatoes. He came up sputtering and gasping for air. About that time, Grumpy firmly twisted Pike's right arm behind him again, and I heard a loud crack. I discerned that Grumpy, somewhat out of control with his pent-up anger, had broken Pike's wrist.

"Don't fight us, Pike, don't fight us or more hurt's on the way." I placed my handcuff on his left wrist and after he still struggled violently for several minutes, we were able to cuff the other wrist and lock him down.

As I was dragging Pike from behind the table, Grumpy said,

Frank-3 Enroute

"Randel, stop! Look! Around his neck. That's Tilly's ring. I bet that's Tilly's ring!"

I straightened Henry Pike's head by pulling his hair backward and looked at his neck. There was a gold chain that had a gold ring bearing the Cracker Jack emblem with a small heart attached to it with the letter 'T'. "By damn, you're right, Sikes. That's Tilly's ring all right."

"I'm gonna jerk that off you, you SOB, then I'm gonna cut you!"

"No, Grumpy, no. We need to have good pictures with that hanging around his neck. Easy now, we haven't even read Mr. Pike his rights yet. We don't want to mess this up because this bastard is going away for good. Read his rights to him." Grumpy got back into the swing of things and did not want to make any mistakes so he took his Miranda Card from his own wallet and carefully spoke each word verbatim as he read his rights to Mr. Henry Erwin Pike.

Pike refused to acknowledge that he understood his rights. We asked Jade and the cook, Manuel, to come out, and Grumpy re-read the Miranda Rights with them as witnesses so that we could verify that the rights had been read. Finally, Pike admitted that he knew his "F…n' rights.

During this time, I used Denny's phone to call dispatch and asked them to send a patrol unit and to call Criminalistics to have someone come to take pictures of everything. I especially wanted pictures of Pike wearing that Cracker Jack ring. We were going to nail his sorry ass for all those Breakfast Burglaries.

The next thing I knew, Maggie was on the telephone. "Randel, what you got?"

"Hey Maggie. We have a guy here that likes to eat breakfast at other people's houses. Isn't this your day off?"

"Yes, but it's yours too! Rod, you really got that dirt bag? I'll be right there."

"Yeah, Grumpy and I were having lunch and that bastard walked in and sat down next to us. We couldn't believe our luck. God is good! How did you receive the call?"

I was already in my office doing some cleanup on old reports when dispatch called and said that it was you. I know how important this case is to you so I took the call. I'll be right there."

Grumpy started outside with Pike so that we would no longer disturb Denny's business. As they neared the cashier, Grumpy stopped and asked, "Excuse me, ma'am. How much was this man's bill?" Sikes reached into Pike's jeans pocket and pulled out a twenty-dollar bill. When the cashier told him that it came to $8.79, Grumpy turned and handed Jade the twenty and told her to keep the change because she deserved it. I was proud of Grumpy at that moment. *He was very generous! Of course, it wasn't his money either.* But I was still proud of his thoughtfulness.

When Maggie arrived, she confirmed, "Sure it's my day off, but I'm here for you and those old folks that this guy has hurt. What can I do first?"

"Maggie, I really appreciate you're coming. I'm so damned excited about this arrest that I sure don't want to mess up anything. Do it by the numbers. We need pictures of Pike, especially that gold necklace and ring around his neck, his torn ear and his clothes. I know without a doubt that the ring belongs to Ms. Tilly. So, take some close ups from all sides before you take it off his kinky-haired chest. I want pictures without his hat so we can see his hair. I don't want the defense attorneys to have any reason to have this case thrown out. Henry Erwin Pike needs to go away for good.

The patrol unit arrived and heralded us for our capture and said that they would help handle everything for us. Grumpy stated, "Randel, I'm gonna ride in the back seat with this SOB so that I can make sure he doesn't try to escape." Scowling at Pike with all the anger and hate he could muster, Sikes said, "I just hope you start something, you bastard. I want to cut you long, hard and deep and make you bleed to death for all that you have done to our old people, but I'm a police officer and I won't do anything to a handcuffed man, unless of course, he's resisting me and trying to escape. So, just give me a reason, any reason at all, Pike. I do not like your sorry ass."

"That's enough Sikes, I stated. "Remember, we want this as clean as possible. I'll follow you just to make sure he doesn't give you any trouble." I looked at Pike, giving him my evil eye and reiterated, "This is one of Las Vegas's toughest policemen. He's not afraid to cut anyone to pieces if he hates them bad enough and I'm here to tell you, Pike, you had better tow the line or you just might be fish bait by the time they arrive you at County Jail." The other officers scoffed as I closed the door on Pike's side of the car.

I went to the parking lot and started my Camero, waiting while the patrol car pulled out. Maggie came to my side window and I rolled it down, thanking her again for all she had done. "Randel, I'll have those pictures for you within the hour. It's gonna cost you though."

"Name your price, Maggie, I'll gladly pay."

"How about that dinner you promised the night that you were crashed into? You still owe me for that one."

"That's a good deal. And, I'll even take you to a good movie or a play of your choice. You say when, and I'll be there."

"We'd both better check our schedules, Rod, and make sure we can keep a date free. Give me a call. Oh, by the way, you can probably take that necklace and ring once you clear it with Lieutenant Germain. I have taken plenty of pictures for evidence. I know that Grumpy really is hot about taking it back to Ms. Tilly. She will be so excited when she sees it. Talk with you later, Rod." She smiled sweetly and left me sitting there with my little heart pounding. *That is one nice woman,* I decided. *I'm looking forward to our first date.*

As we were booking Mr. Henry Erwin Pike, ID #162991, another prisoner was also being booked. He called out to Pike, "HEP Cat! Brutha', I see they finally caught you for all those burglaries."

I turned to him and asked, "What did you call this man? And what did you say to him?"

"HEP-Cat! That's what we all calls Pike. We all knows he's the one that breaks into those houses on Rexford. He be braggin' 'bout it all the time."

I asked Lt. Garcia if we could get statements that the prisoner had said that to Pike, because it would improve our case. The prisoner, Jangles, said he didn't owe HEP Cat anything and that he would tell us again what he said.

HEP Cat Henry Erwin Pike, glared at the man and snarled, "Shut the f...up. I don't know you, but I'll see you inside ass wipe."

After we took the prisoner's statement, the correction officers decided that he should be placed in isolation where he would not have to confront Pike. We all felt more at ease about that, and I figured that they were going to let him off easy for his help. *We might need him alive as a witness,* I thought. Other people that were around signed statements to the effect that they had heard the first man, Jangles, confront Pike, call him by his nickname and challenge him as the Breakfast Burglar. Grumpy booked him with pleasure on fifteen accounts of burglary and two attempted murders. To my surprise, Grumpy said, "Randel, I'll do the reports on this myself. I want to make sure that we don't miss anything; we're gonna take our time and make sure we get this guy."

I went to the officers that did the strip search on Pike and told them that I would need everything that he was wearing so that I could place it into evidence. Grumpy made sure that he received Tilly's gold chain with the heart and the ring. *Man, I haven't seen Grumpy this happy in a long time, not even when he rescued the black bitch and her puppies. Damn, I love that big guy. Now, I'm gonna make him even happier.*

As Grumpy sat in the passenger seat of my Camero, he said, "Let's go together to take Tilly's ring back to her, Randel. She and Oscar are gonna be so happy. Can we go now? Damn this feels good!"

"Sure, Sikes," I assured as I headed for Sahara.

"Where the hell we goin'?"

"You'll see." I parked tin front of Christiansen's Jewelers on Sahara. "Come on, we're going in here first."

"What you got in mind?"

Inside, I asked for Rholph, who came from the back and greeted me. "Officer Randel! How nice to see you. What may I do for your today?"

I explained briefly about the return of Tilly's ring and asked if he would possible have a nice little padded jewelry box that we could place it in to take it to her. He took the ring to the back and returned shortly with a four by six-inch, black, velvet, snap-shut jewelry box with gold trim. He opened it and showed us a highly cleaned and polished chain, ring and tiny heart that were professionally encased in the inner, black-satin cushioned case. The set looked exquisite and brand new. Grumpy gingerly took the container in his giant hands and stared down at the Cracker Jack ring. *I think this big lug is gonna cry,* I thought. "Randel, look at that; just look at it. Thank you, Mr. Christiansen. Ms. Tilly will really be happy about this. How much do I owe you?" he asked as he reached into his pocket for his money clip. *He doesn't even care how much it costs. He'd pay anything to see that little old lady happy.*

"Officer Sikes, you and Officer Randel do so much for all the downtown merchants. Please let me make a little contribution to make a sweet little lady happy. Take this to her with my best wishes, and you have a nice day."

"Thank you, sir," I praised when I noticed that Sikes was suddenly speechless. "You have made our day."

Back in the car, Grumpy held that black jewelry box as if it were solid gold. We skirted the traffic and headed to the Rexford area. We approached the house slowly, checking out the entire neighborhood. As I pulled along side the curb, I looked at the front of Oscar and Tilly's house. My heart sank to the bottom of my chest. On the front door hung a single black wreath. I took a deep, painful breath and cleared my throat. "Look at that, Sikes. What do you suppose has happened?"

"Oh no. Shit! Just drive on, Randel. I can't handle anything else today. This isn't the time to take back the ring. I can do it some other day."

"Well, let's at least check it out and make sure that whatever is going on, no one needs any help. Come on, Sikes, you can handle it, buddy."

Sikes set the velvet box on the seat of my Camero as he exited, hiked his dress jeans, tucked in his shirt, straightened his jacket, and then slowly turned toward the door. That black wreath loomed ominously before us as we slowly and painfully approached the house. Somebody had died. Our greatest fears were certain to be realized. There would be no happy reunion for sure.

I rang the doorbell and waited patiently for an answer. Grumpy was standing on first one big foot and then the other, probably thinking that he should turn and leave. At last, the door slowly opened, and

Oscar stood before us. "Officers how nice of you to drop by. Did you know that we had a death in the family?"

I modestly answered, "No, Oscar, we were in the neighborhood and thought we would drop by and see if you needed anything. Then we noticed the black wreath on your door. We are so sorry for your loss."

"Come in, come in, gentlemen," he invited quietly and humbly. "Make yourselves at home. Please have a seat. It's been a rough few days." We walked inside and selected seats on the antique floral sofa. Sikes was fidgeting, his head down, his mouth more southbound than his chin. I looked around taking in all of Ms. Tilly's womanly touches. There were heavily starched doilies on the coffee table and end tables. There were ceramic figurines pleasantly placed around. I noticed that there were plenty of masculine memorabilia set so that all could tell that this home was for two people that had always been close, loving partners.

"Can I bring you something to drink? It's pretty hot out there. It was sweltering this morning at the cemetery. I thought I would have sun stroke, but the good Lord watched over me." As Oscar turned to go into the kitchen, the doorbell rang. He shuffled to the door and opened it, allowing a middle-aged man to enter. "Officers Sikes and Randel, this is my nephew, Bertrum. He was nice enough to come and take us to the gravesite. Bert, these are the nice policeman that came when our house was broken into."

"Oh yes, and I believe that you went to my father's home when he was burglarized. Do you remember him, Bertrum Warner?"

I concentrated, *Bertrum, was that the name of one of the people whose home was broken into? I can't remember.* I allowed, "Why yes we do. How's he doin'?"

My dad is Uncle Oscar's younger brother, and I'm Bertrum Jr. Unfortunately, my dad was not strong enough to recover from the trauma caused by the burglar. He never was able to return home."

Oscar interrupted, "Excuse me a minute, gentlemen. Bert, can you fetch the officers something to drink?" Oscar headed toward the bedrooms. In a couple of minutes, he walked out with... *Ms. Tilly* on his arm. In shock, I thought, *Thank you, dear God. What a wonderful surprise!* I almost yelled out, I was so happy, especially for Grumpy.

"Tilly, honey, look who's here. It's Officer Sikes and Officer Randel." Then to us he commented, "Bless her heart, she's not getting any younger. She needs to rest a lot now."

I thought that Grumpy was going to jump straight out of his skin with joy. He rose immediately and clambered over the edge of the coffee table, his number 14's almost tripping him. "Ms. Tilly... I was afraid that you... I thought that... Oh, never mind. How wonderful to see you!" He rushed the few steps to her side, and gently lifted the tiny lady off the floor and swung her around, placed her back on the carpet, and kissed the top of her gray head. "I have some wonderful news for you, ma'am. I didn't hurt you did I?"

"Oh no, dear man, you could never hurt me." Taking his giant hand in her tiny one, she continued, "We could use some good news with Oscar's brother dying unexpectedly like he did. He was only a couple of years younger than Oscar, but his heart was weak, and when that evil man tried to strangle him with his own sock, he just couldn't gain the strength to get better. We kept praying for him to improve. We've been sitting up with him almost every night and now, he and Oscar and I can have some well-deserved rest. He has gone all the way home, and we buried him today. Poor Bertie is left all alone now. But we'll keep care of him, and I'm sure he will tend to us." She patted Grumpy's hand before she let go of it. "Now, Officer Sam, what is the good news?"

"Just you wait right here, ma'am. Randel, toss me the keys to your car. Ms. Tilly, I'll be back in a second. Don't you go anywhere," he pleaded like a little kid afraid that his parent would leave him. Bert returned with large glasses filled with fresh lemonade. Sikes was out the door and back in a flash with his grand prize tucked in his giant fist, and a smile as large as the Cheshire Cat's. "Ms. Tilly, please have a seat in your favorite chair. I told you we would catch the man that burglarized your home. And we did, just few hours ago. Unfortunately, Oscar, not soon enough to protect your brother, Bertrum. I had not put your two last names together until just now. Please accept our sincere apologies and condolences for his death. But, Ms. Tilly, look in the purty little box. I think that you will be surprised and happy." With that, Grumpy snapped open the case, revealing the Cracker Jack ring, the necklace and the tiny heart with the 'T' that stood for Tilly.

"Oh, praise the Lord, praise the Lord," she exclaimed, clapping her hands together. "Where did you ever find it, Officer Sam?"

"Pike, the burglar that we arrested this afternoon was wearing it around his own neck. That's why we could never locate it in a pawnshop. He must have thought that it was really special and didn't want to give it up. We took it off him, and Mr. Christiansen at Christiansen's Jewelers cleaned it and boxed it for you with his best wishes. I'm so happy that I was able to bring it back to you, Ms. Tilly. When I make a promise I try my damn.... Excuse my language, ma'am, I try my darndest to keep it."

"Lean down here, you big sweet man. Let me give you a kiss. You are the nicest policeman I have ever met. Your heart is as big as a lion's, and so is your growl, but I love you and thank you from the bottom of my heart. Oscar and I are so happy to have our little love momento returned to us, aren't we sugar?"

Grumpy turned several shades of red after she kissed him, and he stammered as if he were tongue-tied. "Thank you, Ms. Tilly, Oscar. Well, we'd better be goin', Randel. It was a pleasure to meet you, Mr. Warner."

We said our good-byes and returned to the scorching heat inside the Camero. "Damn, that felt good, Randel. I haven't felt this good in a long time. It's a shame about Mr. Warner though. We didn't do enough, did we?"

As I started the engine and slipped out of the parking spot, I commented, "No, we probably never do enough, Sam. Maybe we should have gone back to the hospital and checked on him from time to time. But I had no idea. We've been so intent on catching Pike that maybe we were neglecting our other seniors." I drove to the corner and turned onto Oakey.

"Where we goin', Rod?"

"I'm goin' over on Sahara to the Tiger Lily Flower Shop."

"What you gonna do, buy posies for Cheyenne?"

"Nope. I'm gonna buy a snappy bouquet of flowers and we're

gonna make a call on little Gracie Echstein. What better thing do we have to do on our day off, Sam?"

"We need to stop back by the County Jail and change the charge to one attempted murder and one murder."

"Sam, we did our jobs. Tomorrow's another day. That Breakfast Burglar has eaten his last free breakfast!"

"Amen to that, Randel!"

HANGIN' AROUND

I HELPED MYLINDA OUT OF THE gutter and she rested on the curb. This was not the first time, and I didn't figure it would be the last time I rescued her pretty little ass from the hazards of the Las Vegas streets. At twenty-seven, she looked forty. Her mossy-brown hair was thinning and stringy, her eyes were glazed, the pupils fully dilated, her nose ran constantly, her teeth were rotting and she was as thin as a rail. Her arms and legs and between her toes showed track marks from using every kind of drug you can imagine. She sported bloody bruises on her forearms and on her shins, products of her frequent falls, and anemia. Mylinda wore dirty, ragged, cut-off, blue-jeans shorts, a tank top without a bra and floppy sandals. Her fingernails and toenails, however, were perfectly manicured in the French Silk fashion.

"Mylinda," I softly spoke, "Come on baby, Grumpy and I will call home for you."

"Hell no, Randel, I don't wanna go home. My dad will be mad if he sees me like this. Please don't call him."

"Miles, the only other option is to run you in. You can't stay on the street like this. You need some groceries in that empty belly of yours, and a place to sleep. Come on, baby, sit up straight, now." I hailed a cabby and gave him her family's uptown address and twenty bucks to see that she made it home safely. I tacked a note to her tank top to have her father call me at the station. We needed to figure out a plan for Mylinda.

"Damn," remarked Sikes, "That is one messed up chick. How'd she get so mixed up? Can't her parents help her?"

"They do, Grumpy. They've paid for every kind of treatment and cure known to man, but she'll be out of one of those centers for a week and she's back on the streets buyin'. Her family is great. Mr. & Mrs. Grayson are two of the nicest most giving people you could hope to find here in Vegas. Her brother and sister are top-notch, youngsters, college graduates, and then there is the older sister, Mylinda, for whom there seems to be no hope. She's had everything and every opportunity to survive and to do well, but for some reason, she just can't seem to make it. I know that meth-heads and crack-heads seldom ever completely break loose, but some do and live good lives. We need to help this woman if we can."

"Hell," grumbled Grumpy, "I'll help her out of her misery. I'll cut her long, hard and deep and watch her pale, pink blood ooze to the gutter. I ain't got sympathy for dopers, Randel, so don't ask me to help you."

"Shut the hell up, Sikes," I countered, "or I'll shoot off your arm and stick it up your ass, before you can draw your first knife. You don't have to be involved with Mylinda, but I want to help her folks. They're always there for us cops and anytime I have asked for a donation at Christmas or for equipment for the kids in the projects, Mr. Grayson has always been very generous. They're good people and deserve better."

"You don't know that for sure, Rod. Do you know where his big bucks come from, huh? Could be one of the biggest drug dealers in the county for all you know!"

"Wrong, Grumpy, he makes his money in airplane parts and rocket and jet fuel. Selling drugs would not be worth his time, and he is a very religious man."

Two days later, I received a call from dispatch. "Frank-3, copy this call." It was time for our lunch break, and Wells and I had just checked out with her. She was a new woman on the switchboard, and she had a lot to learn about police work. Cheri' never called us during our breaks if she could help it, but she knew we would go if we were needed.

"Go ahead, Nita, what do you need? We're on our break."

"Someone just called in and asked for you to go to their home. They were informed that address is out of your area," she replied sharply. "However, 513 has granted permission to leave your area and head to 5027 Mockingbird Lane, in Pattern Valley." I could tell she was thinking, *I don't care who you are, but you think your so special, Randel. She was right.* "A woman was found hanging from a wooden beam in the family's great room. You need to go now."

"Switch Channels, dispatch." From there, I informed Nita, "Mark us down as **Frank-3 enroute** in ten minutes. Willy and I are stopping for lunch first."

"I can't do that, Randel. You're either enroute, or you're not. Which will it be?"

Listen, bitch, I thought. *I'm swingin' through Mickie-D's for my two Big-Mac's, fries and an iced tea, and you can kiss my butt.* "I'm at the drive-thru, waiting for our lunch. That woman will still be hanging when I get there. Oh, hell, **Frank-3 enroute**."

As I approached the Pattern Valley exit, I began to visualize that I was headed for the Grayson mansion. I knew the address; I knew the house. My heart sank as the realization that the hanging woman was more than likely Miles Grayson. What the hell was I going to say to her folks? As I circled into the covered arches of the mansion's drive, I saw the coroner's vehicle among the police cars and an ambulance. I advised dispatch to arrive us, and we alighted from our patrol car. At the ten-foot high, double door a gentleman in a butler's garb met us and ushered us into the great room.

There surrounded by officers of the law, the coroner, homicide detectives, and family and friends, hanged the emaciated and very dead body of Mylinda Grayson. She had been dead for some time. Petechia, the breaking of small blood vessels, had set in on her face, leaving a ghostly-blue hue, and her ankles and feet were a blackish-blue as the blood settled to her lower extremities. Rigor had not completely set in, but it had obviously been several hours since she had hanged herself. She apparently had planned this event for the late evening. She was cleanly bathed, and her hair was shampooed and neatly combed. She wore makeup that added gory shadows to her death mask. She had applied expensive perfume, and had dressed in high-fashion black tights and a black, silk and lace blouse. She had not, however, known about or planned for the last body excretions that would take place when she jumped from the ladder. She had left a vulgar and smelly mess running down her legs and onto the expensive carpet below.

I went directly to Mr. Grayson who shook my hand and thanked me for coming. He told me he knew that I was good to his baby girl as she had talked about me to him and his wife. He asked if I would make sure that the police took good care of her for him. I said I would, although other than to comfort them, I would have little to do with the case, or so I thought. I felt small and ineffectual as I expressed my sympathy to Mrs. Grayson, and could read the torture and sadness in her tear-filled eyes. Willy and I remained until the body was removed and all had taken their leave. The Graysons felt reassured that everyone had done their utmost for Miles. They thanked me again and again, until I finally felt I was going to be ill if I did not take my leave from there.

"Control, Frank-3, clear us."

"Frank-3," came back Nita's call, "You are to report directly to Lieutenant Dan Arnold's office. He said he doesn't want to hear any excuses and that he expects you ASAP."

"Okay, Nita.... What for?" I asked politely.

With a barbed tongue she ridiculed, "You'll find out when you get there, Randel."

What frog's up her butt, I wondered. *Am I gonna have trouble with this new bitch?* "**Frank-3 enroute**." I could not imagine what the hell Arnold wanted with me. *Here we go again. He's always trying to place my ass in a sling over any small thing.*

"Randel, do I have to go with you?" pleaded Wells.

"Of course, you do, Willy. You're my front man. I can't face Arnold alone."

"Oh shit! My career's on the line again, and I know I'll be havin' nightmares."

"Hell, Wells, you have nightmares over work? I sleep like a baby. No problems."

In his office, I greeted Arnold amicably and he bluntly told us to sit down. "Randel, you were insubordinate and out of line over the air. You made a mockery of a hanging victim's predicament on the radio, and you will be brought up on charges for that. Do you read me?"

I responded with my most polite inflection, "No, Lieutenant, I don't."

"Did you or did you not tell Nita from dispatch that Miss Grayson would still be hanging around whenever you got to her house?"

"I believe that I answered her correctly, Lieutenant. I did not intend to slur the sweet young woman who died today."

"Well, what you said went over the airways, and anyone could have listened in on your conversation. We can be sued for such smart-ass comments, Randel."

"Well, sir, I believe that if you check, we were on Channel 5 when I spoke privately with dispatch. I did not use a name because dispatch did not call one out. However, If I erred I will try to make amends." *Personally, you ass-wipe,* I conjured in my mind, *you can kiss the rosy-red cheek of my sweaty ass before you get anything from me.*

At that moment, Lieutenant Gene Germain stuck his head into Arnold's office. "There you are, Rod," he spoke in a friendly manner. "I heard you might be experiencing a problem with dispatch so I dropped by and spoke with Nita. We agree that you simply repeated back to her the exact words that you heard her say. I can see no wrongdoing. As far as my department is concerned, Lieutenant Arnold, there is no dilemma. Randel, I'm headed to Sam's Town for dinner. You and Wells want to join me?" Germain looked at Arnold with no other words spoken, not even goodbye, and I felt that Wells and I had been vindicated and that only Arnold had been left hanging.

WILD THING

WELLS AND I WERE SITTING IN IHOP at Boston and Las Vegas Blvd. on a Sunday morning, about 9:00 a.m., and we had ordered breakfast. We were just beginning to eat when the dispatcher called and reported a 416 with three adult men in an altercation. Cheri' knew that Wells and I always answered calls that others wouldn't take, and that she wouldn't call us if we were on break unless it was necessary. When Cheri' asked, "Frank-3, can you respond?" Willy and I left our food and as we say were TCB, Taking Care of Business, because it was in our area.

"Frank-3 enroute."

On this particular day, I was in my own patrol car and Willy was in his; sometimes we worked the same area that way. I shot down Fairfield, and drove the circle around Fairfield where the park is. Cincinnati is the last street before Sahara Blvd. On the 200 hundred block of West Cincinnati lie a bunch of apartments, and in front of each apartment is a nice lawn and large trees. I noted as I approached, that the apartment complex was set far back from the street.

On the grass, three guys were goin' at it pretty hard, so I hit the lights and I turned on the siren. I drove right over the sidewalk and onto the lawn. As I jumped out, I turned off the siren because it was earsplitting. These three were still fightin' and not payin' any attention to my presence. So I took out my baton, (my PR-24) and grabbed the guy closest to me. Not wanting anyone behind me, I kept him in front of me, with everybody else on the other side of him. I reached up and grabbed him by the hair and I brought my baton back. When I grabbed him by the hair, he went down and I was left holdin' some fuzzy object.

Astonished, I yelled, "What the hell?" I wasn't sure what I had, so I slung the damned thing. As I was throwing the furry item in the air, Willy arrived. He jumped out of his car and pulled his gun; he saw some kind of animal, so he thought, and he was gonna shoot it as it hit the ground.

When the crowd saw that, someone hollered, "Hey, he jerked Charlie's hair off!" Then I figured out it was a toupee, definitely the worst hairpiece I'd ever seen in my life.

Instantly, poor old Charlie screamed, "My hair, my hair, don't shoot! Please don't shoot my hair!"

I yelled, "Get down, get down, now!" I threatened all three with the baton and everybody went down on his stomach. Willy and I hooked 'em and I looked at this older guy, Charlie, somewhere in his fifties that lost the toupee, and shook my head.

He cried, "Officer Randel, would you put my hair back on?"

I instructed Willy to return the toupee to the man's head and to frisk the three men. "Why does it have to be me? I don't want to touch that thing."

"Because you're Willy," I replied. Poor Willy returned to his squad car for his gloves. He dejectedly retrieved the hairpiece, and laid it on the bald head, patting it in place. It wasn't on right; it was pathetic, like a bird's nest on a chimney, but Wells left it just as it was.

Charlie with his hands cuffed behind him whined, "Please, Officer Randel, fix my hairpiece. It's not right." I readjusted the toupee, and it honestly did not look any better, but Charlie seemed more pleased, thanking me munificently and graciously.

Before we took the men away, a lady came around and asked old Charlie, "Would you like me to take care of your hair until you get out of jail?" She lived in the same apartment complex and obviously knew him as a neighbor and in the middle of all the confusion she was concerned about his toupee.

Charlie responded fretfully, "No thanks. Officer Randel or Officer Wells will take care of it for me at the jail."

Willy and I were doin' our reports, lookin' at poor hairless Charlie, and we were laughin', not out loud, but inside to ourselves, knowing that Willy almost shot that damned toupee. Then we took them to jail where they were charged with disturbing the peace. That was about all I really could do. I didn't even have to book them, but after runnin' them up and seein' their rap sheets, I decided on disturbing the peace. Charlie asked me at the jail if I would turn his toupee around so it would look better. So I did…. It still didn't look better. It looked a little like some rumpled wild thing sitting on top of his head. The correction officer that was processing Charlie asked, "What the hell is that on his head?"

I simply replied, "This is Charlie, and that is his hairpiece."

He shook his head and responded under his breath, "Oh my gawd!"

As we were booking them, it suddenly dawned on me there could be a complaint filed on behalf of Charlie's hair. So I told Willy to take Charlie's hair, bag it, impound it, and place it into evidence. Charlie was not at all pleased with this circumstance. When he went for his pictures, he pleaded to have the photo with his hairpiece. It was decided to take photos with and without the toupee. When Charlie was photographed without, he was crying because he felt naked and exposed. As Willy and I were leaving the jail, Charlie called out, "Thank you, Officer Randel, for fixing my hair."

As we walked out the door, Willy shoved my shoulder and teased, "I think Charlie likes you, Randel."

I retorted with the usual, "F…you."

We didn't see Charlie for about another thirty days when we received a call at the substation and the girl said, "Officer Randel, there is a call for you, some person named Charlie." I went out and took the call. Charlie said that he had been told that he could come to the station to retrieve his hairpiece but that he had had a problem when he went. He asked me if I could meet him there and help him. I wasn't anxious to see him, but I met him. He had the correct paperwork that he presented to the clerk.

The clerk reported that she had not been able to locate the evidence. I politely asked her to search one more time, and she did. Eventually, she located the box and asked what was inside. I told her she didn't want to know. With a blank stare she replied, "Okay."

Charlie quickly took the box, opened it, withdrew his toupee and plopped it on his head. He said, "Thank you, Officer Randel, thank you!" Charlie promptly left the premises.

I turned to the clerk and said, "Another satisfied customer." She gave me the same blank stare as before. I left the substation pondering the case of the flying toupee. In reflection, it's a little scary jerking someone's hair off his head.

GEORGE AND THE ALIENS

IT WAS ONE OF THOSE MISTY, winter nights in Las Vegas. Not too much was going on for Christmas time. Of course, there was the occasional convenience store holdup, purse snatching at the mall and liquor store disturbances, but all together it was a quiet night for December 23, 1983. Willy Wells was still riding with me and in training. He'd been with me for several months, but was still pretty green about some things. However, his training was going along as planned. We were patrolling Fremont Street between 9 p.m. and 10 p.m. when we heard the dispatcher send out a call.

"All units in the vicinity of Seventh and Fremont. George just called for the third time tonight. He sounds desperate. Aliens are after him again. Units respond that can take the call."

Officers of several units called back and said reluctantly that they would check on George when they finished what they are currently doing. It so happened that Willy and I were so close to Seventh and Fremont that we could smell the stench in the gutter. I went on the radio and came back, "Cheri', Frank-3. I'll take the call, and I'll see to it that George won't be callin' in again about aliens."

"Randel, you won't hurt him will you?" I could hear the anxiety in Cheri's voice.

"Switch channels, Cheri'. Go to channel 5 where we can speak freely without others listening. Cheri', how long has George been callin' in afraid of aliens?"

"At least once a week, for a couple of months."

"Okay. I don't know what goes on in his head, but we'll take care of George."

"Promise me, no rough stuff, Randel!"

"No rough stuff, Cheri'. I'll check in again as soon as we finish with him. Arrive us."

I eased the squad car to the curb in front of the apartment building. George lived on the second floor, room 205. I hesitated a moment, then said to my partner, "Willy, whatever I say or do, you go along with it. Got it?"

"What do ya mean, Randel?"

"Just play along with me." I could see that Wells was a little apprehensive, being new to the game. I wanted to reassure him, but this is what it's all about. You go into a situation and you never know what you will find. Maybe aliens right? However, good training and trust with your partner is imperative. I gave him a few minutes. I checked my gun, fumbled with the radio, squared my uniform, checked my hair and my teeth in the mirror, and then opened the car door.

Willy as I said, was a bit far sighted, so he had to wear glasses, and I swear his eyes were glued wide open as he looked at me. We charged up the stairs two at a time then stopped dead still at the top of the landing. It was a typical apartment building for people on their way down. Brown, shabby carpet, graffiti on the walls, bare, twenty-five-watt light bulbs hanging from water-stained ceilings. We reached 205, George's home, and I reminded Willy to go along with whatever I did before I knocked.

The door flew open and a fiftish-year-old male dropped to his knees and threw his arms around my legs. In a grateful voice, he declared, "Thank you, thank you! You've saved me. I haven't slept for three days or nights."

"It's okay, sir. We're here to help you." It was obvious that George had not slept for a long while; his eyes were bloodshot, his hair disheveled and his clothes were rumpled and soiled. "Let's step back

Frank-3 Enroute

into your room, George." I helped him up and felt his trembling arms. Once inside, my partner was watching my back. George backed into the middle of the room and I looked around. I noticed that it was a studio apartment that hosted a pulled out sofa bed and a four-shelf bookcase with a hot plate on top. There was one large sliding-glass window that looked over the mist-covered street below. Next to the window was one over-stuffed chair that could use more stuffing. There was a bathroom off to the side, and I looked inside. All clear. Continuing around, there was a small bureau, a round table with two chairs, and an open closet with a curtain across its opening. I signaled Willy to come in and shut the door. George paced from the bathroom to the window, looked out and paced again. I felt sorry for him and his predicament.

"So, George, you say that aliens are after you. Is that correct?"

He entreated, "Yes, yes, can't *you* see them? They're everywhere!"

I looked around searching for one, and suddenly stomped my foot about two feet from him. "Yeah, Willy, did you see that?"

"See what, Randel?"

I rolled my eyes at Willy, *remember what I said about going along with me,* I thought, and shook my head slightly. "That little alien bastard that I just squashed."

"No, Randel."

I stomped again. "Well, Willy, you saw that big one didn't you?"

"Oh, yeah I saw that one; a big SOB wasn't it."

George was looking at Willy and then me. He implored in a trembling, frantic voice, "Don't let them get me, please?"

That's when I saw the answer to George's problem. *The Gold Can!* It was sitting on the second shelf from the floor in the bookcase. "George," I asked, "Do you ever have roaches or ants?"

"Sure do," his shaky voice responded, "but I kill 'em with bug spray."

"So why don't you use the *Gold Can* on the aliens?" I shook my head in affirmation, hoping my partner would play along. "You use the *Gold Can* at your house don't you Willy?"

"Oh, you can bet on that," replied Willy. I wanted to hug him for catching my drift.

"Now George, think about this. You know who Superman is, I'm sure. What protects him from Cryptonite?"

"Uh," he's thinking… "Is it lead?"

"You damned right it is. So what can we use against these otherworld pricks? If lead protects Superman, why not use *The Gold Can* on the aliens? You already have some here, George. All you have to do is use it." I grabbed the can of *Gold*, AKA, Pledge and I sprayed it around the window edges, along the floor and around the door. "There you go, George. No more aliens will come into your apartment. We'll sweep up the rest of the ones here, and you'll be just fine."

But George didn't look fine yet. There was a wild look of wonder and uneasiness on his face. I took in his unshaven countenance, his hunched 5' 6" frame, his black belt, which held up a pair of pants that was two sizes too large, brown shoes covering feet that wore no socks, and I understood that George was not all right. He might never be. But I could only do so much as an officer of the law. "George, when was the last time you ate, buddy?"

"I don't know, two, three days ago, I think."

I took out a ten and handed it to Willy. "Wells, go to Mickie-D's and bring back a burger, fries and a…Do you like chocolate, George?" an affirmative head shake…"and a chocolate shake." Wells followed my lead, while I sat at the small table and started writing a report. George sat for the first time since we entered the room and seemed to relax ever so slightly. He watched as I wrote: *all aliens have been extracted from the premises. Gold Pledge has been applied to all exposed entrances. The resident now feels safe and secure. He will eat, bathe and have a restful night's sleep. He has been instructed to spray all openings twice a week to alleviate the alien problems.* I signed: Officer Randel, Las Vegas Metropolitan Police Department. At the bottom, I scribbled 'Merry Christmas, George.' I tore off a copy for George, who folded it and stuck it in his shirt pocket, afraid to let go of it.

Wells returned with the burger and fries, and George started in on them with a ravenous appetite. While he was chowing down, I told him to lock the door behind us and to spray under the door one last time for safety.

With his mouth full of burger, George mumbled, "Thank you, Officer Randel, thank you Officer Wells. I'll never forget you guys."

We actually hoped he would, so that he wouldn't keep calling our switchboard. We said good night and headed for the squad car, another citizen served. I checked in with Cheri', and told her how we solved the problem. She laughed and told all the other officers how Randel and Wells cleared the aliens.

I haven't seen George for a long time. He used to wave at us when we drove past as he walked on Fremont Street, and he would holler, "You guys are the best!" Occasionally, he would drop by the sub-station with store-bought cookies or a cake and treat everyone. Recently, I heard that he took a job as a janitor at the airport and that he had moved to a nicer apartment. He reported a break-in and burglary and the police were called. The on-duty officer reported that a television and a small radio were missing, but he affirmed that there was a case of eleven gold cans of Pledge sitting just inside the front door, and one can sitting on the kitchen counter. George has never found it necessary to call about aliens again so I feel certain that he is finally rid of his alien attackers. *Amazing, what we 'can' do for the citizens of Las Vegas.*

CHRISTMAS

THE PAST WEEK HAD BEEN HELL for everyone on the police force. We were all mad as hornets about the disappearance of Carrie, Jeff's wife. No news had come from any source, neither the police, nor the FBI. Carrie's photo had been broadcast across the nation with no results. There were no calls from pranksters or from sickos wanting to claim credit for her disappearance. There were no leads to follow, no tire tracks, no fingerprints, no ransom notes, and no phone calls. Literally nothing! How could a woman vanish without a trace?

The only clue available was the theory of the tan colored van. Yet, no such vehicle had been spotted around Las Vegas. Every police officer was certainly keeping a keen eye on the look out for such a van.

Family and friends all said that Jeff and Carrie were a very happy couple. The new baby had been the joy of their lives and they had been blissfully involved with him in parenting classes and at their church. The police had already ruled out Jeff as a suspect, as he was at home with the baby waiting for the baby sitter when she vanished.

Christmas Eve, 16:00. My squad was present and ready to start handing out baskets with addresses as each patrol car came. Rookie Roscoe had come, even though she was not working with us, but was assigned at another station. She told us that she didn't know of any other group that was giving out baskets from the Metro Police Department. She had organized each delivery by area and street and made sure each basket was properly identified by name.

Jeff Riley was there again to help. I said that it was not necessary, but he commented sadly, "Carrie would want me to do this for us. We had so much fun, and she talked about how happy all the people will be when they receive the boxes that are so pretty. I can feel Carrie's presence, Randel, and I know that she is here with me."

Sad for Jeff, but with false bravado, I cleared my throat and spoke gruffly, "Okay, Riley, then help us load up those patrol cars." I was forceful. "We don't have all day! Grumpy, get your ass over here and help out. Or are you gonna stand around cleaning your fingernails all evening?"

After the deliveries were made, I called Cheyenne and asked her to meet me at the Blue Mule. Hell, it was Christmas Eve and I didn't have anywhere to go, or any last minute shopping to do. I was sure glad that I had someone to go with to drown my sorrows. I was shocked when Ben advised me that it was last call and that he would be closing at midnight because it was Christmas morning. Cheyenne invited me to her house. She challenged, "Randel, I have a roll of quarters that says I can beat your sorry ass at poker."

I reached into my pocket and extracted two quarters and replied, "And I have two quarters that say I can take that whole roll of quarters from you before the night is over, Missy." I staggered out of the Blue Mule and left my Camero where it was parked, feeling it was safe because of my buddy, Grumpy. "Merry Christmas, to all, and to all a Good Night," I hollered as Ben locked the door. I slipped into Cheyenne's hopped-up, red Corvette, and did not remember anymore about the night.

It was 10:45 Christmas morning. I was lying on Cheyenne's couch, my face buried in a pillow, my right arm and leg hanging on the floor. Cheyenne was shaking me, and I thought I would throw up. "What the hell? Let me sleep, damn it."

"Wake up, Randel. Wells and Riley will be here in a few minutes to pick you up. You're serving Christmas dinner at the Salvation Army at 11:30."

"No I can't. I'm hung over. My head hurts and I need to sleep. Leave me alone."

"Here, drink this V-8. I'm going to cook some eggs and toast. They'll be ready in a few minutes."

"Over easy, please. Oh hell, I don't have a clean shirt. Shit, Chey, I can't do this."

"Yes you can, Rod. Willy's bringing you a clean shirt and underwear and you can jump in the shower before they get here. I'll check your pants when you undress. Now get your lazy butt up and get busy. By the way, Merry Christmas!"

I could not believe how bossy that woman could be. I did see a whole stack of quarters lying on the floor at about hands-reach, and I wondered if I had actually won them from Cheyenne playing poker. I had no memory whatsoever. I slid off the sofa and got on my hands and knees and eased my body into an upright position. Man, my head hurt and my mouth felt like I had been eating cotton balls. I couldn't find my boots and I hollered out, "Who the hell took my boots?"

"You lost them to me last night. I'll sell them back at a high price. Get in the shower, Rod. I'm putting the eggs on now."

"I don't want any cold damned eggs. Wait a minute," I yelled as I took a leak. I left the bathroom door open so I could breathe. Cheyenne came in behind me and started the water. She watched as I undressed and handed her my pants.

"I never realized that you had such a cute little butt, Randel," she chided. "The rest of your package is well above average though." She swatted me on the rear as I stepped into the shower, closed the door and leaned my head against the tile, letting the cold water bring me back to life.

The day after Christmas, I was back at the briefing. Sheriff Morgan was there and had a list of names of the officers that would receive a half-a-day off during the next week. Other officers questioned what that was all about and the sheriff pulled no punches when he informed them that they were all given an opportunity to help fill the baskets. Some complained that they were there to deliver the baskets and should be given time off too. He informed them that they were only there because he had ordered them to be. Otherwise they would have been left to their own devices, and would not have done anything for the community or the department. He tried to impress upon them that the people of Las Vegas judged the police department on how they helped the city and that included helping the homeless and the less fortunate. He elaborated on reports that had come back to him from officers and from phone calls stating how grateful folks were to receive such nice packages. "And, only those officers that helped to fill the boxes will be given extra time off. Next time I ask for volunteers, maybe you'll listen up."

"Sir," stated Gilmore, as he stood. "I would like to give my day to Officer Riley."

"Thank you very much, Officer, is that Gilmore?" The sheriff looked closely at his badge. "Duly noted. If there are others that would like to follow suit, please feel free to do so."

Jeff Riley rose, "Sir, I would like to thank you all, but I really would like to be here and to be with my brothers on the force. Carrie would want me to stay busy and to do my job. You don't know how much your gesture means to me, Gilly. Thank you."

"Sheriff," Gilmore continued, "Then is there anyway we can donate our time to make calls or to follow up on missing persons that might help to find Mrs. Riley?"

"Check with Officer Randel, Gilmore. He and Riley are riding together this week, and I know he can help you figure out what we can do. Thank you officers. Lieutenant, back to you." As Sheriff Morgan left, I felt the weight of the world descend on my shoulders. How the hell could I help Jeff, help Carrie, and help my buddies and brothers to find the sons-of-a-bitches that had taken her.

SCARED

WILLY AND I WERE MEETING GRUMPY at the ARCO station for a break. We had circled once and pulled along the side of the building, facing out when we noticed two young boys, about ten and eight, mount their bicycles and light out quickly from the parking lot. The lady, Janice, who ran the day shift, scurried out the door and yelled after the boys, "You thieving little brats had better not come back in this store. I know who you are, and where you live, and I'm gonna tell your folks the next time they come in." She turned to go back inside when she noticed us. "Officer Randel, those kids stole a pack of cigarettes from behind my register while I was stocking shelves. This isn't the first time, either. They sneak in here when I'm busy with something else and steal candy, or sodas or whatever else they can. I can't leave the store to chase them, and they know it."

"That's okay, Janice," I said kindly. "We'll handle this. Grumpy is on his way here. Tell him we'll be right back." With that, I headed in the direction that the boys had gone, and I could see them riding their bikes up Fairfield, and I followed slowly for several blocks. Finally, one of the boys looked back and saw me, and the two took off like streaks of lightening. The first child suddenly made a left into an alley, and the other child followed. However, the first boy hit a patch

Frank-3 Enroute

of gravel and went down. The second boy ran his bicycle into the first one. They righted themselves and were quickly gone again, as we turned into the alley just before Boston. I rolled down my window. "You boys stop there. Don't make me chase you."

That was the wrong thing to say! They dropped their bikes and immediately climbed over a six-foot, stained, redwood fence, trying to make their escape. Wells was out of the car and in hot pursuit. He climbed over the fence behind the boys before I could stop him. I heard Willy utter an expletive as he bounded over the top. *Hell, I thought, he should just wait right here until those boys come back for their bikes. If I know kids, their bikes are their prize possessions, and they don't want to lose them. That is of course, if the bicycles belong to them.* I called control, opened the trunk of the patrol car and loaded the bicycles. I drove through the alley and turned toward the street just as the boys ran across that street in front of me, and into the next yard. Stopping abruptly, I jumped from the patrol car, and yelled, "Stop, or I'll sick my dog on you." The two little boys froze. Placing their hands on their knees, they were panting from the ride and from running. I walked up to them just as Willy hurdled over the lower, front fence and ran toward us. "Wells," I stated, "call off the attack dog. These boys have given up." When he looked at me in wonder, I said. "It's all right if Rex stays with the bicycles. But, call him off the chase." I thought, *the boys don't realize that I have the bikes.*

Finally realizing that I had used my invisible guard dog, Elvis, again, Willy cautioned, "Right, Officer Randel, I'll tell Officer Sikes to take him. Don't you boys move until I call Rex back, or he'll chew you to bits." *Willy's gonna make a good cop in time. He's a quick learner.* Wells turned and went back the way he had come, only to return before I had finished talking with the two boys.

"You boys live around here?" I asked. Scared stiff, and standing at attention, they both shook their heads affirmatively. "I can't hear those loose marbles rolling around in your heads, men. I need a real answer, and a polite one."

The older boy swallowed hard, and croaked, "Yes, sir. We live on the next street. This is my brother, Chuckie, and my name is Freddie Watson." I was thinking, *what are these kids, characters from horror stories? I have just stopped Chuckie, the doll, and Freddie Kruger.*

"Please don't tell our mom or dad that we stole the cigarettes. We took them for our big sister. She always sends us to ARCO for whatever she wants and if we don't get it for her, she's real mean to us."

The eight year-old chimed in, "And my dad will whip us hard with his belt, mister. He's meaner than Theresa is. Mom'll just cry; that's what she always does."

I could see neighbors peeking out windows and standing on porches to see what the commotion was about. Strangely, there were no barking dogs. Sternly, I commented, "Well, I should arrest you boys and take you to Juvie where you'll find out how really bad 'mean' can be." I scrunched my eyes and glared at the smallest one. "They'd maybe eat you for dinner, Chuckie." I scrutinized the boys. They were of Asian decent, were clean, and dressed in shorts, muscle shirts, and Adidas tennis shoes with socks. Their black hair was closely crew cut, and it looked like they were clean behind their ears. Their hands and knees were skinned and dirty from their falls on the gravel. Otherwise they looked well enough kept. "Get in the car, boys," I said gruffly, as Willy reached us. Without a word, the boys, shaking and holding on to each other proceeded to the car. Wells opened the back door, and gave me a questioning look. "I don't think we need to handcuff them, do we boys? You're gonna behave yourselves, aren't you?"

"Yes sir, Officer Randel," Freddie assured.

Chuckie, his black Asian eyes as big as the original 'Chuckie's', reiterated, "Uh huh."

I called control giving mileage, and Willy told the boys to put on their seatbelts. We drove around the corner and down the street to the ARCO station. Wells was amazingly quiet, seeming concerned, but not about the boys. When we arrived, I notified dispatch, gave our mileage, and told Cheri' we were going inside for a break. Sikes had arrived and was waiting for us. "Listen up," I warned, "That's Officer Sikes standing over there; we call him Grumpy! He's one tough police officer, and this is his area. He doesn't put up with children that steal from people in this neighborhood. He eats them! If he knew that you took cigarettes from Ms. Janice, he would skin you both alive." The boys, releasing their seatbelts, peered out the window, their little heads barely over the doorframe of the patrol car and observed Grumpy cleaning his nails with his six-inch knife as he waited. Sinking back into the seats, the boys diminished themselves as much as possible.

Chuckie murmured, "Is he the one with the big attack dog, too?"

"That'd be him. Now, I'm gonna take you inside so that you can talk with Ms. Janice. She'll have to identify you both and tell me what you have done. If she wants to press charges, then I'll have to run you in. Understood?" Not waiting for answers, I opened the back door and watched as two very little, and very scared kids scooted off the seat. Freddie had the pack of cigarettes in his hand and tried to hand it to me. "I can't take that, Freddie (*Kruger*), it would be accepting stolen property, and I don't want to get into trouble. No, you have to take it back." I opened the glass door to the store, as patrons turned to see what we were doing with the children. People at the gas pumps were moving in slow motion so that they would not have to leave until they saw what was going to happen. I waited while the young boys moved to the counter where Janice was tending the cash register.

"Ms. Janice, I... I... I forgot to pay for these cigarettes for my sister. Can I bring some money back later?" *Lyin' little piece of shit*, I thought.

"Freddie Watson," Janice scolded, "shame on you. I already called your sister and she's on her way down here with the money. Anyway, I put it on your mother's tab. But you boys know better. Next time, I'll call these nice police officers and they'll arrest you. Give me those cigarettes, and I'll save them for your father." Janice looked imploringly at us, letting us know that she did not want to do anything to the boys. *Man, what a friend they have*. Of course, we didn't know the family dynamics, but I wanted to talk with that big sister, Theresa.

And here she came. She was about four-foot-nothing, and trying to be too grownup. I figured she might be all of thirteen. Wearing short shorts, a halter top and flip-flop high heels, she was 'dolled' up. Her shiny blue-black hair was twisted and held with combs and sparkles, she wore long dangling earrings, deep-red lipstick and false eyelashes, mascara, rouge, pan-cake makeup and fake nails that were long and painted. She wore bangled, wrist bracelets, ring, ankle bracelets and toe rings, and she smelled of cheap cologne. When she saw the police, she looked sheepishly embarrassed and I could tell that she was thinking about leaving. "There she is! That's my stupid sister, Theresa," shouted Chuckie.

"Miss Watson, I am Officer Randel, ma'am. These two boys have stated that you send them to the store for items that you want. In the future, you will have to accompany them, or they will not be allowed to enter the premises. Ms. Janice does not want to have any trouble with these nice little boys, and I want them to grow up as good citizens. Do you understand, ma'am?"

Miss Watson half-bowed in the respectful Asian way and affirmed that she understood. She thanked us politely, thanked Ms. Janice, and left the store without the cigarettes and with the boys in hand. Wells removed the bicycles from the trunk of the patrol car. Theresa admonished the boys, "Just look at what you did to your new, Christmas bicycles. Mom and Dad will be furious with you."

Grumpy heard what she said, and inquired, "Do you boys have those new bikes registered and licensed? No, I see that you don't. What's gonna happen if someone steals them? How are the police gonna help you find them? Officer Wells, make a note to have a bike registration set up in Adam and Frank areas right after the first of the year." We watched as the boys rode away, leaving their high-heeled, sister, Theresa to walk the distance home.

"Oh, I don't want to see what happens to those boys when she's through with them," Janice stated, shaking her head. "That is one mean little witch. She is so cruel to those boys. I never say anything to her parents, and I just put what they take on their bill. Their folks never question the price, either. I wish they had a different sitter, but that's what happens when both parents work."

"Well, I think that Theresa is going to have to find another way to get what she wants. I intend to speak with her parents later. Let her know that the next time she comes in, okay, Janice."

"That will be fine, Officer Randel," Janice said as she handed me my iced tea. "I doubt if Theresa will dare to send them to steal again, and I think that you put the fear of the Lord in Freddie and especially Chuckie."

I smiled inwardly, *Kruger and The Doll*. I couldn't stop making the comparison. *What the hell were their folks thinkin' when they named them.*

Grumpy was chuckling as he stood outside the door smoking a cigarette. "I don't think those little rick-shaw rats will steal again, Randel. I told them that if I heard anything more about them that I would skin them alive. Hee, hee, hee. I can't believe that they would risk their new bikes for one package of cigarettes."

Wells caught up with me and said quietly, "Randel, I think you need to see something that I saw in the alley where I chased those boys. Can we drive back over that way? It's by that 7-11 at Boston and Fairfield Circle."

"Yeah, let me check in with Cheri' and tell her where we'll be.

SKINNED

WELLS AND I RETURNED TO THE same alley where we had chased the boys and Willy pointed to the same high fence they had climbed. I did it the easy way. I pushed open the unlocked gate. Willy gaped at me, "Well, I'll be damned," he exclaimed as he realized he had not thought of that before. "Randel, go look in that shed and tell me what you see."

As I entered the back yard I observed a beautifully kept oriental garden with a trickling waterfall that spilled out of three lion's-mouth spigots, each with different colored lights reflecting onto the water. There was Chinese bamboo around the edges of the small pond, and lily pads in the water. Away from the water's edge, the flowers and plants changed to desert blooming plants that could withstand the intense Nevada heat. They were well done in an array of colors from deep purples, to spiked, crimson reds, to thorny, saffron yellows, brisk, deep-olive sage, and with wide-leafed and lithesome lime-green sprigs of desert plants and cacti. Someone in this house understood about horticulture and the southwest.

I went around to the large shed with open doors and observed many potting buckets with plants, potting soil and gloves. There were shovels, spades, rakes, hoes, clippers and many gardening tools, all neatly oiled and hung. There was a table that held small Bonsai plants in attractive, colorful ceramic dishes. Then, I saw what I thought to be stretched skins at the back. I entered the shed, walked to the rear and counted seven various colored and quality cat skins, including heads, with teeth but missing eyes, stretched tightly on racks and held with twine. Those skins looked amazingly like some of the cats that Grumpy had mentioned in the last few weeks. Neighbors had reported their cats missing, but no one had found or reported having found cats. *Hmmm! I think I can figure this one out.* I turned and left the shed.

"What did you see, Randel? Did you see what I think I saw?"

"Willy, it looks like we have found a cat skinner. Those are cat hides stretched out to dry."

"Oh dear God, what do you think it means, Randel?" Wells wrinkled his nose and his face in disgust. "Is it some kind of voodoo magic or kinky stuff?"

"Asians live in this area, and they eat cats. They also eat dogs. You won't see any strays in this area." *That's why no dogs barked at the little boys.* "No! Un Uhh. Dogs are especially prized as good to eat."

"What are we going to do? Isn't this against the law?"

I called control, "This is Frank-3. Be advised we'll be at the house on the Northwest corner of Boston and Fairfield Circle. Reference a 425, suspicious cats."

Cheri' acknowledged and said, "Randel, what are you up to? Go to five." I switched to five, "I can tell by the sound of your voice that you're up to something."

"Well, Cheri', we have cat hides here, do you need one?"

"Cat hides?" she questioned.

"Yeah, they're dryin' out so you can make things out of them like fur collars, hats and muffs."

"You're sick Randel!"

Laughing heartily I replied, "Really? You think so? No we're here at an Asian's house. They eat cats, so we have to talk with them."

"Do you need backup?"

Cleverly, I reiterated, "Nah, I don't want Grumpy down here with his knives. He might cut these hides loose and we'd have a major incident on our hands. We can handle this by ourselves. This neighborhood seems quiet. I'll have Wells call you if we need assistance. Thanks, Cheri'."

"All right, we'll be waiting to hear a code 4 from you."

Willy and I parked the car on the front of the street about two houses down. As we approached the house, I explained to Willy, "Let me do all the talking, Wells. You need to understand that these people are Asian and they have different customs and culture than we do. We don't want to have this blown out of proportion." I knocked softly on the door and stood back as a young Asian-Americanized girl approximately seventeen years old opened the door. The sensuous smell of Jasmine incense wafted out the door. The girl was wearing clothes appropriate for a private school and her long, ebony hair was French braided, hanging over her shoulder and was held by a single, jaded, floral barrette. She wore no makeup. Speaking gently, in a lowered tone, I questioned, "Do you speak English?"

Bowing slightly, the young woman spoke respectfully, "Yes sir, I do. How may I help you?"

"Is your Mama-son or Papa-son home?"

Before the girl could answer, Mama-son appeared behind her in her native dress. With her eyes diverted to the floor she very daintily queried, "Yes, can I help you, plee..ze?"

"Yes, ma'am. I am Officer Randel of the Metro Police." Her eyes shot up and she looked wonderingly at me with her deep, black Asian eyes. "I need to speak with the head of the house. Is anyone else here?"

"One moment, plee..ze," she replied as she respectfully bowed and backed away from us as she spoke. She quietly disappeared into the house.

Willy whispered, "Why didn't you just tell her what we want?"

"That would be disrespectful to the head of the house, especially if it were her husband. If however, there were no one else here, it would be appropriate to speak directly with her. But I think she has gone for her husband."

The young woman was about to ask us to enter the foyer when a small, gentlemanly well-groomed Asian man appeared at the door. Very courteously, he asked, "How may I help you?"

I responded loudly with, "**Hie!**" Willy almost jumped off the porch as I did so.

Smiling in greeting, the man boisterously returned, "**Hie!**" That is hello and goodbye in Oriental cultures. "I am Hsu Tham. Welcome to my home."

"May we speak with you outside, sir?"

Bowing slightly, and sharply, he placed his stockinged feet in his outdoor shoes and silently came outside, carefully shutting the door. We walked off the porch and stood beside his heavily laden lemon tree, on his front lawn that looked nothing like the backyard. It had grass that was full of empty, brown spots, and matched the rest of the neighborhood. "We just chased some children through your back yard and Officer Wells noticed that you have some cat skins in your shed. I need to talk with you about that."

Thinking that he had done nothing wrong, he smiled and asked, "You want to buy?"

"No, I do not want to buy. Where did those cats come from?"

Looking at my badge he said, "Offica *L*andel, we eat cats in our country. There are many cats in America. We eat velly well."

Willy started laughing and I turned to him and asked him to bring the car and park in front of the house. I did not want to disrespect the gentleman. "Sir, Mr. Tham, we don't eat cats in the United States. It's against the law."

"We sell hide, get money."

Trying not to laugh, I smiled and said, "No, you sell hide, you get jail."

He looked confused and so I explained to him that in America cats are domestic pets and people do not eat them; the law protects them. "In the past few weeks, neighbors have reported that they are missing their cats, but no one has found those cats. However, some of the hides that you have in you shed resemble the descriptions of those cats. I suggest that you not do this anymore because if your neighbors file complaints, you are going to have a lot of problems. Do you understand, Mr. Tham?"

"What if cat in my yard?"

"No sir, cats are known for roaming the neighborhood and then returning home."

"Good owna no let cat outside. What about dog?"

"The same goes for dogs, sir." I was afraid he still had a problem with his culture versus the American culture. "No eating cats or dogs."

"Thank you velly much Officer *L*andel. You numba one police offica. Thank you velly much."

"You are welcome, sir, and I believe that you are a man of your word, so, if you tell me that you will not kill or eat anymore cats I will let this be the end of the warning."

"Offica *L*andel, Tham house no eat no cats again." With that, he motioned to his wife, who was watching curiously through their living room window, to come join him.

Mrs. Tham pleasantly bowed and shyly asked, "Evelything okay?" Mr. Tham spoke with her in their native Vietnamese tongue, some of which I could still understand, explaining that they could not kill or eat cats, or sell the skins. "Velly solly, Offica *L*andel, no happen again." All the time, Mrs. Tham was softly and affectionately stoking a pure white Persian cat with sky-blue eyes. I thought that it was ironic that these people would keep a pet and at the same time eat the same species.

As I was bidding the Thams goodbye, Mrs. Tham whispered something to her husband. He stepped forward and quietly asked, "Mama-son wants to know if pigeon is all *l*ight to eat?"

Though I tried not to, I think I did chuckle when I replied, "Papa-son, only if they are your pigeons."

The young girl came from the house with two small plants wrapped in paper towels and in plastic. "Please accept these Friendship Plants as our apology, Officer Randel, and Officer Wells. Place them in some rich soil and they will bless your homes for many years. My honorable father works for the Tiger Lily Floral Shop on Sahara. He is a landscaper for them. He knows a lot about plants. In South Vietnam, he was a general in the army, but now he takes care of plants." Knowing that it was not our policy to accept gifts, I could not however, refuse the plants, because to do so would have been an insult to the Tham family and I did not want an international incident. Thanking them, I bid them farewell as I politely gave a semi-bow and backed away from their home. They bowed deeply to us, showing the utmost respect, and shyly waved as we drove away. *I wonder if people will be missing anymore cats in the area, or will Mr. Tham tell all his friends and neighbors that it is not an honorable custom to eat cats in America.*

After we left, I thought about the whole thing and surmised, maybe their culture was not so different from ours. Americans keep pigs, chickens, cows and rabbits for pets and still eat those species.

Willy and I would occasionally see the Thams on the street and they were always very respectful. They felt comfortable with us. Mama-son would come close to me and speak softly with a rising lilt to her voice, "Offica *L*andel, we no eat no cat now!" She would cover her mouth and giggle shyly, but her eyes sparkled as she did so.

I cheerfully replied, "Thank you, Mama-son; thank you Papa-son. Have a good day." They waved and bowed politely as we passed. *I really admire those kind, hardworking people.*

One day, Papa-son Tham invited me to come to his home. He said, with the utmost respect, "You come, hona my house, Offica *L*andel. See my new pigeon coops. Have dinna with us. Mama-son cook velly good pigeon."

THE NEW YEAR

Cheyenne had asked me to dinner at the Cellar inside the Four Queens for their New Year's Eve Party. It was a gala affair and we had convinced Willy to bring that cute little policewoman, Amy Mills, with him. Grumpy and Kate joined us, and surprisingly he even commented, "Not bad for a 100 bucks a couple, huh, Randel? But, that does include dinner, dancing and champagne at midnight."

I thought Sikes might pull his biggest knife on me when I asked, "Oh, was it hundred a couple, I wouldn't know."

"No! You dirty SOB, don't tell me they 'comped' the damned tickets for you!" So I didn't tell him anything. I still hate to lie.

The place was packed and the noise was astounding. There was a good band playing, and the food was fantastic. However, the excitement seemed to be lacking with our little group. As we reflected on the year past, I began to feel that it was a complete bust. So many things had gone wrong recently that I could hardly remember the good things about being a policeman.

Cheyenne asked me to dance and all I could do was step on her toes again and again, until we finally sat down in desperation. Grumpy was imbibing heavily and Kate had turned her attention to Amy who was talking about her life on the force. A fight broke out on the dance floor and I thought, *It's about time there's some decent action in this place.* I watched for a minute, and when no security appeared, I excused myself from the table and went into the fracas. Two women in their forties were fighting over one man named Arnie, one claiming that he was her date, and the other saying they were only dancing. Hair was being pulled, and the women were attempting to wrestle each other to the floor. I stepped up and hollered, "Excuse me, ladies, may I interrupt for a moment. What seems to be the problem?" Both women looked at me and the fighting stopped.

"Well hello, good looking," exclaimed a dyed, chestnut-brown-headed gal wearing a gold lame', skin-tight evening dress.

"I saw him first, Gladys," chimed in the other siren, a dishwater blond, wearing a sea-green strapless gown. "You can have skinny, old Arnie. I want this pretty young guy. What's your name, honey?"

"I'm Officer Randel, and I will arrest you both for disturbing the peace if you don't sit your asses down and act like nice ladies. Do I make myself clear?"

"Well, you don't have to get huffy about it, Officer. Come on, Abigail, he's not that cute anyway. We can share Arnie. I'm sorry, honey," claimed Gladys. Together, arms around each other's waists, the women took their leave to the lady's room to regroup.

As I turned around to rejoin my party, I almost ran head on into Lieutenant Dan Arnold. "Happy New Year, Randel," he blubbered as he staggered past me, holding on to my shoulder as he did so. "Where the hell did those women go," he said to himself.

"What women, LT.? Was one of them your wife?"

"Oh no, I was only looking for some friends of mine." About that time, Abigail and Gladys returned from the lady's room and spotted both of us.

"Oh lookie, honey," said the one with the green dress, "aren't they so cute together. You take your pick, Gladys, but I still like Arnie." *Arnie? Is this Arnie that they were fighting over? Oh shit. He's out with two broads, and neither one is his wife.*

"Randel," Lieutenant Arnold stammered, "I've got to get home. The little wife is waiting up to ring in the New Year. I'll see you at the office." He turned and swayed through the crowd as I called after him.

"Nice to see you enjoying yourself, Lieutenant Arnold. You should loosen up more often. Have a good night, sir. Oh yes, maybe you should call a cab to take you home to the little woman."

Damn that felt good! I'll lay odds that he has me in his office first thing Monday morning trying to make some kind of deal with me to keep me from saying anything about what I saw tonight. Shit, I don't care what the hell he does, but I think I'll jerk him around about behavior unbecoming and officer. Forget him!

I feel like kicking butts tonight. I don't want to sit here and act like I'm having a good time. Maybe Grumpy and I can go cause trouble of our own. Willy won't go 'cause he'll be in fear of losing his job, so I won't ask him. Oh hell, I'll just have another drink and take Chey home and see what happens. This whole year stunk! Maybe there have been a few good things. Cheyenne and I are hitting it off pretty well. And we have solved the Breakfast Burglar serials. That bastard will be put away for a long, long time. The Naked City is going to hell, though; too much senseless stuff, like little Juanito Chavez. Of, course we haven't found Jeff's wife yet either, and probably won't. Also, we know that there is a serial killer out there somewhere, working in my area; too many dead young women. Grumpy and I have managed to get old Lieutenant Dan Arnold's goat a few times though. Ha! I'd like to kill that bastard. Maybe I'll go find him and kick his ass tonight. Hmmm....

"Randel, if you're just going to sit there and pout," Cheyenne began, then she leaned over and whispered into my ear, "why don't you take me home and take out some of your aggression with me."

That sounded pretty inviting to me so I downed the rest of my Jack and Coke and we said good night to the others before the New Year rang in. But, I was not disappointed in the rest of the night. I won twenty-five dollars in quarters from Cheyenne before we quit playing poker and went to bed. To this day, I don't know if she knew I was palming cards when we played. But, I taught her that she was not as good a poker player as she thought. However, she taught me a few new tricks too.

"Wake up you sleepy head," crooned Cheyenne. "You gonna sleep all day?"

"Maybe," I replied as I playfully pulled Chey on top of me and mussed her hair. "You have anything better in mind?"

"Yes, and what about you?" We made love again and then lay together, Chey's head cuddled on my shoulder. "Rod, lets go for a long drive. I don't want to waste our first day of the year together. They say that what you do on New Year's Day you will do the rest of the year."

"Wow! We're off to a great start then aren't we?"

Cheyenne kissed me passionately, then rolled out of bed and twisted her sexy derrière for my benefit as she proceeded to the bathroom. I actualized, *she is one knockout woman and one helluva gal.* Placing both feet on the floor and shaking off last night's liquor, I called, "You startin' the shower for me, hon?"

"No, it's for me, but you're welcome to join me." I did.

"Where do you want to go? Can we just drive and then stop at some nice little place for breakfast?"

"Rod, it's one thirty. More like let's have lunch."

"Suits me, but I'm not really hungry yet."

Outside her lavish apartment, we climbed into her cherry-red Anniversary Corvette convertible with her behind the wheel. I still felt a little hung over and did not want to be pulled over. We headed south on I-15, laughing and talking about nothing in particular. Cheyenne's foot became heavier as we drove; at one point I looked over at the speedometer and saw that it registered 110 mph. "What's your hurry, babe," I questioned. "I thought you said we had all day."

"I like the speed, and I like to feel the wind in my face and the sun on my back. How about you?" Before I could reply, Cheyenne stomped on the brakes, almost fishtailing and pulled to the side of the highway. I wondered, *did I piss her off talking about her driving?* She jumped out and started waving her left arm, motioning a black Cadillac to pull in behind us. She walked haughtily toward the vehicle as I alighted from my seat and quickly followed. "What the hell do you want?" she screamed at the two men in the vehicle. She showed no fear, only ambivalence.

"Sorry, Miss Turner," replied the driver of the car. "We have our orders to watch you 24-7."

"Well, you can just turn around and leave me the hell alone. I don't need you watching everything I do." She turned and almost ran over me as I had placed myself closely behind her in a protective stance, with my gun drawn and aimed directly at the driver of the car. "Move!" she ordered caustically as she stepped around me and headed back to the Corvette.

I think she means me! However, placing my revolver behind my back, I reiterated, "You'd better move on and leave us alone, men, or you'll really piss her off."

The car peeled out in front of us, and sped away. I could see the passenger using the car phone to make a report. Back in the car, I questioned, "What the hell was that all about?"

"Oh, Daddy has his goons following me everywhere I go. He's so afraid with all the women disappearing and winding up dead that something could happen to his only little girl."

"Doesn't he think I am capable of taking good care of his little girl?"

"Is that a proposal, Rod?"

"Hell no! I'm not the marrin' type, Chey. You know that already."

"Just trying to get a rise out of you, brat. I'm not interested in marrying any man, especially not a cop. I've been there and done that. I was married the first time at sixteen. I dated a sweet sergeant from Nellis Air Force Base. He was a twin and I thought it would be so cool to have twin babies so when he wanted to have sex, I told him not until we were married. As soon as Daddy found out, which was the next day, he stomped into Nellis and told the Air Provost Marshal that I was only sixteen and that Danny was twenty-seven and he wanted him charged with having sex with a minor. I had lied and Danny thought that I was eighteen. The marriage was quickly and quietly annulled and Danny was stationed elsewhere with no charges against him in return for his never contacting me again.

"Then I married when I was twenty-one, a free, white, adult woman, and I made a terrible mistake. That scumbag, John Baker, a Metro police officer, beat me and locked me away and would leave me for days at a time with no food and no way out. There were bars on all the windows and the doors were all double locked. Did you know him?"

"No, I didn't. Go on, baby."

"One night when he was asleep, I swiped his house key. To this day I don't know why I didn't take his car keys and just leave. Instead, I left the house and walked to a neighbor's and pleaded with them to call the police. I think they were afraid of John. Anyway, they called him instead, and he came for me. I couldn't walk or see for a week when he was finished with me. One day, Daddy dropped by and John gave me an evil look and almost dared me to say anything. I did though. I cried, 'Daddy, I want to go home with you. I don't want to be married to John anymore.' That was all I had to say. Daddy heard my anguish, recognized my fear and could see some of my bruises. We left the house and I never went back. Daddy had all my things moved home, he arranged the divorce and I have never seen or heard of John since. He may have disappeared or be dead for all I know, and do you know what, Rod, I don't care." Cheyenne's foot was heavy on the pedal again as she shared her story, and I felt compassion for her, and glad that she was not afraid of a clean relationship, even with a Las Vegas Metro cop.

Cheyenne braked and pulled into the Whiskey Pete's. We sat closely together, with her hand pressed firmly in mine while we waited for our food. She locked her fingers into mine, and raised our hands to her lips. Kissing my fingers, she shared, "I love you, Rod. Please believe that I do. But you and I both understand that our relationship will never go farther than companionship and friendship, don't we?"

"Whoa, girl, you really know how to let a guy down. It's all right, honey, I love you too and I understand the parameters of our relationship. I'm happy and content with things as they are. We always have a hellava good time together, and you're very easy to be with. I don't like it much when you beat the socks off me at poker though."

We were laughing at ourselves when our food came, and we ate silently. When Cheyenne finished eating, I sipped the last of my iced tea, paid the bill, and we rose to leave. Chey said, "Rod, follow me to the bathroom, please."

She can't be afraid to go to the john by herself. Out of curiosity I followed her, holding her hand that she had stretched behind her.

When we reached the door, she opened it, checked inside to see who or what was there, and then pulled me inside and locked the door. We had the best, most frantic, rowdy sex I ever had in my life, for a quickie. When we exited the bathroom, two middle-aged women were waiting outside and gave us the most disgusting looks you can imagine. Cheyenne smiled at them and spoke casually, "Don't you just hate it when they don't supply condoms in a restroom? It's so inconvenient, especially when you're as horny as I am."

The women's mouths were open wide enough for a Mac truck to pass through as they stared blatantly at Cheyenne. I calmly stated, "Have a nice day, ladies," gave them a nice smile and we walked hastily from the restaurant. Cheyenne bent over laughing so hard that she could hardly get her breath.

Finally she gasped, "Did you see the look on those women's faces? What do you think they were thinking? Oh well, it doesn't matter, we'll never see them again." With that, she handed me the keys and asked if I would drive because her side hurt from laughing so much.

"How can I drive when I don't even know where we're going?"

"Just drive, you idiot. You'll know when we get there."

So, I drove until we passed into California and were on our way to Barstow. Chey finally said that we were going to Calico, an old ghost town. We had to take a trolley up the side of the hill so we had to wait for the next one. Who should arrive to take the same trolley that we did? You guessed it; the ladies from Whiskey Pete's. They tried not to look at us, and they never spoke to us, even though we smiled pleasantly at them. Cheyenne whispered, "I think they look like a couple of old prunes, don't you?"

When we were at the top, Cheyenne surprised me saying, "Come on, Rod, I'm going to buy something expensive from the most expensive store in the area." We went into an old general store where she picked out a pickax, a miner's hat with a light on it, a handkerchief for around my neck, and a bucket for all the gold. When she was thoroughly satisfied, she purchased a little camera and took pictures all over the town and back down the hill, photographing me doing every silly thing she asked of me. We even caught a few pictures together when other tourists would take them for us. When we returned to the trolley waiting area, I asked her to wait for a minute while I went to the restroom. However, inside the general store, I browsed for a few minutes and decided to purchase a key chain that had an actual gold nugget hanging from it. It wasn't much, but it was the thought that counted. Cheyenne was thrilled with it. Smiling at her genuine pleasure, I surmised, *with who she is, with as wealthy as her family is, and with all she has, she's the kind of woman that nothing is truly good enough for, but who is not too good for anything. That's one of the many virtues that I like about her.*

We stayed at Calico until they closed the place down for their winter hours. Driving back down the red rock hills, we talked about the impressive dry caves, our failure to find gold, and we laughed about the guide that walked backward until she almost fell into an abyss, actually an old tunnel that went about 500 feet straight down. "That scared the dickins out of me," Cheyenne commented. "They should have all those old holes covered or closed."

"Oh they just do that for theatrics, babe. She knew exactly where she was and what she was doing. She didn't even look that scared."

"But, did you look down that hole? It was so dark down there, and I could just imagine old miner's bones and lost treasure. It was fun though. Thanks for going with me."

We were headed down Mountain Pass when I looked in the rearview mirror and noticed the sun setting behind us. I slowed and entered the first pullout I came to and we turned the car around to watch. Holding each other gently across the console, we enjoyed the wondrous red glow of the huge star as it sank behind the Nevada hills. It left a pink and orange glow that we observed as it too slipped away, leaving only the ebbing darkness and the glow of the lights of Barstow some forty or more miles away.

Afterward, we swung into the Madonna Inn for dinner as my experience in the caves and the hiking made me hungry as a horse. We ordered my favorites, soup, salad, steak, baked potato, fresh rolls and cheesecake. I cleaned my plate and Cheyenne ate daintily as usual, and asked for a doggie bag. She was always hungry an hour after she ate and loved the leftovers.

As I drove down the Mountain Pass I was testing how well the Corvette took the curves and winding road. I was speeding along the straight a-way when I saw the flashing light of a state trooper's vehicle that was stopped behind another car. The officer was ticketing the driver of the car. I looked down and noticed that I was going well over 100 mph. as I decelerated and passed him. *That trooper's gonna let that bastard go and he'll be coming after me as sure as grass is green. He's not gonna let this hot little Vette get past him. I'm gonna pull over and see what he does.* A rest area sign came unexpectedly into view, advising me that the next area was two miles away. "Hang on, baby," I crooned to the Corvette, "we're going to see what you can do from here to there."

"Rod, aren't you gonna slow down? You know he'll call ahead and ask for a road block."

"Don't worry, Cheyenne. I'm going to pull in and put the top up anyway. It's getting a little cool." I had no sooner spoken when the turn off appeared. I braked and geared down and cut into the rest area. I was electrically closing the creamy white top to the Corvette when 'Johnny Law' swung in behind me, his reds flashing. He was hot under the collar. Outside the Vette, (I knew I should remain inside the vehicle, but had I done anything wrong?) I was watching the top rise and was waiting for the trooper. As he approached I said, "Howdy trooper!" *I feel a little like a cowboy tonight.*

That didn't fly with 'Johnny Law'. "May I see your driver's license, registration and proof of insurance, sir?" asked the obvious *Rookie* of the Nevada State Troopers. I handed him my license and my badge, and Cheyenne had already given me the registration and proof of insurance. "You realize, sir, that you were speeding! I clocked you at over 100 mph."

"Oh re..al..ly," I replied skeptically. "How fast was I going?"

"About 110. I see that you are a Las Vegas Metro police officer, Mr. Randel. You should know better than to speed like that."

I don't need a wet-behind-the-ears rookie telling me how to drive. I could have avoided him and he would never have spotted me if I didn't want him to. "If that's what you say, Trooper Atkins. You're doing a fine job. I want you to know that I am carrying a loaded piece in the car." I thought he looked a little nervous. "You have all you need in your hand with my badge, sir," I replied courteously.

Judiciously, he responded, "Mr. Randel, I will have to ticket you."

"I figured you would, Trooper Atkins." I stood a respectful distance away from him at the back of the Corvette and watched his skills as he ran Cheyenne's license and registration. He neglected to look at my gun, trusting that I would not use it one him. *Big mistake for any officer, especially with a passenger in the car. But, it isn't my place to teach this kid.* "Mr. Randel, signing this ticket is in no way an admission of guilt. It does, however, say that you will appear in court. If you fail to appear, a warrant will be issued for your arrest."

I signed the ticket, knowing that I would be appearing in a Las Vegas court. I returned to the car, slid behind the wheel and waited for the trooper to leave. That snot nosed trooper waited behind me until I finally returned to the highway. Then the little bastard pulled out behind me, waiting to see how fast I was going to drive. "Are you in any hurry, Chey?"

"No, I have all night, but I know that you have to be at work at seven, why?"

"I think I'll just cruise along at about fifty or fifty-five, take our time and enjoy the ride."

Cheyenne conceded, "Now that the top is up, I'm going to put in a tape. What kind of music do you prefer?"

"Something country, 'cause I feel like a cowboy tonight."

"Maybe we'll go for another ride tonight after we get back home."

"Cheyenne, honey, I can't go again tonight. If I even try, I'll never make it to work in the morning. You are almost too much for me, baby." Cheyenne laughed heartily and we drove slowly all the way to her apartment. 'Johnny Law' followed closely behind, only driving on as we pulled into the gated area. We kissed goodnight at Cheyenne's door and I switched back to my Camero and drove the speed limit to my house. I reminisced as I prepared for bed, *this was a great day, in spite of the ticket; as a matter of fact, it's the best day I've had all year.* I laid back, turned out the lights and slept like a baby.

THE CALL

It was just after 06:00 hrs. when I was stepping out of the shower. I heard "…airplane of Senator Maitlan Devereaux has been reported missing after the senator, his wife Darlene and their daughter Caitlan left the Las Vegas airport on a 2:30 a.m. flight. The last call was a 'May Day' from the senator, at 2:51, but he did not give his heading. It is feared that the 1984 twin engine Cessna may have gone down over the snow-covered Charleston Mountains. Search and rescue teams are already looking for the missing couple and their daughter."

Well hell, another politician bites the dust. That can't be all bad. Nah, Rod, that's not a good or wise way to think. Wonder if the asshole was drinking or on drugs when he took off? I guess we'll find out soon enough. I went about my daily grooming and dressing while I listened to the sports and weather, then left in time for briefing.

I had no intention of arriving one minute ahead of time and Grumpy and I would probably test each other to see which one could slide in closest under the wire. Like Cheyenne said, what you did on the first day of the year, you would do all year long. *I wonder if the second day works the same?* 06:59:51 hrs. was as close as I could time it, as I was never, well almost never late. Sikes was already in his seat at the back of the room and I slid into mine just as the lieutenant took front-and-center.

"All right, listen up. Some of you are getting complacent and lazy. You're not doing your jobs. Randel and Sikes do more in a day than most of you do in a week. Now, Rice and Spalding, I need a drug bust. Jason and Martin, bring in a felon if you can find one. It's a new year and we're going to hit this town hot and heavy and bring down all the scumbags we can. Randel, I want two felons from you. Sikes, two prostitution busts, understood. The rest of you hit the streets and see what you can do rather than sit in your cars and eat." I mentally cursed, *why the hell don't you put some pressure on the other officers, LT. No wonder everyone thinks Sikes and I are hard asses.*

When we left the briefing, Wells asked me, "How in the hell are we going to suddenly find and arrest two felons, Randel?"

I gave him my standard answer, "Watch and learn, Willy, watch and learn. Check out an unmarked car, follow me and I'll show you how it's done. Let's stop off for some iced tea to take with us. It could be a long morning." We each drove to the back of the Restaurant Association Union Building and I drove slowly past the vehicles parked there. I radioed Wells, "Take the first car's license, I'll take the second. Run your plates and see what you come up with. I'll do the same until we check all the cars here and find a couple of winners. Then, my boy, we sit and wait."

"What are we looking for, Hawk? Or do I want to know?" His young voice was reaching a high pitch, "You know how to make trouble more than any other officer I have ever heard about and I drew you for a partner. I just know it. Here goes my career!"

I chuckled, but not over the radio. *Hell yes, we could get into trouble, but we can have more arrests and convictions than the rest of the squads put together. This is an old trick that I learned from my FTO, Dave Mantooth, back when I was a rookie. Old Dave, was quite the old cowboy. 'Just get 'er done' was his adage.*

Sure enough, we came up with a couple of vehicles that were registered to felons wanted both in Nevada and Colorado. Wells then understood that we would wait to see who came to either of the vehicles. If it were a wanted person, we would approach and make an arrest. It wasn't long before a white male and an Hispanic woman came out together and walked to the car that I had tagged. I waited until the couple was in the vehicle and then I pulled my patrol car behind their car, blocking their exit. Wells was right beside me, his weapon drawn. I cuffed the man and pushed him over the hood of his car. Wells had the woman outside, watching her.

When we checked their identities, we found that they were both wanted on multiple charges. Wells cuffed the woman, who was cursing him in Spanish, of which he understood nothing. I called for backup, and Adam-12, Grumpy stated, "Adam-12, enroute, about two minutes away."

From my patrol car, I heard, "Frank-3, copy a call."

I hesitated leaving my prisoner so I dragged him with me. "Control, Frank-3. I'm making an arrest. What do you need, Cheri'?"

"Contact me as soon as you're free, Officer Randel."

"Sure thing, control."

Adam-12 arrived and I left my prisoner in his tender loving care and called dispatch. "Control, Frank-3. Adam-12 has arrived and I am free. What do you need, girl?"

"Switch channels, Officer Randel."

When I was on channel five, Cheri' said, "Rod, Lieutenant Arnold wants to have lunch with you. You are to meet him at the Peppermill and he said that he is buying."

"Oh shit! Excuse me, Cheri'. I know what this is all about. Let him know that I'll be there at 12:00 sharp. Steak and shrimp, here I come!" *That little weasel wants to work me about New Year's Eve. I know it. He wants to know if I'm gonna file a report on his behavior. I hope he's been sweatin' it ever since it happened. Ha! The shoe's on the other foot, Benedict, you slimy bastard.*

Wells, Sikes and I booked our felons and I helped Sikes run in a couple of hookers and we were finished booking them way before lunchtime. "Wells, turn in your unmarked. You have learned a cherished secret for making arrests while barely leaving your vehicle. Remember it well." *I think the kid is learning the ropes and he'll do well when he's on his own. Of course, he's learning from the best. What more can I say?*

I received a call from Cheri', "Frank-3, copy a call. Lt. Germain wants you to sit in with Mrs. Devereaux as she tells us what she knows about the plane that went down early this morning. She specifically requested that you be there. He said it won't take long; he knows you are to meet Lt. Arnold for lunch."

"**Frank-3 enroute,** Cheri'. Go ahead and arrive me, I'm pulling in now."

Mrs. Luella Devereaux, the family matriarch, relayed the story to me and to Lieutenant Germain. Tearfully she explained that it was about 1:30 a.m. when Maitlan Devereaux downed the last of the smooth scotch on the rocks as he sat on the bed fully dressed in clothes that he had worn for the past two days. She sat in the overstuffed chair in the hotel suite listening to his sorrows. "He said, 'I lost $600,000 over the holidays at the tables, but our family had a good week in Las Vegas, our suite and all expenses were comped. Mother, you, Darlene and Caitlan, were happy at the poolside, shopping and having your hair and nails done daily, weren't you? You all spent untold hours in the spa and really enjoyed the massage therapy given by Xavier. And I saw you, Mom, at the gaming tables. Did you win or lose? No, never mind. The money is no problem Mother; I can make a few calls and checks will roll in from certain people and I can cover my losses in no time.' Of course, I was put out with Maitlan for his big losses, but I was more concerned about his deciding to fly home in the middle of the night after drinking so heavily. But no one could tell Maitlan anything once he made up his mind about something. Maitlan went on about having good connections and told me not to worry. It bothered him that those sons-of-bitches at the private poker party took a third mortgage on his multi-million-dollar house to hold for security. He knew it would piss off Darlene, but she didn't need to know anything about it. He asked me to say nothing to his wife, and assured me that everything would be taken care of within the week.

"I begged him to sleep of his drunk and head for home in the morning, it would only take an hour and one half, but he was too agitated to sleep. I told him that the girls, Darlene, Catlain and I would stay and catch a flight the next day.

"Maitlan ran his hands across his unshaven face and through his greasy hair, he was such a mess," Mrs. Devereaux commented sadly, "then he leaned over and shook Darlene, telling her it was time to dress and leave for the plane. He poured another scotch; it didn't matter that there was no ice. He poured another. He had plans to fly back at 2:30 a.m. so that he would be back in his law offices at 10:00 a.m. I told him that I was not about to leave with him, even though he insisted that we all go. He called the valet and waited while his wife and daughter dressed, then they took a limousine to the airport where he would pilot his private Cessna. That is the last I saw of my son, his wife and my granddaughter, Lieutenant. Maybe I should have gone with them. Maybe I could have saved them."

The lieutenant said, "No, Mrs. Devereaux, you did the right thing, and sometimes our best just isn't good enough. Can I offer you something to drink, ma'am?"

When the interview was finished, Grumpy and Willy were still at the station. We talked briefly about the plane crash. "I hear that you're having lunch with a friend, Randel. Give him hell for Wells and me. If you need any help, give me a quick call."

I left my best buddies to meet my archenemy, Lieutenant Arnold, at the Peppermill. Arnold, his long, skinny body, his high forehead, gaunt face and his dark, devious mustache that hid a weak mouth, reminded me of Ichabod Crane from Sleepy Hollow. The image was uncanny. I thought his wobbly knees and his bowed legs were going to fail him before we reached our table. Dee, the attractive blonde waitress and my long-time acquaintance, had my frosty, iced tea waiting.

"Officer Randel," Arnold began, "I know that we've had our differences in the past. But, with the new year beginning, I thought that you and I should come to some kind of understanding about the department and what's going to be best for it, and the officers in all the squads."

I did not speak, but thought, *yeah, like conduct unbecoming and officer. How many times have you tried to write Grumpy and me up for useless shit and been overruled? I know what you want, you bigot.*

Enjoying his captive audience, he continued, "You and I both know that the other officers look up to you and to Officer Sikes, and a lot of them try to emulate you. So, if you do your job by the book, they're going to try to do the same things, too. I'd like to put a stop to officers being written up all the time for small violations of policy. You could be a big help if you are so inclined."

I pondered his statement, thinking what smart-ass comment I could give as I noisily clanked the spoon in my tea, stirring in the copious amount of sugar. *Hope he finds this irritating.*

"Maybe you shouldn't use so much sugar, Randel, and you would be in better health, not so antsy all the time."

"Better health, what do you mean, Lieutenant? I haven't taken a day of sick leave in years, sir. Anyway, sugar and beautiful women sweeten our lives, don't you think, LT.?" I lifted my eye brow and my iced tea in an all-knowing manner. *Squirm, you little worm. You know what women I'm referring to. Ha! Gotcha! This is perfect.*

Dee came to our table with a portable phone, excused herself and reached across our booth as she plugged it into the wall receptacle. "Officer Randel, you have a telephone call; if you would like, you may take it here. I can transfer it for you."

"Thanks Dee," I replied, lifting the receiver and waiting. Arnold was picking at his food while he eavesdropped. "This is Officer Randel. Yes, Lieutenant Germain. The sheriff and the undersheriff, the captain, you and me at 2:00 in the undersheriff's office? Yes, sir. I'm having lunch with Lieutenant Arnold now. No, sir, I won't. Thank you, sir." I cradled the phone in its receiver and started eating my shrimp.

"What the hell was that all about, Randel?"

"Can't say as I know, LT." I didn't either. I had just been told to report there as instructed and to say nothing to anyone. I wouldn't.

Lieutenant Dan Arnold paled, and by the look on his face I sensed that his sphincter muscles had tightly clinched, and he acted as if he needed smelling salts. "Why haven't I been informed? If you and Germain and the captain are meeting with the sheriff and the undersheriff..." He paused, sucking in his breath, then expelling it angrily, "Hell, I have a right to know what's going on in the department." He squirmed uncomfortably in his seat. "What the hell do they want? Is this about me, Randel?"

"Couldn't say, sir." I used my napkin to wipe my mouth and

mustache, hiding the smirk on my face. I continued, "Sorry, Lt. Arnold, I don't know. How's your hamburger, sir?"

Arnold rose haughtily from the booth and stomped out, complaining, "I have a right to know what's going on. I'll get to the bottom of this right now, Randel, or my name's not Lieutenant Dan Arnold!"

"Thanks for the lunch, sir!" He never looked back and I knew that I would have to pay. *That's Officer Randel to you, sir, and you are Lieutenant Dan (Benedict) Arnold to me!*

What the hell is all this hush, hush shit with 'Mean' Gene and the sheriff? So much is goin' on that I don't even know what anyone wants anymore. I paid, left Dee a generous tip and headed for the office. All I could think about and wonder about was 'The Call.'

Norma Hood, a retired business owner and a former New Mexico State Legislator, is the mother of four fantastic and successful children, and the grandmother of a baker's dozen, plus one great-grand daughter. She is an accomplished writer of poetry and prose. Collaborating on their first novel together and developing a wonderful friendship has been an exciting experience for Norma with Rod Harris.

Rod Harris is a Veteran who served his Country in the U. S. Marine Corp in Vietnam. Semper Fi! He is also a twenty-six year plus Veteran of the Las Vegas Metropolitan Police Department. His adventures have turned into the first of the delightful series of Frank-3 Enroute novels written by Rod Harris with Norma Hood.

THE CALL

The next exciting book of the FRANK-3 ENROUTE series. Coming the summer of 2011